W9-DAN-488

NOBODY DIES IN A CASINO

ALSO BY MARLYS MILLHISER

FEATURING CHARLIE GREENE

It's Murder Going Home
Murder in a Hot Flash
Death of the Office Witch
Murder at Moot Point

OTHER NOVELS

Michael's Wife
Nella Waits
Willing Hostage
The Mirror
Nightmare County
The Threshold

NOBODY DIES IN A CASINO

MARLYS MILLHISER

ST. MARTIN'S PRESS
NEW YORK

For information, address St. Martin's Press, 175 Fifth Avenue, New York, N.Y. 10010.

Library of Congress Cataloging-in-Publication Data

Millhiser, Marlys.
Nobody dies in a casino / Marlys Millhiser. — 1st U.S. ed.
p. cm.
ISBN 0-312-20344-6
I. Title.
PS3563.I4225N63 1999
813'.54—dc21 99-12859
CIP

First Edition: May 1999

10 9 8 7 6 5 4 3 2 1

For my sister members of Femmes Fatales,
with whom I share a newsletter,
a Web site (http://members.aol.com/femmesweb),
and a very special bond.

Charlie Greene and her author would like to acknowledge the help of Tony Fennelly on astrology, Gail Larson on blackjack, Jay Millhiser on Vegas and aircraft, Lloyd Boothby of the Hilton in the title, and editor Kelley Ragland for a patience that surpasses all understanding.

And to Caryl, Pat, Terry, and Barry and Terry in Dallas—they know who they are.

NOBODY DIES IN A CASINO

CHAPTER 1

CHARLIE GREENE DECIDED it was a sign of the times.

Just off a jet, she walked along a concourse at McCarran International Airport beside her boss and between rows of bleeping, blinking, whistling slots. Her notebook computer in her briefcase so she could send and receive office E-mail, one man passing her talking on his cellular and another approaching her doing the same.

She didn't know about the guys on the cellulars, but Charlie was on vacation.

Sure didn't feel like it.

The men on the phones wore shorts. The one coming at her looked into her eyes without seeing her, his vision directed to his conversation. He was a hunk. The one passing her said, "No, Benny, I keep telling you—in Vegas, it's gaming, not gambling." This man was not a hunk. But he did have an air of prosperity.

"Merlin's Ridge?" The hunk's face suffused with an anger that would have made anyone else ugly. "Never heard of it."

"Babe," her employer burst into her thoughts. "Baggage claim's this way. Pay attention. What am I always telling ya?"

Charlie turned to follow him just as the hunk said, "What I do in your plane is your business. I wasn't flying Yucca on your time. You fire me and I'll open up—"

"Hello?" Richard Morse, head of Congdon and Morse Representation, Inc., stood nose-to-nose with Charlie. Congdon and Morse was a talent agency in Beverly Hills, Charlie its lone literary agent. "Anybody home there?"

"Did you hear what he'd open up?"

"Did I hear what who would open up?"

"The hunk on the phone." Charlie pointed to where the guy, his cellular, and Mr. Prosperous had been replaced by a whole new crowd.

I knew I needed a vacation, but eavesdropping on strangers and then getting worked up over it?

"Knew you needed a vacation, but jeez," Richard all but repeated her thoughts—which was even scarier. "No hunks for you tonight. Room service and sleep. Boss's orders."

Charlemagne Catherine Greene checked into the Las Vegas Hilton, unpacked, and stared out the wall of window at the blinking, sparkling, blatant Vegas night. A blimp in the sky sported garish advertising that zipped in flashing lights across its side. An acquaintance had once remarked that Vegas took tacky to an art form. Too true.

She slipped into a long knit dress with a slit up the side, matching jacket, and sandals and headed for the lobby shuttle that would take her the few blocks away to the Strip.

Charlie, probably a little over half Richard Morse's age, knew vacation for her didn't mean sleep. She'd have her room service in bed for breakfast. At about noon.

If everything in one's life had some meaning, which Charlie highly doubted, Richard must function to reinforce her resolution to remain a single mom who seeks fulfillment in her career.

Winning at both the slots and the blackjack table at Bally's, she paused at the Flamingo Hilton's snack bar for dinner and played video poker at the booze bar over a free margarita—

postponing losing all her winnings in the next round, people watching.

Funny, how you could enjoy being alone in a crowd.

"This your lucky night?" a suggestive voice suggested behind her. An arm slid around her waist.

Charlie removed it and drained her margarita. "Apparently not."

Well, you're the one who had to wear a slit in your skirt that opens up a whole new side of you. Damn near to your navel.

It does not come to my navel.

Your underwear then.

Charlie slid off the stool, no longer deliciously alone, and came down hard on the foot belonging to the suggestive arm.

"I suppose I can be thankful you're not wearing those damn high heels."

"Evan." Wonderful. Charlie had just snubbed a client. "God, I'm sorry. I wasn't expecting to see you until, what, Tuesday?"

"Apparently not," he mimicked. Evan Black, with his sleek ponytail, a black ninjalike outfit, dark eyes in an olive-tanned face, a boyish smile, and round tinted eyeglasses. "Just out looking for trouble and spotted you the minute I walked in."

"I thought some creep was trying to pick me up."

"I am. I mean, he is." He nodded to the bartender to bring her another margarita, ordered a beer for himself.

Evan had a home here and one in Beverly Hills. The umbilical cord linking L.A. to Vegas was charged by proximity, smog, jet contrails, cash, the flight from taxation, cash, lack of snow you couldn't sniff, entertainment talent and its money.

Evan—screenwriter, director, and producer of low-budget specialized features—had cleaned up at the film festivals and often on the megabuck-proven story formulas at the box office, as well. So the studios making them had begun to court him and he'd sought out Congdon and Morse to represent him.

Maybe because in the world of rapacious entertainment conglomerates, Charlie's agency was relatively small potatoes too.

Evan could bomb in the hundreds of thousands instead of hundreds of millions. But when he hit, it was mostly profit. He could attract star talent for peanuts because he offered memorable scripts that taxed and excited them.

A brand-new client worth the earth. And she'd stomped on his foot.

"So, how much have you lost?" He kissed her neck, forgiving her.

"I've been winning, smart cheeks, and I've got the rest of the night to lose it. Wanna help?"

In the spirit of Robin Hood, they decided to hit the Barbary Coast and Loopy Louie's because she'd earned her winnings in the posher casinos.

They were at the craps table at the Barbary, losing, and she'd paused to watch the rippling lights on a keno board ripple across the lenses of Evan's glasses when, over his shoulder, she saw the hunk from the airport. He was in earnest conversation with a blonde in black leggings, high-heeled boots, and a vest that almost hid her nipples.

Evan turned to follow her stare. "That's Caryl. She's my pilot. Cute, right?"

"I was looking at the guy. He's a pilot too. She looks more like a bar girl." With the empty tray wedged against her hip, she looked exactly like one.

"Young pilots don't make much money. Too many people wanting the fun, glamorous jobs, so the pay sucks until they get mucho hours. Unless lightning strikes, they need a day job. In Caryl's case, a night job."

Charlie lost interest in the pilots when Evan's luck changed and the dealer began shoving chips his way. But when his winnings had piled into neat rows of some height, Charlie's client decided he would cash them in.

"You can't do that—you're on a streak, you idiot," she let

loose before she could talk sense to herself. She'd become so involved in his winning, she felt like a participant instead of a bystander.

"She's my agent," Evan explained to the fragile woman next to him. Her head shook with palsy in sync with her diamonds strobing back the flashing lights that careened around a DOLLAR DELUXE sign above a bank of slots.

She squinted up at Charlie and patted Evan's hand with jeweled fingers. "You should look into a manager, honey."

"Hey, in the spirit of fairness, Charlie," he said on the way out, "I have to lose my winnings from the Barbary at Loopy's."

They'd reached the delightfully tawdry entrance to Loopy Louie's—it resembled the entrance to a harem in Cecil B. De Mille's seriously senior-citizen dreams—when she saw her pilot hunk again. He was exiting the harem's blue-pink-and-gold doors—tastefully rendered in neon and mirrors—with a somber muscleman on each side. Shoulder-to-shoulder on each side. Without them, the pilot in the middle might be staggering. These guys weren't eunuch harem guards. One had a shaved head, the other shoulder-length curls. The pilot looked bewildered, half-aware, in the process of swelling up around the eyes and neck, but the swelling had not yet discolored.

Mind your own business, Charlie. "Evan, did you see that? The pilot who was arguing with your Caryl, and those goons muscling him out the door?"

"No. Maybe he was counting cards. Come on, agent mine, you have a duty to help me lose money."

Charlie, mind your own business.

"Evan, they've hurt him." But she'd no more than said that than she lost sight of the three too.

The sidewalk was very nearly a solid mass of people, like the sidewalks of Manhattan at morning rush hour, but without the rush. These people sort of slushed instead, slowly pushed for a better view of the "volcano" erupting at the Mirage. It sounded more like a hot-air balloon than an eruption, more of a whooshing noise than an exploding one.

Fire, rising on rather obvious natural-gas jets, but no rocks, spurted thirty to forty feet into the night from a mound in a pond. It erupted on waves of canned music and creative lighting that reflected off upturned faces even here across the street.

She found the three men again because they stood at the curb and took no notice, even when colored lights on cascading water pretended to be flowing lava and steam hissed up out of the pond. The air filled with the scent of stage smoke and raw natural gas, of car exhaust and beer-laden human breath.

The mysterious beacon of the Luxor's pyramid sliced into the heavens, where countless jets, wingtips flashing, circled the landing pattern at McCarran or soared off to find reality. A Steven Spielberg brainstorm run amuck.

And down at Charlie's level, an ambulance tried silently to thread traffic too packed to get out of its way. Traffic moved, but in a slow, solid mass, as if welded by headlights and taillights and blaring horns, side-road and pedestrian traffic ignored until the eruption ended. Interest in this extravaganza that played every fifteen minutes after sunset and alternated with the pyrotechnics of exploding pirate ships next door at the Treasure Island Casino attested to the turnover of tourists and money on the Strip.

The three men at the curb stood so close, their shirts could have been sewn together at the shoulder seams. "What do you bet they're going to try to force him into a car?"

But her client had gone on through the harem doors without her.

Charlie was pushing her way to the curb, her eyes on the three heads not turned toward the volcano at the Mirage.

When the head in the middle disappeared.

The other two moved in opposite directions. If she could get the license plate of the car they'd jammed him into, she could report an abduction to the police.

But they hadn't jammed the hunk into a car. They'd pushed him *in front* of one.

Charlie lost her margaritas in the gutter next to the part of him not still under traffic.

CHAPTER 2

CHARLIE'S SKIN STILL tingled from a hot shower when room service arrived with poached eggs on a bed of corned-beef hash, little bottles of catsup and jam, thick slices of toast, a huge glass of fresh orange juice, and a *big* pot of coffee.

She settled back into the king-sized bed, an abundance of pillows bunched behind her and the tray on her lap. Life and all its little upgrades seemed incredibly precious this morning.

It wasn't noon, as Charlie had planned, more like 8:30. But, for a vacation night, she'd gone to bed early. And not only had she slept, she was hungry.

It had taken forever to get the ambulance through the traffic last night to pick up the body. Somebody from Loopy's came out to cover it with a gaming-table cover. The cops gave up and threaded the crowd on foot. One of them managed to get through on a bike.

Charlie broke both yolks and let them run over half the corned-beef hash, refusing to associate her food with any images of the grisly gutter, even when she topped the mess on her plate with the red catsup.

You made a mistake getting involved to begin with. Stay out of the whole thing.

I thought you were my conscience.

I'm your good sense. This is Rambo's world, not the Good Witch of the West's.

She ate slowly. Hell, she had all morning to fight with her demons and seriously sluggish conscience. Besides, she hadn't kept much down for the last ten hours. It takes strength to face reality.

She really had irritated Congdon and Morse's hot new client this time by insisting on explaining what she'd seen in some detail to the skeptical bicycle cop, the only one who even consented to listen to her. Evan Black, who had come back out when he realized that she hadn't followed him, nudged with his elbow, pleaded with his eyes, and finally told the policeman, "We have to go now, Officer."

The officer had simply nodded with relief. Charlie ate half the hash mess while puzzling Evan's reaction. She finished off the juice, splurged on a piece of toast with the first cup of coffee, and made the mistake of reaching for the remote.

Just in time for the news.

After informing the population of the wonderful weather and not-too-terrible smog, the morning anchor turned to his lovely partner and said, "I understand there was another pedestrian error on the Strip last night."

"Error? He was pushed."

The local newswoman ignored Charlie's outburst and went into a patient but lengthy recounting of the numerous accidents resulting in death on the heavily traveled Strip when pedestrians jaywalked instead of waiting for traffic lights at the corners.

"He wasn't jaywalking. He could hardly stand up."

The guy anchor also ignored Charlie and explained the efforts of the mayor's office to educate tourists on the dangers. "You know, Terry, visitors get so caught up in all the fun and excitement here—they don't mean to break the law. It's such a shame."

"He wasn't a visitor, he was a pilot, dickhead." Charlie spilled coffee down her front.

You know he was a pilot. You do not know he lived here. And we do not say dickhead, even when alone.

"Oh, shut up, all of you." Charlie squirmed herself and the breakfast tray across the expanse of the kingsize.

"Right, Barry, a tragic shame, and the pedestrian error last night is no exception."

"It was murder, you—" At this rate, she'd need another shower before getting dressed.

Remember, we have an ulcer and a daughter to raise.

Libby is raising herself in spite of us . . . ohmygod, now it's we, us. "I'm too young for Prozac."

Charlie was talking to herself in the mirror, the front of her scanty robe dripping with coffee. Terry was talking on the television about how the poor victim had yet to be identified.

"Shit, I can identify the murderers. What more do you need?"

When the phone rang, Charlie watched it instead of the TV. If it was her boss next door or teenaged daughter back in Long Beach, Charlie would lose her corned beef for sure. If she didn't keep something down, she'd be too sick to care if some poor unidentified pilot's murderers got away with pedestrian error or not.

She finally picked it up, relieved when it was Evan, the client, producer, director, writer.

"Charlie, I hate to do this to you, but Caryl won't listen to reason. She's determined to talk to you."

"Caryl."

"Caryl Thompson, my pilot? The bar girl at the Barbary Coast? We're downstairs. Charlie, it was her brother who died last night. I don't think she's going to take no for an answer."

Charlie slipped into shorts and a shirt while Terry and Barry turned their attention to Yucca Mountain, where the nuclear industry and the military hoped to conceal and ignore the deadly residue of their trades. Hadn't the dead pilot mentioned Yucca Mountain in his phone conversation at the airport? And a ridge she couldn't remember the name of.

The news team went on to relate apparent security breaches—mainly tourists trying to get too close—not only at Yucca but also at Area 51, or Groom Lake, some ninety miles out of Vegas. Here, the air force did not disclose it had a top secret installation to test new aircraft, and so popular myth accused it of concealing everything from the latest time machine to alien body parts. The world was such a loony place the way it was, Charlie couldn't figure why anyone would worry about woo-woo stuff like that. *They* were everywhere. Not the aliens, but people who seemed to have an inexplicable craving for woo-woo.

She'd once had a close encounter of the carnal kind with one of the more famous of these people and could personally attest to the strength of their beliefs. Fortunately, this particular guy had a few other strengths, not the least of them a fantastic back.

Barry and Terry didn't pretend Area 51 was nonexistent, and they warned that security forces in restricted areas, "armed response personnel," were highly professional, heavily armed, and authorized to use deadly force.

Evan Black arrived disheveled and sweating, and Caryl Thompson was crying. How could anybody's pilot be that young? Obviously, Evan didn't share Charlie's fear of flying.

Charlie fought guilt. He was wearing what he'd worn the night before, along with a morning beard, uneven in length and patchy. He had not slept well like she had. He bent to pick up a flyer somebody had slipped under her door.

A sky blue flyer with a golden cross and an unlikely cloud formation in the background that spelled out "REPENT!"

". . . should not be allowed to advertise brothel services in the city," Barry said.

"You've got to tell me everything," Caryl said.

"I already told you," Evan said.

"I want to hear it from her."

"FOR THE TIME IS AT HAND," the inside flap of the flyer said.

Caryl hadn't changed her clothes either. Charlie got them seated on the couch under the window, where the sky backdrop was blue but the few clouds weren't spelling out anything.

She tossed the tumbled bedclothes toward the headboard to cover the suspicious stains spilled coffee had left and ordered up juice, coffee, and bagels. Just as she reached for the remote to get rid of Barry and Terry, Terry said, "Yes, and although the crime rate is high in Las Vegas and gaming is often blamed for it, did you know there has never been a murder in a casino?"

"Hell no, they just walk them outside and push them into traffic while everybody's watching a frigging volcano," Charlie answered her.

Caryl's face crumbled into Evan's shoulder and he sent Charlie a beseeching look.

"Well, folks, now that you know where the safest places in Vegas are," Barry reassured them, "go out and have some fun."

Caryl Thompson made no effort to keep the vest in place and her nipples played peekaboo with the atmosphere. She and her brother had been born in Vegas. Their parents divorced and moved to opposite coasts. "But Pat and I both had work flying the ditch and were building hours, so we stayed. And now, now I don't have anybody."

"The ditch?"

"Grand Canyon."

Charlie described the three men on the sidewalk and her suspicions to Evan and a calmer Caryl. Their breakfasts came and both claimed a lack of appetite, then proceeded to pack most of it away.

"You'll just have to go to the police and tell them who the victim was and that he'd lived and worked here all his life. They're convinced he was a tourist, too excited about the wonders of Vegas to watch where he was going," Charlie finished.

"I know, pedestrian error. There is a lot of that going around."

"Caryl, it was wall-to-wall traffic. If you'd wanted to jaywalk, you'd have had to hop from one car hood to the next. They must have waited for the light to change and cars to begin creeping again and timed a shove to get him to street level at all. He was definitely not himself."

"I can't go to the cops."

"Caryl—" Evan warned.

"You have to. Your brother was murdered."

Charlie, stay out of this. It is not your business. And you don't *know* the dead guy was her brother. And Evan's looking funny. Vegas may be a great place to have fun, but it's a bad place to get involved.

"You're right," Charlie told her common sense.

"She is?" Evan looked from Charlie to Caryl and back again.

"I am?"

"Absolutely. I've told you all I know about your brother's death. And the police too. It's up to you now. Would you believe I came here for a vacation?" Charlie stacked their dishes back on the tray, pointedly opened the door to the hall. To hell with her conscience.

"You mean you're not going to do anything?" Caryl was youthfully plump in only the right places. It gave her a healthy innocence, hard to square with the vest.

"Hey, he wasn't *my* brother."

Evan Black and his lovely pilot left, obviously disappointed in her. What did they expect?

They were trying to use her.

Charlie applied a trace of eye shadow, tried to improve on her hair, and grabbed her purse. This time, she would listen to common sense and leave well enough alone. If poor Pat the pilot's sister couldn't talk to the police, Charlie sure as hell wasn't going to. Evan Black wasn't telling all either.

"I'm on vacation." Charlie yanked the door open to a

blonde who stopped just short of knocking on Charlie's forehead.

"I am too." The blonde withdrew her knuckles, tightened her tit and ass lines, and walked into the room as if it were hers. "How'd you know? I mean, that I was outside the door before I could even knock?"

"I was on my way out."

Charlie's visitor looked around the room, checked the bathroom. "Are there two of you?"

Actually, sometimes there are, me and my common sense. "Not at the moment."

"I'm Tami." Tami reached into a back pocket of her jeans and withdrew a tightly folded note. "Are you Congdon and Morse, Inc.?"

"Uh . . . I'm part of it."

"I understood this was going to be a guy gig, but I'm flexible." Tami stretched a well-muscled body to prove her point. Her eyes were an even deeper blue than Caryl's.

"He didn't tell me you were coming."

"Hey, got it. You're a couple who want to go home with fantasies to keep things hot for months, right? Well, I'm your girl."

"Poor Richard."

"I can take care of poor Richard anytime." Tami dropped herself to her knees, and her halter to her waist. "And you too."

Tami reached for the snap on her jeans and for Charlie's crotch.

CHAPTER 3

It was still early. There was only one blackjack table operating in the Hilton's casino downstairs, where acres of crystal hung from the ceiling, at odds with the arcade decor below it.

Charlie made a third player at the table and accepted a free Bloody Mary from the breakfast cocktail server. This was party-twenty-four-hours-a-day town. Right?

Besides, Charlie'd earned it, rescuing herself just in the nick from a fate worse than death. She'd convinced Tami the body-builder to hurry next door and relieve Richard Morse of his anxieties and no doubt a good portion of his cash. The agency didn't cover Tamis as an expense, surely. Did Tamis take Visa?

Charlie might be on vacation, but she had an early dinner date with a local book author at an outdoor restaurant at the Flamingo around six and she was determined to enjoy the rest of the day before that, no matter how many people were struck dead around her. One always dined with Georgette early because the author was in bed by 8:30. Charlie had the feeling Georgette Millrose was not going to be a happy date.

There were six decks in the shoe—a clear plastic box with a ramp on its face that delivered one card at a time—all mixed up together. Dealers rarely played the shoe down much over halfway. Treasure Island had the reputation for dealing down the farthest. With three players at the table and ten burn cards shoved into the discard box, she couldn't know how many face cards and aces had already turned up.

An intense guy on one side of Charlie played a roll of hundred-dollar bills, three at a time, instead of chips. The woman to her left sat whimsically relaxed, seemingly daydreaming, checking her watch as if passing time until a companion arrived to take her to breakfast. But blackjack is a fast-moving game, and her signals to the dealer were on time and to the point.

The dealer was of the silent, stoic variety Charlie preferred. She found the chummy, garrulous types a distraction.

Lights flashed, zipped, and careened around the room, glinting off crystal facets. Metal tokens clanked into slot trays, and a few levers ratcheted. Whistles, calliope bleeps. Vacuum cleaners buzzed before the true crowds descended again. And this was one of the more staid of Vegas's casinos. No wonder nobody died in these places. No quiet place to do it.

Charlie's overly acute hearing, the result of her inability to indulge in loud music as a teen due to tone deafness, could be both a boon and a vexation.

Her aging, horny boss, her close call with his lusty entertainer, even what they could possibly be doing at this moment, the body in the gutter last night, Evan Black the important. Had he insisted Charlie talk to the police again, she would have. But he'd acted disappointed that she wouldn't and reluctant to have her do it. Granted, by the time Evan saw the pilot, he was not readily identifiable. And Caryl with the peekaboo nipples—they all faded as the game took hold. Mercifully, the background noises blended, then receded.

And yet Charlie registered the pit boss's belt buckle, silver and turquoise, with a finger ring to match, the hair on the back of his hands as he turned to keep watch on the dealers at various games around him. The way those hands flexed at his side as if surreptitiously exercising, the crooked seam in one pant leg.

The low cards were playing out. And the kings.

The eye in the sky, circled with crystal lashes, kept watch on the pit boss and the placing of chips at the tables. Charlie did not have the memory to be a card-counter, but with a six-deck shoe that would probably only be played down four decks anyway, she didn't know how anybody could tell how many face cards might be left.

The black globes pocking the crystal and two-way mirrored ceiling offered a decorative contrast, reminding Charlie of alien bug eyes. They held camera eyes instead, taping people and activities in the crystal cavern. No wonder there weren't any murders in the casinos—they'd be documented in the process.

The best places for blackjack were downtown on Fremont, the original Glitter Gulch, where there were casinos that advertised single and double decks. That's where the dedicated locals played.

The reason Charlie and Richard and everybody at Congdon and Morse used to prefer to stay at the Vegas Hilton was the relative absence of children. Now, with the new Star Trek Experience wing, there were more families evident. But here in the old casino, one rarely noticed them. And Richard had some kind of deal on rooms at this hotel. Even if she lost money gaming, it was a cheap vacation.

Charlie was aware on some level of the odors of stale tobacco, spilled beer, dead perfume, sweat, and the chemical deodorizers out to kill them all.

The guy next to her ran out of hundreds and left the table, muttering something about this "filthy town" and the "blasted world." Charlie couldn't tell if he was a Kiwi or an Aussie. She'd never doubted she could lose at gambling. But she also thought she could win. Gamblers are optimists. The shoe was emptied and refilled with brand-new decks, the pit boss peeling the cellophane wrappers off himself.

After the next deal, Charlie, with an ace and a five, scratched for a hit and so did the woman on her left, but by pointing at the table in front of her. She wore her bangs heavy to cover the wrinkles on her forehead, had her hair colored that sandy brown so popular these days, and sported a bemused smile that only toyed with her lips but fairly sparkled in her eyes. She dressed in loose-fitting cream slacks and jacket over a cream silk shell, gold chain necklace, and earrings. The only contrast, the deep tan of her skin and the blue shading on her eyelids.

The woman in cream and gold began to win and she began to play with two and then three black chips at a time and then stacks of the hundred-dollar tokens. The bemused smile turned to silent laughter. She straightened in her chair.

The dealer grew more tense than formal now. The pit boss settled behind him and stayed.

Everybody's guilty until proven innocent in Vegas.

Charlie figured most of the cameras behind the bug eyes overhead were zooming in on this table too, to make sure nobody on either side of the table cheated the house.

This was a hot shoe. There was a streak going here.

Even the security rooms and halls in "that other casino" have cameras taping everything that goes on. Charlie knew, because a few years ago two cops were taped beating a purse snatcher caught in a casino. They were taped beating and threatening to sodomize him with nightsticks. God, you couldn't even die in that mysterious security area all casinos have without being documented.

In fact, Charlie had never heard of anyone just dying in a casino, simply dropping dead of something. Older, and often hugely overweight, people were common in these places.

Charlie's other mind was making money. But nothing like the cream-and-gold woman, who laughed, never making a sound.

"It was awesome," Charlie told her boss as they lay side by side on webbed deck chairs by the pool. This recreation deck on the third floor was also awesome. All eight acres of it.

"She counting?" Richard sprawled on his back, trying to hide the bruises forming there.

Charlie would save Tami for later ammunition. Tami had apparently not mentioned Charlie. "I don't think so. It's like when the shoe changed, she knew it would be hot. Like she waited for it to get dealt down less than maybe a fourth of one deck and got interested. She kept checking her watch though. Wonder if that means anything."

"Sounds like you made your move then too. You're supposed to be the psychic—maybe she was watching your reactions."

"No, she started it. I just went with the flow." Charlie'd come out about thirty thousand dollars richer, thanks to the woman of the silent laughter, who must have made more like several hundred thousand. The dealer, pit boss, and hard-faced suits that gravitated toward the pit weren't laughing. "And if I were psychic, Richard, I'd be rich by now. It's not like this is my first trip to Vegas."

"Just don't spend it all in one place." Richard the Lionhearted, as he was known around the office, had a hickey.

"It's all going to the college fund."

Richard raised to an elbow to wipe the steam off his sunglasses with his towel. He had protruding eyeballs that gave him a certain air of authority for no good reason. "What, she's changed her mind again?"

"That, she's good at."

Libby Greene, seventeen, had been waffling about college for the last three years. One time, she wanted to be an astronaut, another an archaeologist, then a stripper, then a doctor in sports medicine, your regular model, movie star, even housewife. She'd been through many careers in her mind, for most of which, neither she nor her grades qualified. Actually, Libby Abigail Greene's qualifications for model and movie star grew more apparent by the month.

Charlie would rather the kid find some rewarding skill to keep her satisfied, fed, happy, and as independent financially as she was temperamentally. Charlie had a life. She hoped the same for her daughter. "She gets her braces off next month."

"Oh, Jesus. Don't waste your money on the college fund."

"Think I'll get it wet."

The water was just cool enough to refresh at the weeny end, cooled enough at the deeper end to be invigorating without being uncomfortable. I won thirty thousand dollars this morning. Saw a murder happen last night. And don't remember when I've enjoyed life more than I do this day. Something's wrong with the script here.

"You look better when you're all wet, know that?" Richard Morse told her when she returned to the lounge chairs. "Now don't get huffy on me, babe. Because I been thinking about your problem."

"Which problem?" Charlie gathered her things, her "all wet" chilling in the dry October breeze up here, and headed for the concrete Grecian Jacuzzi, Richard trotting along behind her. Built to fit twenty-four, according to the sign—you could have crowded in another ten easy. Formed and rounded in mysterious ways to accommodate couples, the molded underwater bench rimming the tub suggested the sign meant twelve couples.

There was only one man in the Jacuzzi when they arrived, bubbles foaming almost to his chin.

She and Richard crawled down into the couple niche farthest from the man in the circle, as people do when they have all the room in the world.

"The thirty thousand problem—wait, is this before or after taxes?"

After—and I don't believe it either. "Before."

"Oh, well . . . still, Charlie, you know what you should do with it?"

"Gamble it away?"

"Stock market." The wise man with the Tami hickey nodded sagely and slid down into the frothing hot water up to his chin too.

"Same thing, right?"

"Not at your age, babe. You think you're independent because you have a job and a mortgage. Take those away and you're on the street, and your kid too. Time you began to think about compounding."

Richard Morse, the second bane of Charlie's life, her mother being the first, was nothing if not mysterious. Her daughter was just young, and there was always some hope for improvement in that quarter. "Compounding what?"

"Dividends. DRIP. Face it, babe, we're in a risky business here."

"Who isn't?" Take your hunk pilots, for instance.

"Yeah, but we know it. We need to plan for the future. Charlie, you listening to me? What's wrong with you?"

Charlie belatedly figured out what was wrong. That other guy in the Jacuzzi with them? He was one of the two heads who'd walked away from a murder on the Strip last night.

CHAPTER 4

"GEORGETTE, HOW WONDERFUL to see you again."

The outdoor café at the Flamingo Hilton had real flamingos in a garden-pool-courtyard paradise and other exotic feathered and leafy things. It also had paths and nature signs for the educationally inclined and trash music that drowned out miniature waterfalls and surviving birdsong. They sat at a table shaded by the monstrous backdrop of the Flamingo, an umbrella, and a wilting palm imported from California.

Georgette was Georgette as always, bones and skin, with occasional lumps that identified her gender and osteoporosis. Bright red hair and a face that had given up on its lifts, leaving the boldly capped teeth to go where her expression could no longer follow.

"So? I understand you put this kid's manuscript up for auction," she said around the prominent caps. "Reynelda somebody? She was nobody—she's from Colorado, for godsake. And boom, now she's rich and famous." Georgette raised her martini and the rocks in her rings sent facet flashes jumping all over the underside of the umbrella. "Never in all these years has an agent, including you, put a novel of mine up for auction."

If seeing the thug in the giant Jacuzzi spa hadn't wrecked her mood, Charlie knew she could count on Georgette. Last time, it had been that her publisher was not accurately reporting her sales and was stealing her blind and it was all Charlie's fault.

"It might be Reynelda Goff's first novel, but the woman's in her mid-fifties, Georgette. She just got lucky." And, believe me, there wasn't anybody more surprised than I was. "How did you know about the auction?"

"Lucky because you put her novel up for auction. And I knew about it because I read *Publishers Weekly,* young lady. Don't think I live in Vegas because I'm dumb enough to gamble."

How did Georgette afford her lifestyle? And goddamn *Publishers Weekly* anyway. Authors should not be allowed near it.

The thug in the pool had stared at Charlie and finally left the spa. He was the one with curly hair. His presence had to have been a coincidence. But Charlie hadn't stopped looking over her shoulder ever since. She'd wanted to tell her boss about the pilot's death and the man who had left them alone in the spa, but Richard was too busy waxing poetic about dividend reinvestment and compounding.

"She was lucky that certain newsworthy events made her manuscript suddenly marketable. It was like winning the lotto. I mean—I thought you were loyal to Bland and Ripstop after all the years they've published you." Bland had sent a sheaf of detailed material on the status of Georgette's sales at Charlie's request, all pretty much indecipherable, but most publishers wouldn't have bothered. Although her sales were brisk, they were mostly "special sales" to chain stores that discounted books heavily because they could get high-volume deals, which pretty much dried up the author's trickle.

"I'll remind you that three of my novels have been optioned repeatedly by Hollywood production companies. Why are my books never put up for auction?"

Because Hollywood's dumber than New York even. They'll option half of anything that makes it to bound galleys. To date, all but one of Charlie's book authors had at least one option—mostly for cable TV—but still . . .

Only one of her book authors had ever made it to actual produced feature film, and that author had been long dead when she hit. Her heirs were making out splendidly, however.

Charlie dearly loved being a literary agent. She used to be a New York literary agent, but now she was Hollywood. She'd just as soon dump her book authors and concentrate on screenwriters, but things never quite worked out that way. For one thing, most of her book authors wanted to write screenplays so they could quit their day jobs or get a divorce or whatever. Most of her screenwriters wasted too much time writing novels nobody could sell.

"Georgette, lightning could still strike you like it did Reynelda Goff, but I can't put you or any of my authors up for auction until I know more than one house would be interested. She was an unknown commodity and things just clicked."

"And I'm just a shopworn old frump—is that right?"

No, you're just a midlist author. Among book authors, there are four kinds—self-published, prepublished, no longer published, and published. Among the last, there are two—star authors and the vast majority, midlist authors. There is no low-list author. "Of course not, you have published, what—twenty novels in hardcover?"

"All but one of which is out of print. I'm not even selling paperback rights anymore."

"The paperback market has really constricted. I can't control the marketplace. I mean, it's not like you're starving."

"No thanks to my agent. It so happens, miss, that I invested large portions of both my late husbands' estates in the stock market. The marketplace works very well for me except with my writing. I want to know why." Enlarged knuckles pounded on the menus their waitperson had left and which neither had bothered to open.

"Okay, send me a proposal on the next book and I'll hand it around to see if I can stir up enough interest for an auction.

But I'm warning you—there's nothing more embarrassing than throwing a party and nobody comes. And Bland and Ripstop is not going to be happy about this. We're risking a lot here."

"No, my dear. *We* are risking nothing. Because *you* are fired."

✣

Charlie sat staring at Georgette's empty chair and martini glass, so stunned she ordered a hamburger with fries and a glass of merlot from the waitperson and didn't realize she'd been forgetting to look over her shoulder until someone startled her from behind.

"Well, for heaven's sakes. It's my partner in crime. May I join you?"

Charlie hadn't heard anyone say "for heaven's sakes" since *Father Knows Best* on Nick. She'd have minded, but it was the woman in cream and gold. This was the first time Charlie had heard her speak.

"I'm Bradone and I feel like I've known you forever." Her voice fit her perfectly—moderately low, pleasant, mellow, personal.

"I'm Charlie and I—" And I don't know what to say—"Charlie Greene, and yes, please sit down." Charlie'd never been fired before. She'd parted with clients, but never like this.

"Know what?" Bradone put down the menu. That laughter Charlie sensed, barely below the surface. "I'm going to be deliciously naughty and have a hamburger and fries too and a beer."

"Why are we partners in crime and how did you know what I'd ordered?"

"Our crime was all that money we won at the other Hilton this morning. I was seated at the table behind you here and overheard your order. And wasn't that Georgette Millrose who left in such an unseemly huff?" This Bradone—she pronounced it *Brad-own*—was striking—in her way, almost beautiful. "And

I know that because I've seen her photos and read several of her books. So there."

"She just fired me," Charlie blurted, knowing better. Then, of course, she had to explain in what capacity she'd been fired and admit to her occupation, which she never did to strangers.

Charlie tried to cut off her urge to confide.

Bradone was Bradone McKinley, and when Charlie asked what she did for a living, Bradone McKinley swirled the end of a naughty french fry into a puddle of naughty catsup and laughed out loud before taking a bite. It must be wonderful to be so happy all the time.

"I play blackjack and sometimes baccarat. I travel the world. I read the stars."

"Are you a card-counter?"

"I'm an astrologer."

"Did you know it was going to be a hot shoe?"

"Not really."

The music had mercifully paused for a while and imprisoned nature was quacking and squawking and cawing and squeaking. The birds must have had their wings clipped, because nobody took wing but sparrows looking for french fry bits.

"Do you always play blackjack so early in the morning?"

"Only when the timing is right and Venus is making good aspects." They both managed to put away about half of their burgers and a fourth of their fries. Bradone ordered wine and coffee for herself and Charlie too. Much as she wanted to get on with her life, Charlie found the woman mesmerizing.

"Works wonderfully, but not always, and it's fun. Works well enough though, that I have to be careful to lose money about a third of the time."

"I don't believe you." Charlie realized she was grinning. In the last twenty-four hours, she'd witnessed a murder, sat in a Jacuzzi with one of the killers, and been fired by a client for the first time—and she was grinning.

Be careful. She's probably setting you up to look at a book

proposal for astrologers who want to gamble.

Evening had softened the sun and the breeze was dry and cool, sweet with tropical plants blackmailed somehow into living here. Children splashed and chattered in a swimming pool on the other side of a hillock.

"I know you don't believe me, Charlie. Nobody does. That's the beauty of it. I've been doing this for years. It's a fabulous life. Monte Carlo, Malaysia, Macao, Alaska, cruise ships, Latin America—the world is very literally my oyster."

"Do you have a home base?"

Bradone Mckinley had a home in Santa Barbara, where she retreated when the stars were not propitious for gambling. "And to rest and to study. Astrology takes a lot of study."

She salted away a third of her earnings after taxes, made a point of losing a third—usually at baccarat, because it was faster—and spent the rest for living and traveling expenses. "I love travel, astrology, blackjack, my home in Santa Barbara. I couldn't be happier."

"Any family?"

"Just my cats and a houseboy."

"You should write a book," Charlie said, testing her.

"That's too much work. I already have plenty of money." As if to prove it, Bradone insisted upon paying the tab for both of them. "Notoriety, I don't need. I like my life the way it is. And I so enjoyed watching you winning this morning. You're great company when you're not too intense."

Charlie had enjoyed it too, and the dinner, and the company. She felt a little lonesome when they parted ways on the street outside.

She should head back to her room and check her E-mail. Call Libby. But she turned up the street toward the Treasure Island Casino instead, crossing Las Vegas Boulevard so she wouldn't have to pass the place where the hunk pilot had died. She passed the statues of a triumphant Caesar, out to sack your bank account instead of Gaul, and winged angels lauding the idea by blowing silent trumpets from their pedestals along the drive of Caesar's Palace.

The courtyard of the Treasure Island was red with stage smoke as a pirate ship defied a brig of Her Majesty's Navy with phony cannon shot and firecrackers over the heads of the assembled tourists crowding an enormous wooden gangway entrance to the casino. The brave Brits fired back and many a stuntman on either side met his demise in the broiling waters of battle.

Yes, it was silly, but it made Charlie happy again. If Hollywood was the reality you were trying to get away from, it took something as bizarre as Las Vegas to do it.

She battled her way through the throng—let Mr. Thug try to follow her now, har, har—to get inside to the blackjack tables, where she happily lost and won and lost again thirty dollars that would never compound or DRIP or whatever.

By the time she made it back to the Las Vegas Hilton, her stomach remembered to turn sour over her fat-drenched dinner and the wine. So she stopped by the twenty-four-hour café for milk and dry toast.

Her stomach might feel bad—it was a grouchy stomach anyway—but she felt pretty good.

Until she glanced at the headlines of the *Las Vegas Sun* left on the seat next to her.

A cop on the Strip had been found murdered. No question of pedestrian error here. This was an obvious hit-and-run. His name was Timothy Graden. Timothy Graden left behind a wife and two young children.

There was a picture. He was the bicycle cop who wouldn't believe her at the scene of another murder last night.

CHAPTER 5

CHARLIE WOKE UP the next morning much as she had the one before—early, rested, hungry, guilty. She was on a roll here.

Nothing like murder and being away from home to get some quality sleep. She ordered a bagel, coffee, and milk in deference to her type D stomach. A proud and efficient type A personality, Charlie had been saddled with an underachieving digestive track.

I was too sick and tired to do anything about the bicycle cop last night, she told her other self. I mean, what good does it do to kill myself when it wouldn't make the cop, or Pat the pilot, rise from the dead? I am not God.

You are a woman of elastic morals.

I am a survivor in a totally fascinating but corrupt world.

So was Attila the Hun.

Charlie crawled into bed with her diminished breakfast, drank all of the milk first, then turned on the news. Good old Barry and Terry filled her in on a few details of the bicycle cop's demise but didn't report if it had happened on the Strip like Patrick Thompson's. Terry mentioned briefly that investigators were looking for a black limousine, license number unknown, and went on to workers at the Yucca Mountain site who were claiming a cover-up in the investigations into their charges that grains of radioactive sand had been discovered in their baloney sandwiches.

"The DOE's Yucca Mountain Project Office," Barry assured Terry and Charlie, "has pointed out once again that, though the mountain is being prepared to store radioactive waste, no significant amount has been delivered as yet and also that the workers' sandwiches were assembled elsewhere. Workers maintain that large quantities of various forms of hot waste material is even now being tested inside the mountain to determine the facility's usefulness as a safe storage area for the literally infinitely hazardous stuff."

"Meanwhile, that other area is in the news again today too," Terry added, unaware of the bright smear of lipstick on a front tooth. "The apparently unlimited curiosity of tourists in the supersecret government base shown on the maps only as Area Fifty-one caused trouble again yesterday both at tiny Rachel, the closest town, and on an unmarked dirt road that leads off across the vast uninhabited desert. Two hunters from Michigan claim they were forced to turn back by armed men in aviator sunglasses and dark leather jackets."

Terry had gotten the news of her unsightly tooth, probably from the little receiver behind her ear, about halfway through the first sentence. It dimmed her smile drastically. Charlie could see her relief just as the taped interview with the two hunters from Michigan replaced her on the screen.

Officer Graden probably died because of you. He probably made forbidden inquiries about Pat the pilot because you insisted Pat was murdered. So, how safe are you—the star witness?

So, what are you saying? I should have ignored Pat's murder, let it pass for pedestrian error?

Why had Pat been flying over Yucca Mountain? If it was being dug to form storerooms for the bad stuff, what would anybody be able to see from the air?

The hunters from Michigan drove a snazzy Ford Expedition,

shown hanging from the end of a tow chain. They were particularly angered that, on the way back toward Rachel on the dirt road, all of their heavy-duty tires had been slashed.

Charlie ate the bagel dry and wondered how "tiny Rachel" could support a towing service. Maybe by putting sharp things in the road after a tourist vehicle had set out for Groom Lake. And she'd read somewhere that the mysterious guards of Area 51's borders wore camouflage uniforms.

She turned off the TV, poured her coffee, and, for penance, took her Toshiba notebook out of the safe in the closet to check her E-mail.

Type A types may sleep better away from home, but they do not vacation like other people.

There was a message from Larry Mann, her assistant, one from Ruby Dillon, Richard's office manager and right-hand woman, one from Mitch Hilsten, superstar. Nothing from Libby—both a comfort and a worry.

Libby Greene had an old car, a new computer, a new boyfriend, and a new part-time job. Charlie didn't know where to expect trouble next—she just knew to expect it.

Libby has made it to seventeen without screwing up major. That's more than you can say.

Ruby wanted to know why the hell Richard wasn't answering his E-mail or her phone calls. Richard, determined he and his subordinate would get away from the office, had refused to bring his pager or cell phone and insisted Charlie do likewise.

Larry hoped she was having a good time and getting some rest. Reynelda Goff was giving her publisher trouble over revisions to *Bewitched and Bedeviled in Boulder,* which, if you knew Boulder, sounded more like a nonfiction book than a historical novel. (Reynelda was of the age to say "an" historical novel.) The title had almost nothing to do with the story. But it did relate to last year's news event in Boulder, which related to why Pitman's Publishing paid such a ridiculous price for it. Reynelda had turned artistic on them—not an unusual happening when big money makes one suddenly famous. But the news event and the fame had faded by now and the book still hadn't made it to the printer.

There was an analogy between publishing and Las Vegas here that Charlie Greene didn't want to think about.

Larry had a few more office details to relate, one a promising query on Sheldon Maypo for a possible writing job at an ad agency. Pitch a treatment for a feature film and get a job writing commercials. Hey, anything's better than nothing, and Shelly wasn't getting any younger.

Charlie finished off the coffee while responding to Larry's questions and warned him of the problem with Georgette Millrose. She was tempted to answer Ruby Dillon's post with Tami the bodybuilder, but Charlie liked her job. She did not mention the two murdered men and her growing concern that the two thugs were responsible for both and that at least one knew she was staying here.

Mitch Hilsten wanted to know why she didn't return his calls, why he'd had to go on-line to get in touch with her. Charlie just didn't know, so she didn't answer his E-mail either.

She locked the computer back in the safe, showered, dressed, and sat on the bed. She had to tell someone of her suspicions about Officer Graden's death. For someone with elastic morals, she was great at guilt.

She checked her electronic Day-Timer. It was Tuesday.

She knew that.

She had a luncheon appointment with Evan Black.

She knew that too. Somehow, she didn't figure he'd show. But she'd be there in case. She had about two hours to kill at blackjack, or finding out which police station housed the bicycle cops, or wandering around openly to see if the goon in the Jacuzzi was following her, or she could just do nothing.

Charlie had lost the skill to just do nothing years ago, when she realized she was a kid with a kid to raise. But Richard

Morse saved her the need to make a decision.

"Charlie, I'm in love," he breathed over the house phone. "I need your help."

"Whoa, I don't think I can help you there." I barely fought off Tami myself. "I've been around, but not that far."

"But you're a woman."

"That's not the answer to all problems, Richard. I mean, it's not like compounding or anything." But she agreed to meet him down by the gleaming black Dodge Stealth in the lobby.

"So where's"—she almost slipped and said Tami—"this wonderful new love?" Surely, Tami wouldn't accost Charlie in all this public.

But Richard led her around the Stealth, a prize for some contest that offered yet another opportunity to part with your money, and through the rows of bleeping, blinking slots to the blackjack tables. He pointed to Bradone McKinley.

She played at the same table as yesterday, the same pit boss keeping watch, the one with the clenching fist. Suddenly, he was watching Charlie too.

"Is that class or what? I took one look at her, Charlie, and knew. I just knew. Like in them dumb romance novels. Me, Richard Morse, can you believe it?"

Richard, who'd never read a novel, let alone a romance novel, often talked like a truck driver, but he always dressed well, everything tailor-made just for him, and not in Hong Kong either. Most agents dressed like used-car salesmen. Today, he was suitably dressed down in a tan blazer and shirt open at the neck. Charlie had seen this outfit before, but she'd never seen his face so radiant.

"Richard, that's the woman who turned a hot shoe into a fortune yesterday morning. Remember, I told you at the pool?"

"Can't be—she's losing like a just cause. But look at her—serene and happy as a lobster anyway. That's—"

"Class. I know." Losing is what she's supposed to be doing now. Or lose her livelihood. But Charlie had to admit Bradone

McKinley was a whole flight of stairs up from Tami. Richard's dapper outfit included a silk scarf like film directors used to wear in black-and-white movies. It mercifully concealed his Tami hickey. "Richard, you've been divorced three times." And survived our bodybuilder. "What do you need me for?"

"This is different. I wanted you to get to know her. Find out if she is married, involved, you know."

"I had dinner with her last night. She's not married. She has a houseboy. I don't know if she's involved." And she's no kid. Probably no more than fifteen years younger than you, which is not your style, boss. "I do know she travels a lot and is very independent. She's a practicing astrologer."

"I don't care if she's an astronaut. And as long as you know her, you can introduce us."

"Let's wait until she's done losing, okay? She's also very serious about blackjack."

They didn't have long to wait. Bradone was one of two at the table, the other player—an Asian gentleman. The house cleaned up. Bradone rose and bowed slightly to the dealer and her partner in loss, an almost-smile on her lips.

"Just look at that," Richard the smitten effused. "That's elegance. That's Greta Garbo meets Julia Roberts, right?"

Bradone, in powder blue with navy accents today, walked toward them, the grin turning unmistakable, the eyes in full satisfied hilarity. To Charlie, she resembled more Faye Dunaway meets Agent Scully.

"Charlie, how nice to see you again." The mesmerizing voice took hold of Charlie as before and Bradone took her arm, overlooking Richard Morse completely. "You know, I realized after we parted last night where I remembered seeing you. You're a very close friend of Mitch Hilsten, right? You lucky girl. And you didn't even mention it. I told you all about me."

"She doesn't love him anymore," Richard said, taking Charlie's other elbow and squeezing hard. "Hi, I'm Richard Morse. Of Congdon and Morse? Charlie works for me."

"I never loved him. I still like him as much as I ever did." I just don't know what to say to him.

"Bradone McKinley." She reached across Charlie to shake his hand, and he had to let go of Charlie's elbow to take it. "Have you two had breakfast?"

"Yes," Charlie said.

"No," Richard said, and actually bowed. "But allow me the pleasure."

"Allow me the pleasure?" Charlie stared at him, but he ignored her.

So did Bradone. "No, I insist. You must come up to the penthouse."

The penthouse put Richard's pseudo-Tudor mansion in Beverly Hills to shame. Marble columns, a butler and a cook.

"I'd heard about these," Richard whispered. Poor Richard, he only had a suite. And they'd come up on a totally different elevator. "These are only for the mega–high rollers. What's she doing playing down in the casino with the riffraff? And blackjack to boot?"

The butler, Reed, poured them coffee. The cook, Brent, was off in the less formal regions, preparing something Bradone claimed would amaze them. They were already amazed. And they were from Hollywood. Bradone was off either making or taking a telephone call.

"You mean there's more than one of these penthouses?"

"Oh yeah, three anyway." Richard sat, visibly deflated, on the edge of a billowy couch like he was afraid it would consume him if he relaxed. "You got—what?—eight acres of pool and tennis and putting range deck down there, there's gotta be a lotta here up here." This was the same man who'd said, "Allow me the pleasure"?

Charlie should have enjoyed his discomfort. Instead, she felt sorry for him.

Why? He puts *you* down every chance he gets.

"Richard? I have a problem. I need help."

"*You* have a problem?" He snorted and gestured to the walls of window that looked out on Vegas and beyond. "Look at this. What chance I got with this woman?"

"Richard, Georgette Millrose fired me yesterday. And I witnessed a murder the night before. And I'm fairly sure it had something to do with a cop dying in a hit-and-run later that night. I'm worried the killers might think I have the same information the cop did. All I know is what the guys who committed the first murder—which the cops still think was an accident—look like. And I saw one of them here at the hotel."

"Well, it probably was an accident. Charlie, you don't want to get involved in murder in this town. And has Millrose ever made the *New York Times* best-seller list? After all these years? You're better off without her, and so is Congdon and Morse. Just help me figure out what to do about *my* problem." He gestured around the room again.

"Evan Black was involved with the first murder victim and he's acting very funny about the whole deal."

"Charlie, babe, I'll back you on the Millrose thing to the hilt. But we both know Black is bucks. You know? What have I taught you?"

"Back off Black?"

"Good girl." He patted her knee and sat up straight as their hostess entered with Reed, the butler, and the amazing breakfast.

CHAPTER 6

CHARLIE GREENE TOOK a cab to Yolie's to take Evan Black to lunch, certain he wouldn't be there. She was determined to enjoy her lunch anyway, to put off going to the police—she never had much luck with them somehow—and to get the taste of the amazing breakfast out of her mouth. It had come in a glass with a long spoon and looked, smelled, and tasted like yak curds. Not that Charlie had ever tasted yak curds, but she knew.

Yolie's smelled of mesquite, cilantro, garlic, and grilling flesh.

To her confusion, Evan Black rose from a table to greet her. He was having a martini. Up. Like Georgette Millrose had last night. Uh-oh.

Evan was shaved. His ponytail gleamed, his black silky outfit brightened with some kind of white flower at the throat where other people might wear a tie. She wouldn't ask.

Knowing better, she ordered a Dos Equis. It would take something special to scrape the yak curd crud from her tongue.

Tongue, shmung. You know beer will go straight to your thighs.

"Oh, shut up."

"All I said was hello."

"Evan, I'm sorry. Myself was reminding me that beer goes

directly to my thighs. When I get rattled, I talk to myself aloud. It's so embarrassing."

"Everybody who knows you, Charlie, knows that about you. It's one of your endearing qualities." Behind him, a window across the back wall revealed the biggest indoor barbecue she'd ever seen.

"What, talking to myself out loud?" That's what elderly people do. "Or getting rattled?"

"You pretend to be invulnerable and then blow it every chance you get."

"I do?" I do not.

"It's what makes you so special." Rubber belts drove pulleys that drove something enclosed in stationary horizontal tubes at least twelve feet long. That something rotated three-foot skewers over an open flame. "You try to be tougher than the guys. But you don't have to. You've got the guys in the palm of your hand from the beginning."

"This is some kind of macho stuff." Make her weakness sound like strength so she'll be happy and do what she's told. Been there.

"Such a cynic. Is there no romance in you, Charlie?"

"None." Getting knocked up at sixteen sheds a whole different light on things, trust me.

They spooned an excellent tomato and cilantro–type salsa onto thin, crispy flat bread.

Evan ordered a sampler plate for both of them. She hated when men did that. On the other hand, she did like not having to make the decision right now. When was she supposed to notice this was a vacation?

"So, how's your pilot holding up after the murder of her brother?"

"She's bitter. As she has a right to be."

"Did you know he was flying over Yucca?"

Evan Black had saved the olive in his drink until last. He

sucked it off the little plastic sword and said around it, "Now, how would you know that?"

"I told you I'd seen him at McCarran when Richard and I were heading for baggage claim. He was telling somebody about it on his cellular."

"Did he say anything else?" Her client had gone very still behind those tinted lenses.

"Something about some ridge. He was furious."

The waiter brought lumps of flesh on sizzling skewers, hacked slices off onto her plate. Lamb, chicken, beef, pork—this was after he'd filled the table with salad, potatoes, polenta, rice, vegetables, and more salsa. No yak.

"Brazilian cooking," Evan Black explained. "Everything's marinated for days in wine or beer and garlic and spices."

If this was lunch in Brazil, Charlie couldn't imagine dinner. Whatever it was, it tasted as good as it smelled. But she couldn't get through an eighth of it. This was her third meal of the day and it wasn't even 3:00 P.M.

"I didn't want to get involved in Pat Thompson's murder. It was his sister's duty to go to the police." Charlie tried to see through the dark lenses of his eyewear and into his thoughts, but there was too much light behind him. "She didn't go, did she?"

"No." From a fake banana tree at Evan's shoulder, a dead toucan inspected Charlie.

"And you honestly didn't see Pat come out of Loopy's with those men?" The banana tree was a poorly disguised support column that helped hold the roof out of their food.

"I honestly didn't. We were having fun, Charlie. I didn't really pay that much attention." Brown cloth covered the column/trunk and was embellished with green silk leaves, in need of a dusting, and banana bunches.

"If you knew who he was, why didn't you tell the police after he was killed?"

"Because I had to talk to Caryl first. I didn't know they were brother and sister. I thought they were lovers. But either way, I didn't want her finding out from some cop. I had to take your word that's who he was. And I honestly thought it was an accident, whoever the guy might be. Maybe I still do."

Charlie imagined the dead toucan winked a glass eye at her. "That bicycle cop who at least listened to me for a while?" And you did everything you could to dissuade him. "Have you heard that he's dead?"

"Graden, yeah. Look, Charlie, it's terrible what happened to him, and Pat too. But don't you see what you're doing? You're seeing a conspiracy here. Just because you noticed two guys who turned up dead doesn't mean it has anything to do with you or them with each other."

"In the same night? In a strange town?"

"I saw them both that night, and I don't feel responsible for their deaths."

"Look, I may have elastic morals, and I wasn't there when Officer Graden got hit by that car, but I do know Pat Thompson was cold-bloodedly murdered. And Evan? Yesterday, I saw one of the goons who did it—he was in the Jacuzzi with me and Richard at the Vegas Hilton."

" 'Elastic morals'?" His teeth didn't glint like Mitch Hilsten's but they showed off nicely against the olive skin and the dark clothing. The sight reminded Charlie that Libby's braces came off next month. "Charlie, who told you that? You are a very moral person. You're one of the straightest people I know."

That says something about where you come from, guy.

"Which is why I need to ask you a favor." He leaned toward her so earnestly, the flower at his throat nearly brushed his dirty plate.

"Because I'm morally straight, or because I'm seeing a conspiracy here, or because I'm your agent?" Actually, it took the whole agency to handle Evan Black. But Charlie got to take him out to lunch because he seemed to "interface" with her best. More bluntly, in his short association with Congdon and Morse, Charlie seemed able to talk Evan into or out of things

Richard wanted him into or out of. "And what do I get in return?"

"Now you're talking." He actually rubbed his hands together. "I'm going to offer you some totally free information."

"Yeah, right." Charlie slipped the agency's credit card to the waiter, who seemed disappointed he couldn't skewer them further.

"Charlie, I'm the one Patrick Thompson was flying over Yucca Mountain."

"You?"

"Well, me and Mel, my main man on the camera, and Toby, my second-unit gofer."

"And in return for this stunning piece of information, I am to . . ."

"Take a ride with me and Caryl? And Mel? There's something I want to show you."

"In your plane."

"Right."

"No deal. I hate flying."

"You're on a plane to New York every other time I call the agency."

"That's because I have to for my job. I love my job. This, I don't. So, no thanks."

When they were out in his car, he tried again, "I didn't think you were afraid of anything—fear of flying? Shit, this is even better."

"I'll take a cab back to the Hilton."

But his Land Rover pulled out into traffic. "Charlie, aren't you wondering what this is all about?"

"Well, let's see—two murders, a totally nasty type in the Jacuzzi with me"—not to mention an almost sexual attack by a Tami bodybuilder, and getting fired by a midlist author—"and I've been here what, three days?"

"No, not that—what I'm all about? What am I always all about. Really?"

Charlie had to stop and think. "Your work."

"Hey, same as you. Right?"

"So Yucca Mountain, conspiracy, and all this is . . . the next film?" You didn't use the word *movie* with this type.

"Charlie, come with us. It's not nearly as dangerous as driving the Four-oh-five to work every day. Besides, you love to gamble."

"Not with my life, I don't. Why can't we drive?"

"Take too long."

"I'm on vacation. I have time."

"The roads are restricted."

"Evan, tell me this doesn't have anything to do with the tiny town of Rachel and Area Fifty-one. Please?"

He grinned and pulled onto Maryland Parkway.

"You're kidding. Not you. That's been parodied on every TV network and cable too. It's so old, it's panned in commercials. There are people on the Internet bragging about taking photographs of each other peeing on the black mailbox. That story is a dead story."

Reaching across her, he pulled out a thick envelope from the glove compartment and began sorting through colored photographs as he drove.

Barry and Terry smiled at her from a mammoth billboard sporting the moral ALL THE NEWS YOU NEED, WHEN YOU NEED IT. Terry's teeth were brilliantly clean, but somebody had been taking drive-by potshots at Barry that had pretty much torn away one cheek and drooped his smile like the Phantom of the Opera's.

Evan handed her one of the photos. It showed a lean guy in Dockers pants and backpack clearly urinating against a post, grinning over his shoulder at the camera. You could just make out the tip of his penis at the end of his cupped hand and the lack of graffiti on the white mailbox atop the post.

"So?"

"So, I'm not as out of the traffic pattern as you think. So, I have a very good reason to want to involve you in this new project outside your wonderful agenting skills—two reasons, actually. And so"—he turned a quick grin to her before returning it to the traffic—"if you knew about the brouhaha on the Internet about the desecrating of the sacred black mailbox, you had to have been interested enough to go looking for it there, right?"

"But you'll be the laughingstock of the industry. Why would you do that to yourself? And this is a white mailbox. I know you, Evan, and your work. You are not into alien abduction and that kind of stuff." The black mailbox belonging to a rancher was the only sign on a least-traveled road that told the woo-woo nuts where to turn off to the undisclosed Groom Lake air base, and peeing on it had become a sort of in-joke.

"Forget the fucking mailbox. It's probably been painted orange with blue daisies by now. What is the one constancy in my diverse works?"

"The critics seem to think you have different themes . . . all presented with dark humor." Charlie had to be very careful when it came to talking "English lit." That was her major in college, and everything she'd learned had been turned inside out once she'd hit live publishing in New York, where she'd worked until a little over three years ago. She could still spout the jargon, but without much conviction. "At least you have themes."

"Exactly. And my theme in this project is conspiracy."

"That's a theme?"

"People's use of and need for it is. You are obviously a subject to explore, since you hold to the conspiracy theory on Pat's and Officer Graden's deaths. You are determined that you are a connection and somehow partly responsible. And you checked out Rachel and Groom Lake on the World Wide Web."

"Didn't Mel Gibson do this a couple of years ago?"

"We'll use a different title. And I have still another request to ask of you."

"I haven't granted your first request yet."

"We are making progress though—I've got you up to 'yet.' Charlie, I want to approach Mitch Hilsten about this project. What do you think?"

"You know damn well there isn't an actor in Hollywood who wouldn't give his swimming pool to work with you and get to go to Cannes and Telluride and all. I would assume it would depend on his schedule. But Evan, you don't want him."

"Of course I do. Who wouldn't?"

"He believes in this stuff. Really believes. Do you hear what I'm saying?"

"Yes, darling. That's why I want him." And the Land Rover swirled into the Las Vegas Hilton's multilaned and curving "landing strip."

"Well then, ask his agent."

"I prefer to approach his girlfriend."

A gorgeous uniformed kid opened her door. "I am not his girlfriend, Evan Black. He's a friend is all. I thought you were too. But tell you what—I'll go flying with you and Mel and Caryl if you and Caryl will go to the police station with me."

CHAPTER 7

STARTLED AT HOW smoothly she'd been maneuvered into this, Charlie watched the wind sock whip and the minuscule aircraft taxi from its parking space toward her.

Evan kept his plane at the small airport in North Vegas. And Caryl was his flight instructor as well as his pilot.

Caryl had not gone to the police station with them, but then, Charlie had no intention of approaching Mitch Hilsten about this conspiracy project either.

Charlie hadn't set foot in the Hilton, because Evan took her up on her offer immediately, calling Caryl and Mel on his cellular and telling them to meet him at the North Vegas airport. Caryl had been officially notified of her brother's accidental death and had identified his remains. Charlie swallowed hard at the thought and would never ask how.

At the police station, Charlie repeated her certainty that Pat Thompson had been murdered by the two men who'd walked him out of Loopy Louie's and her suspicion that Officer Graden's death was connected. And that she might be in danger from the same people. "They looked and acted like bouncers."

A pleasant-faced woman took Charlie's statement, keying it in as Charlie gave it, printing it out for Charlie to check over and sign. The officer couldn't be very high up in police hierarchy, because she typed too fast and was able to see them right away. "Maybe Officer Graden believed what I told him that night enough to look into it on his own. Maybe he left some notes in his desk or mentioned it to another officer. I really think you should investigate the possibility."

"Every effort is being made to find the person or persons responsible for Officer Graden's death. Thank you for your help. We'll be in touch." And with a half-smile like Bradone's, the policewoman added, "Enjoy your visit. I'm fairly sure you're in no danger, Ms. Greene."

"That was too easy," Charlie grumbled when Evan whisked her off to North Las Vegas. "And you weren't any help."

"That one is your conspiracy. Remember?"

"Isn't it a little late to be taking off now? Can't this wait till morning?"

"My aircraft may not be big and luxurious, Charlie, but it will actually fly at night."

It certainly wasn't big and luxurious. Charlie always took the aisle seat when flying commercially, so she wouldn't see how far away the ground was. There were four seats in this plane, and they were all window seats.

She absolutely would not encourage Mitch Hilsten to take part in Evan Black's conspiracy project.

At least Evan didn't offer to fly the plane himself. Caryl Thompson, her nice nipples well clothed like any pilot's should be, might be younger than Evan but at least she was an instructor and not a student.

Charlie, however, took no comfort in the woman's swollen eyes and faraway expression. Could grief overcome her pilot training and endanger them all? And Charlie still could not fathom why her own presence should be important on this trip.

This was one of those planes where you had to climb up on the wing and then into your seat by bending your body in ways bodies don't bend. Those in back had to get in first. Charlie was the first to board and the gyrations she had to perform to get into the fourth seat made it pretty clear that the only way she could get out was by plane crash.

Charlie would handle this situation by fantasizing she was somewhere else.

Mel Goodall, the main-man cameraman, crawled in back beside Charlie, took one look at her, and broke up—his long face scrunching into a short one. "It's okay, sweetheart. Old Mel will see nothing bad happens to you."

Old Mel was the angular guy with the penis tip and the backpack in the photograph Evan had shown her. He wore tan Dockers today too and looked more like an engineer than a cameraman. He was probably in his late forties—old enough to know better than to be on this rattletrap.

The pilot crawled in (literally) next and Evan last. Over the sound of the revving engine, hysterical propeller, and violently vibrating fuselage, the producer/director/writer bellowed back to Charlie, "You know my secret, Charlie? The rest have concept—I've got theme."

Jesus, God, Allah, and Buddha save us from the artistes of this world and me from this one in particular.

The artiste put on a headset to match the pilot's and tossed two more over to Mel, who stuck one on Charlie.

Buffeted by gale-force crosswinds, the tiny aircraft hurtled down a too-short runway and made it into the air despite rolling balls of attacking tumbleweed. Charlie's client let out a triumphant whoop, sort of a cross between Tarzan and a football fan.

Charlie Greene closed her eyes.

There was no wind, only warm sun bathing the recreation deck of the Las Vegas Hilton, no nerve-jangling music, no screaming children to splash water and wash out her contacts. Just peaceful adults swimming laps or talking quietly on white lounge chairs. Charlie slipped out of her sandals and net swimsuit cover and stepped to the side of the pool. Her—

"Charlie, open your eyes. That's Yucca Mountain down there," Evan Black shouted in her earphone, then began ordering pilot Caryl to turn and dive.

The midget plane was suddenly on its side, circling like a vulture, Mel manipulating a handheld mini through his window, which was a lot clearer and less scratched than hers. Up front, Evan manipulated outside cameras and watched the result on a monitor.

A flurry of clipped indecipherable messages in a male voice came from the headset.

"Radio contact," Caryl said softly. "Next stop, Dreamland."

"Dive," their leader commanded.

Jesus, instead of slipping into a heated swimming pool, Charlie was about to get shot out of the air by her own government. She hadn't wanted to be here. She'd have taken off the headset, except the rickety plane's noise was more frightening than the cockpit communications.

She'd always been astonished when the flight attendant on an airliner announced passengers could listen to the cockpit communications on channel whatever through the headphones at their seat. It was terrifying enough *not* knowing.

"Charlie," Evan said, "note that we are going in a straight line from Yucca Mountain to Groom Lake."

You are going in a straight line. I are going to lose my Brazilian lunch and yak crud.

"Open your eyes," Mel yelled, and shook her shoulder. "Or you'll get sick."

Tell me about it.

But she opened her eyes. They couldn't be more than twenty feet off the ground. Which was fine if the ground stayed flat. The ground did not stay flat. Charlie lost it. Not the lunch, but her control. "What are you guys, fucking nuts? Flying this low—don't tell me about going under radar. They can pick us off with a BB gun from here."

Then she lost her lunch. Mercifully into a plastic bag Mel

held under her mouth and closed quickly afterward. The cockpit still smelled awful.

"Reminds me of flying Vomit Airlines over the ditch." Caryl sounded almost nostalgic.

Here was Charlie Greene, scudding along the uneven ground with a bunch of loons.

"Everybody keep watch for roads, installations, stray vehicles, and buildings to avoid," their pilot instructed, taking over the command. "I've got all I can do to keep an eye on the landscape and the wind. This could get serious here."

Charlie could see the plane's shadow whipping over gullies and sagebrush and scratchy-looking bushes. Charlie was not fond of deserts in general, but southern Nevada was the meanest, ugliest of them all. The sand looked more abrasive, the rock more scoured. Even the mountains were deserts.

They almost crawled up the side of a low, sullen mountain range and dove down the other side, along a valley, and then up and out and over again.

Charlie closed her eyes. Had Pat Thompson been murdered for doing just what she was doing now?

"Almost there," Caryl said.

Charlie opened her eyes without meaning to.

"How much time can you give us?" Evan asked the pilot, and swung back to his monitor.

"Not much."

"We don't need much, got good stuff last time. Ready, Mel?"

"Loaded and ready."

"Start your cameras, boys." Caryl took them over a rise, barely, and Charlie caught a glimpse of runways wider and longer than anything she'd seen at Denver International, and immense shedlike buildings.

Then an orange light flooded the cabin. It didn't seem to bother the others. Charlie couldn't figure out why.

✣

"Charlie, open your eyes. This is stupid."

"You sure she isn't dead?"

"She's not dead. She's warm. Feel her."

"We're all warm, with that fire. Doesn't mean she's not dead."

"First piece of civilization we meet, we get some food in her. She lost all her Yolie's. At least it didn't go to her thighs."

Charlie lay flat out on the hard sand, except for her head, which rested on Evan's lap. A scratchy bush next to them waved its branches in the wind stirred up by the burning plane. Mel gathered tumbleweed and threw it into the flames. The smoke went straight up, leaving most of the sky dazzling with stars—a few of them shooting. Burning plane? "Did we crash? Am I hurt?"

"I don't think so. Try to sit up. No, we didn't crash." Evan sounded high, hyperexcited.

Charlie made it to her hands and knees. "Did we all make it out?"

But he had left her to help Mel throw tumbleweeds on the blaze. Its warmth felt good in front. Her behind felt frigid. Nothing felt injured. She made it to a wobbly standing position. "Where's Caryl?"

"Right here." The pilot walked past with armloads of dried tumbleweed. "Thanks for caring, Charlie."

Charlie stumbled closer to the fire's warmth. "If we didn't crash, why is the plane burning? Are you trying to make a beacon so search parties can find us?"

"No, we're destroying evidence," Mel explained with glee.

This guy needed help.

"And here's our second-unit gofer with the van now," Evan said, just as happy.

Distant headlights bobbed toward them.

"God, let's pray that's Toby." Caryl sketched a sign of the cross between her nipples.

"Women are so damned negative," Evan told Mel. "Why is that?"

"Damned if I know. But here's the cameras and Charlie's purse. Better get them and our asses out of here. Our trackers have to have seen this fire by now."

"What if everything doesn't burn?" Caryl insisted as the men rushed her and Charlie toward the approaching lights.

"Too late to worry it now. Life's a gamble, right?" Evan did his victory whoop again.

Charlie was glad to be alive. But she could do without that whoop.

"See how easy conspiracy is to manufacture, Charlie?" Evan bit into his Big Mac while she stuffed a bite of Ronald's Filet-o-fish into her mouth. The van sat in a far corner of a McDonald's parking lot.

The ride had seemed forever. The driver, Toby, remained cheerful even though Mel and Evan teased him endlessly about his lowly gofer status and about all his uncles. He'd dowsed the headlights, but the farther they got from the burning plane, the more the starry night illuminated the landscape around them. And probably them to anyone looking for them.

"How did you manufacture the orange light?" Charlie asked. That had impressed her.

"What orange light? Anybody else see an orange light?"

"Stop making fun of me, Evan."

"I don't know about any orange light. I do think you got a little overexcited."

"Overexcited, hell—she blacked out on us," Mel said.

"I saw an orange light," Charlie insisted.

"She's remembering the plane burning."

"That didn't look orange to me."

"Don't let these jerks get to you." Toby had a lopsided grin and dark curly hair cut short in back and on the sides, but curls tumbled down over his forehead. He sucked the last of his cola through the straw and started up the van.

"Hey, Tobias," Mel said, "what's your uncle Louie going to say about tonight?"

"Why should he even know? He doesn't have anything to do with this."

"You tell him everything, don't you?" Evan did his boisterous guy laugh.

"Is he in for a surprise tonight." Mel joined his boss in the hilarity. "Isn't that right, Charlie?"

"Planes can't just disappear." Charlie didn't know what was going on, but she didn't find the whole thing a bit funny. "They'll have search planes out looking for it when it doesn't come back."

"All records have mysteriously disappeared, right, Toby? And all records of my ownership too. Damnedest thing."

Toby apparently had this friend who worked at the little airstrip in North Vegas.

"Yeah, our gofer here's got friends in high places and too many uncles."

"What I got, Goodall, is contacts. You're just envious."

"Clear as the skies were out there, some airliner will spot that fire and radio it in," Charlie persisted. She'd gotten involved in real trouble here. "You can't walk off and leave a whole plane. They'll find some identifying thing in the ashes, some metal gadget that won't burn. And they'll come after you, Evan. Why burn your own plane? Why not just fly off with it?"

"Because then they'd have had time to scramble and blow us out of the air. This way, they know where the plane is and all trace of any of us better be burned off what's left of it."

"Why are you so hot to involve me in this?"

"I wanted your take, as a conspiracy freak, on Groom Lake.

And I wanted you to be able to tell Mitch Hilsten what you saw firsthand. Simple, right?"

"Wrong, Evan. Serial numbers and things like that don't burn. The original owner at least has got to be on file somewhere."

"What can I say? Life's a gamble, Charlie." But everyone had grown suddenly somber. "All we really need is a little time and some magic will happen—won't it, Toby? And everything, including you, will be safe as grass, Charlie."

The van turned onto a heavily lighted parkway, and for a second a teardrop glinted in a free fall from Caryl's face before it was lost in her dark clothing. She hadn't joined in the teasing and laughter. More tears formed on her lashes, but her voice came more vengeful than sad. "The plane was listed originally in my brother's name. Nobody can go after Pat now."

CHAPTER 8

CHARLIE STILL FELT strange as she stepped up to the Hilton's glittering entrance. For once, it wasn't her stomach. The McFood seemed to have settled peacefully. More her head—not an ache exactly. Maybe it was just her anger at how Evan Black thought he could use her. It would take more than magic to get them out of this.

"Holy shit," a man said behind Charlie, and she turned at the door, to see him stepping out of a cab. The inside light and the cab's headlights sat in a sea of night under the immense marquee. All the lights and the razzamatazz at the fountain and the rows of lights under the marquee had gone out.

A bell captain passed her on his way to the luggage the cabbie was unloading. "Talk about blinding night, huh?"

It was spectacular. Charlie had an errant thought: If all the lights went out in Vegas, would it still exist? Like, if a tree falls in the forest and nobody sees it . . .

Get thee to bed, Charlie G, you're all done.

For once, we agree.

The elevator quit on her a floor below hers, but at least the door had already opened to let her out. None of the elevators seemed to be working up or down, so she took the stairs one flight to her room, flicked on the lights, flicked off her clothes, and stepped into the shower just as the lights went out. She showered by feel and managed to find her nightshirt and the bed by the light of the Vegas night outside the window.

But then she couldn't sleep. It had been one hell of an unvacation day. And the room was stuffy without the ventilation fan blowing canned air into it.

Finally, Charlie took her frustration to the wall of window and, kneeling on the couch to face it, reassured herself that life was indeed still normal, fully aware of the irony in that. She had no idea which direction Yucca Mountain and Area 51 and the smoldering ruins of a claustrophobic little airplane might be—but she was alive, warm, fed, and well. And she decided she must have imagined the orange light, a vestigial smear of which she imagined still lurked somewhere at the back of her eyeballs. Which didn't mean the United States government was collecting her DNA from a portion of the plane that hadn't burned.

The electricity might be out in her room and parts of the hotel, but the lights of the Strip drowned out the star show that played over Area 51. Closer in, the immense Hilton sign still had juice. It flashed alternate messages across the night—WELCOME AMA and MOST CASH BACK and TWENTY-FOURTH CENTURY IS NOW.

Across the street, BOYZ R US. A block up the street, the spindle of the Stratosphere's Tower was lighted from below and above, the restaurant on top looking like a spaceship with the crazy roller-coaster lights crawling around its top. Below, a string of Metro Police cars, lights flashing, sirens ominously stilled, pulled into the winding drive of the Hilton. You rarely heard emergency sirens here, peculiar for a city this large and busy. Maybe warning sirens would nullify the party ambience. Had they come for Charlie already?

She waited as long as she could and then crawled back into bed and slept through to noon, like someone on vacation should, the ventilation fan and all the lights on when she woke. And no authority at the door to arrest her. She dressed in front of the TV and Barry and Terry on *Live at Noon.*

Nothing new on the hit-and-run murder of Officer Graden. The man guilty of trying to jaywalk Las Vegas Boulevard had been identified as Patrick Thompson, a local pilot employed by a small "undisclosed local airline." No apology for their having blamed his rash decision to cross a gridlocked street during volcano rush hour on his status as a stupid tourist.

And a mysterious power outage at the Las Vegas Hilton.

"So far, Nevada Power has not identified the cause," Barry told Charlie. "But it affected only certain areas in the hotel and casino—not the entire building."

"Yes, Barry, but people were trapped in elevators, some up to ten minutes. Bets on the casino floor had to be put on hold until emergency generators kicked in, and the probable cause was an apparently successful robbery.

"With the lights out and surveillance cameras temporarily out of commission, clever robbers either took advantage of the outage or planned it to rob the cage at the Las Vegas Hilton's casino. The Hilton has not disclosed how much was taken, but the thieves were gone by the time police arrived. Hotel security is still checking for possible clues, but all guests are assured the building is safe and the casino remains open.

"Sources hint that this was unlike the recent rash of casino-cage robberies by Los Angeles gang members. It appears to have been a far more sophisticated bunch of thieves. Only slight injuries were reported.

"Never fear though—Captain Kirk and Mr. Spock were not affected by the outage."

"Right, they don't operate on electricity. They operate on warp drive or something."

Charlie decided against room service. She wanted to get downstairs, where there would be people. She was in the bathroom doing her face and hair when the TV couple went on to the next story.

This one about a downed aircraft located on the perimeters of the undisclosed Area 51.

"There were no survivors," Terry announced sadly, as well she might.

"Yes, Terry, the plane was incinerated in the crash. Officials are searching local and area-wide airports for clues to the aircraft's point of origin, and they ask anyone missing relatives or friends who might have been flying a Mooney 201 aircraft yesterday to contact local police or the Clark or Lincoln County Sheriff's Department."

"The air force has no comment," Terry added unnecessarily. "And for you UFO buffs, the word from Rachel is that there were no disturbing incidents in the night sky out that way last night."

"Terry, this only goes to reinforce the warnings this station, editorials in the *Las Vegas Sun,* and law-enforcement officials in Lincoln and Clark counties have been repeating for some months now—the ridiculous interest in the vast restricted areas and wastelands in this state can be dangerous, unfruitful, and deadly."

"Right, if you want to have fun, come to Vegas instead."

Charlie had no more than switched off the set than came a pounding at her door.

Jesus.

"Housekeeping?" a frightened voice queried from the hall.

The peephole revealed an Asian woman. Charlie was somehow not surprised when two robust gentlemen in suits entered the room with the housekeeper. Hell, she'd opened that same door to Super Tami, hadn't she?

Totally polite and humorless, one, in the interests of the protection of all hotel guests, asked permission and explained the need for a search of her room—possibility of robbers in the hotel. He went on to question her activities the night before. She lied. Instead of fleeing a burning Mooney 201 somewhere near an undisclosed Area 51, she'd been playing blackjack at every casino on the Strip.

Meanwhile, the other totally polite and humorless suit—

public security folks here wore dark blue policelike uniforms—looked for robbers in her drawers, empty luggage, behind the couch, in the shower, in the closet, and had absolutely no trouble with the combination of the small safe where she kept her notebook computer.

Having determined that neither robbers nor their proceeds lurked in Charlie's room, they solemnly rechecked her identification and went off to secure other areas. She left the Asian housekeeper to do her job and sought sustenance downstairs.

The coffee shop, awash in dangerously aging waitresses, fake red flowers on fake vines hanging from fake-wood rafters, fake trees planted in fake stucco Southwestern adobe–theme planters, was uncrowded for this time of day, and Charlie sat facing the room. Having been here often enough to know the food wasn't even pseudo-Santa Fe, she ordered an omelette and studied those souls on her side of the fake stucco planters who would brave a hotel with electric and robber problems.

No thugs in sight, no commando types from her government—just Bradone McKinley and Richard Morse across the room, in a booth for two, facing each other over the table, coffee cups to lips and postures suggesting her boss had scored.

No way. Charlie was imagining again, like the orange light she and apparently the denizens of Rachel, Nevada, hadn't seen.

Charlie gulped at her own coffee and tried to blink smears from her contact lenses. She'd have thought Richard would have lost interest after the yak crud, and why would Bradone dine here, with her own cook and butler upstairs?

You haven't checked for messages at the desk or E-mail from Libby or the office.

"Well, I have to eat, you know."

"I know, sweetie, and here's your omelette." Her server was considerably older than Edwina, Charlie's mother.

"Thanks, uh . . . this looks wonderful." Charlie determined

to open a retirement account the minute she got home, and added sheepishly, "I talk to myself."

"Don't we all, sweetie?" The elderly server walked off on ankles swollen to the knee. Her name badge identified her as Ardith.

Ardith shouldn't have to be working now.

Yeah, she could be starving instead.

Big tip, right?

The omelette wasn't anything you'd order wine with, but it was smooth and bland and comforting.

"You eat too many eggs, kid." Richard stood over her, Bradone, with that sort of smile, behind him.

"I know." And I had McDonald's last night. What could this impressive woman see in Charlie's boss? "Did you hear about the robbery?"

"Yeah, we missed all the excitement, didn't even notice the lights went out. So how did the lunch with our boy Evan go yesterday?"

A lot better than a little airplane ride later. So, they *had been* together last night. Life was becoming one big mystery. "We need to discuss Evan Black, Richard, and his new project. He's getting himself and me into some trouble."

"We'll be on the pool deck. Check the office messages and come on out when you're done."

Charlie's E-mail had some personal messages as well as news from the office. And the message light on her telephone was blinking. Would there never be time for blackjack on this trip?

The voice mail was from her mother. Funny, Edwina Greene had a computer, but she never E-mailed Charlie. The last thing Charlie wanted was to answer it, but the last time she'd ignored her mother's needs, she hadn't discovered the woman had cancer until Edwina'd gone into the hospital and a neighbor called to inform Charlie of the pending mastectomy.

All in all, Charlie thought she carried her burden of guilt pretty well for the unwed mother of a terrifying teen. She didn't ever expect to get hardened to it, mind you, but she'd managed to make a place for herself and her daughter in this world. Talking to her mother, however, always diminished any pride she might have built up in her triumphs.

Stop whining and call your mother.

Charlie's mom lived in Boulder, where she worked as a professor of biology—rats and bats—at the University of Colorado. Where Charlie was born and her daughter conceived on the wrong side of a tombstone. Charlie's greatest nightmare was that Edwina would move to Long Beach and the world would ask three generations of totally incompatible women to live in the same state.

Charlie loved her mother—she just couldn't stand her.

"Well, it took you long enough." It was as if Edwina had been sitting on top of the phone.

I've been busy, like, you know, dead people, crazy clients, midlist authors on a toot. "So what's the problem now?"

" 'So what's the problem now?' " her mother mimicked, and Charlie took a pillow off the bed to kick. "I'm the problem in this family, right?"

"Edwina? I'm listening. But only through the next three words."

Whoa, is that power talk?

Charlie couldn't believe she'd said it either.

"Three words. Never . . ." and Charlie's mother hung up.

I'm going to kill that woman.

You are not, she merely followed your orders. You do not order your mother.

Charlie punched her mother's number, determined not to begin the conversation with an apology. "I'm sorry. What's wrong?"

"I don't know. How many words do I get?"

CHAPTER 9

LARRY SAYS PITMAN'S has given Reynelda another deadline extension, but this is it, and the book clubs are pissed because their schedules are shot to hell too," Charlie told Richard Morse, who was splayed contentedly on the lounge chair next to that of the lovely Bradone. Bradone, a tad thick in the thigh, could be hiding some corrective-surgery scars under her one-piece, but the woman was firm and shapely for any age. Her houseboy probably doubled as a personal trainer.

Richard sagged some about a middle that had been lipoed at least once that Charlie knew, thanks to documented office gossip. But he looked pretty good compared to gray chest hair nearby. Didn't even bother to hide his hickey.

Richard roused himself enough to ask Charlie, "What's your mother say? She knows this Goff woman better than anybody."

Charlie's mother had claimed on the phone to be on the verge of suicide because of hot flashes now that she couldn't have hormone-replacement therapy. Charlie had told her to sit in front of a fan in her office and to air-condition the house.

Edwina had hung up again. Charlie dialed again. Apologized again. Jeesh—you'd think hot flashes were fatal.

"My mother says Reynelda Goff is suffering from menopausal symptoms and has these panic attacks that—"

"Jesus Christ in a chorus line, is nothing safe from old women in menopause?" Richard sat up and whipped off his sunglasses. "Well, I mean, most broads don't make such a big deal of all that shit," he added weakly when he noticed Bradone had whipped off her sunglasses too.

" 'Broads'? I haven't heard that anachronism in years. You do mean shit like breast cancer," Bradone McKinley said, far too politely. "If she can't take hormones—"

"No, it's my mom who had the breast cancer and can't take hormones," Charlie said, coming to her boss's defense. She *must* love her job. "Reynelda's a neighbor of Edwina's who—"

"Who wrote a book and got menopause," Richard chimed in, but then he added disastrously, "Why can't beautiful, young, sane women write books?"

"I expect they do." There was something reassuring in Bradone's smirk and the possibility that the planets had not stood still for her because Richard Morse scored.

Poor Richard, so insulated by his power status in the positioning of the genders in the Hollywood universe, didn't hear what he really said. He'd even get torqued when Charlie refused to appreciate insulting jokes. And yet he could be so savvy in other ways. Didn't add up.

You're the one who told her mother to sit in front of a fan.

"Ruby is about to implode if you or I don't answer her messages, Richard. And I don't know how to answer them."

Richard decided Charlie could tell him what Ruby Dillon wanted and he could give Charlie the answer and she could tell his office manager. All because Charlie knew how to E-mail.

"I'm not your secretary." But she jotted down a few notes to pass on to Ruby as he tried to impress his new girlfriend with sage answers to mundane office matters.

That was another thing. If you didn't learn the new technology, you'd fall behind at Congdon and Morse. If you did, someone above you in the food chain would use you and these skills to make his more important work easier. Charlie had other serious misgivings with these timesaving electronic devices that ate up all your time to learn and, when you finally did, forced you to upgrade to something new and the "learning" started all over. Libby'd had to help her out more than once. But Libby learned computer-ease at school, far earlier in life than Charlie. Larry, Charlie's assistant, treated it with contempt and deigned only to use E-mail, the word processor, and a spreadsheet to log Charlie's schedule, phone calls, and the script submissions that crowded his cubicle.

No message from Libby today. Libby hadn't contacted Edwina either. Charlie could only hope and swallow a lot. She hoped Libby would contact their neighbor Maggie Stutzman if anything earthshaking occurred. Both Maggie and Libby had instructed Charlie to take a vacation and not call them. They'd call her.

"What about our boy in Folsom?" Richard asked importantly and informed Bradone, "Keegan Monroe, screenwriter, inked *Phantom of the Alpine Tunnel, Shadowscapes,* and *Zoo Keepers.*"

Edwina was threatening to go off tamoxifen—a drug prescribed to block natural estrogen production in her body—because the unnatural estrogen prescribed to head off hot flashes, panic attacks, heart disease, osteoporosis, and old age had given her breast cancer.

Everything Charlie'd read said that synthetic estrogen did not cause breast cancer.

"Actually, Keegan's on chapter ten of his novel," Charlie answered. Which is further than he'd ever gotten before.

"Christ, with all the time he's got on his hands, he could of written three *Moby Dicks.* Tell him to finish the damn book and get back to screenplays that make money."

Edwina, who smoked, had said, "Well, tobacco companies used to say cigarettes don't cause cancer too." She'd sent Charlie a folded insert that had come in the box containing an old Premarin bottle. It listed, in minuscule print, breast cancer as a possible side effect.

Now Edwina had found a new wonder drug on her own. Something she called "snake oil."

"Snakes don't make oil, right?" Charlie asked, interrupting whatever it was Richard was saying.

"No, dinosaurs do." He hated being interrupted. "Snake oil—where the hell did that come from?"

"Edwina called. She wants to go off the tamoxifen and rub this stuff on her skin instead."

"Rub snake oil on—your mother's always been a few bricks short of a bale, but—"

"*Snake oil* is a term used historically to mean a magic elixir, a medicine or concoction that can cure all your ailments at once," Bradone explained. "Hucksters used to sell it at fairs and outdoor markets. They probably still do, but by mail-order catalog. It often contained a good dose of alcohol or a potent drug like cocaine."

"Not even somebody with menopause should rub good hooch on their outsides," the president of Congdon and Morse said with weary disgust.

"She mentioned something about yams too."

"She's going to rub herself with sweet potatoes?" Richard was on his feet. "I'm going to the gents."

"Where did he learn to speak like that? Old movies?" The astrologer watched Charlie's boss strut off and almost laughed.

"Thanks for not jumping on the 'few bricks short of a bale' thing. That was a trap. He mixes metaphor, analogy, and worn-out sayings on purpose. But when he wants to, he can be sort of intelligent."

The astrologer turned her amused attention to Charlie. "I expect your mother was talking about wild-yam cream. The wild Mexican yam root contains natural progesterone and helps to adjust hormone levels at all ages and for both sexes, but I've known women who have been on it for months with no results. It depends on who's making it and how reliably it's standardized."

Because of the aging of the baby boomers, this was the latest snake oil, according to Bradone, and everybody wanted in on the profits.

"Why can't the drug companies make and standardize the cream in their labs? The FDA could test it."

"Because drug companies can't patent natural products. It wouldn't pay them to make and test a drug anybody who wanted to could make. Charlie, I think your mother should think long and hard before disobeying her oncologist. Cancer's not to be toyed with. We don't know that natural hormones react that much differently from synthetic hormones."

Forget the IRA and the DRIP and the compounding. Charlie decided to die before ever reaching the age of the dreaded menopause. She wouldn't want people like Richard talking about her that way.

"Are we done with the sweet potatoes, ladies?" Richard asked with severe condescension upon his return. "Any more agency business I should take care of?" He picked up his towel and glasses case. A signal for Charlie to say there was no more business for today.

Actually, the sweet potatoes thing wasn't the worst. Mitch Hilsten threatened to come to Vegas if she didn't answer his E-mail. "Evan Black and his project, remember? I'm in trouble, and so is he."

"Oh, you're always in trouble. Relax, kid. Catch me later. Got to go now." He reached a proprietary hand down to Bradone, who took it to rise from her lounge chair.

"I'll see you later too, Charlie. I have this delicious secret to share with you." When he'd turned away to the Grecian Spa, she mouthed, "About Richard."

Charlie looked at the pool, where two kids had cleared out the adults with power cannonball dives. Thanks a lot, Captain Kirk. Where were these security types when you needed them?

She hurried to her room and changed into comfortable clothes instead of answering the office business or checking for more E-mail. To hell with Richard, and Evan Black too. Life was short and unpredictable and she'd never felt more aware of that. She wanted to be like Bradone, who knew how to live life to the hilt.

Charlie, catching herself grimacing at the mirrored elevator on her way down, forced her mouth to grin, and took a shuttle to the blackjack tables on Fremont Street. She had thirty grand to lose, since she wouldn't live to see menopause and Libby wouldn't make it to college with her braces off.

Compared to the ever-raging extravagance of the Strip, Fremont Street had gone seedy and become a refuge for locals. Like organized crime of old, organized corporate America had a finger in most pots, and entertainment in all forms was particularly vulnerable to its ready cash. Gambling was a uniquely profitable form of entertainment, and someone up there had looked down on Fremont and seen a bargain.

The street was now a covered mall, hostile to panhandlers and overt lewdity, its dome a state-of-the-art laser show at night, with enough music and panoramic extravaganza to make your neck ache. The spectacle emptied casinos and shops so locals and jaded people like Charlie could slip in and find single-deck blackjack with few other players and not too many nasty rules. But it was daylight and the casinos were crowded.

Mitch Hilsten threatening to come to town. No word on what Libby and her new boyfriend were up to. Whatever they did, they probably couldn't do it in the house. Tuxedo didn't like him. For once, that damned cat showed some sense.

Determined to lose money, probably the easiest thing to do in Vegas, Charlie couldn't.

Blackjack was the one game where you could supposedly beat the house advantage by paying strict attention. She couldn't remember lunch, never mind the cards.

Dumb Richard having his way with savvy Bradone. Wild

sweet potatoes, for godsake. Probably the CIA and the FBI and the IRS, and the armed response boys—they all had to be in cahoots—were looking for Charlie because she flew over Area 51. With all this, nobody could have concentrated. And still she won.

"Lady, you need a drink or a massage, know that? Here you are winning and yet you are not happy," said a man beside her. "What'll it be?"

What would Bradone do in this situation? Lighten up, she could almost hear her new friend say, go with the flow.

"Red zin," Charlie answered the man, and watched the dealer push more chips her way. The only thing Charlie hadn't been worrying about was the Thug.

This occurred to her suddenly because the man beside her, at the moment explaining very meaningfully to the cocktail hostess that yes, there was too such a thing as red zinfandel and she'd best get a glass of it here in a hurry, was the Thug.

CHAPTER 10

When it came, the red zin tasted exactly like the ubiquitous house burgundy, sort of like your well wine. Charlie didn't mention the wine problem to the man who'd nudged poor Patrick Thompson under the wheels of a car. Charlie wondered if that car was a black limo like the one that took out Officer Timothy Graden. Or maybe the same one. How many cars had run over the hunk pilot before Charlie made it to the curb to view the result? How could the people in that first car have missed seeing the act in progress? Or were they looking over their shoulders at the volcano?

No, Charlie didn't think she'd complain about the wine.

Still, she kept winning. Maybe it's better not to concentrate—which she certainly wasn't. And every time she looked up, some people at the bar waved in her direction. Charlie wanted to cash in and get out of the Golden Nugget. She'd have been happy to give it all back to be able to leave for free.

The Golden Nugget, unlike most casinos, did not rely heavily on the color red. Colors here were a soothing plantation white—read cream—with gold trim. Latticework and mirrors. Taupe upholstery. If not for the presence of the Thug, Charlie would have felt comfortable here, would have calmed down, enjoyed herself. And if not for the strange people over at Claude's Bar who continued their unnatural interest in her. An overweight man and two women of girth.

"What you've got to understand, Mrs. Greene," the Thug said kindly, "is that the odds are against us all."

Mrs. Greene. Did that mean he knew about Libby? After the battering motherhood had taken—people still thought of mothers as "Mrs." Charlie took a slug of the official wine of the nonastute. Now it tasted like ashes.

The expanse of his shoulders would make more than two of Charlie's. His suit was gray, his manner overpolite. His dark hair, streaked with gray, hung in curls to those shoulders. Something mesmerizing about the thick lips and uneven teeth. Charlie wondered what Evan Black would think of her conspiracy theory now.

"But here you are, Mrs. Greene, beating the odds. And not enjoying a minute of it. It's obvious, right?" he asked the dealer, who remained noncommittal and nodded at the two cards dealt Charlie. The dealer showed ten.

Charlie waved away a hit without bothering to look at what she had. The three other players scratched for a hit.

All went bust.

Mr. Thug took Charlie's cards and laid them out. The ace and the jack of spades. Charlie smelled a setup.

She would have to talk to Bradone about how to lose. If she lived long enough to make that necessary.

"Excuse me, ma'am?" The overweight gentleman waver appeared suddenly at her side. He wore Bermuda shorts. Yes, they were plaid. Yes, he wore bifocals and a baseball hat and a grin to tear a face apart. "I hope you're not offended, but we"—and he motioned to the two well-stocked women grinning at her from stools at the bar—"wondered if you're that girlfriend of Mitch Hilsten or just a look-alike? I mean, we already seen four Elvises in two days."

Charlie tried to decide whether the setup was Bermuda Shorts or the Thug. Or the dealer dealing her such treasure. Somehow, Bermuda Shorts didn't seem a likely tie to the other two.

"It don't matter. I'm Ben Hanley, and they're my wife and her sister. We'd like to buy you a drink anyway. When you finish your game. We been watching you and wondering. And finally Betty figured out where we seen you before. On television. You know, when you and him fell off that cliff? Mitch Hilsten, I mean."

"How nice. I'd love to join you and the ladies," Charlie gushed, and turned, to find the curly-haired thug no longer at her side.

The Ben Hanleys and her sister not only bought Charlie a drink but accompanied her to Binions and the Las Vegas Club, helping her lose some of her winnings from the Nugget. She didn't see Mr. Thug again that afternoon, but he could have set a stranger on her tail. And there were still all those government types getting ready to pounce.

The type of people Charlie would usually avoid, Ben, Martha, and Betty, the sister, were reasonably good company for shields. They may have saved her life or her kneecaps, and she hoped she wasn't putting theirs in danger.

She took them back to the Hilton and treated them to dinner at the Baronshire. Betty and Martha, motherly types, soon had Charlie talking about her life and her relationship with Mitch Hilsten.

Charlie didn't want to be alone—even in the crowd that was Las Vegas. These people, unintimidated by the dark room and the formality suggested by the decor, were flying back to Wisconsin tomorrow and she'd never see them again.

"Mitch and I are just friends. We don't travel in the same circles—I mean, he's a superstar and I'm a literary agent," Charlie explained.

"That sure wasn't what it looked like on the TV," Betty said, emboldened by martinis. Everybody seemed to be drinking martinis these days. Both sisters did, but Ben stuck with beer. He ate as if there were no tomorrow and all the alcohol had made him quiet and flushed. He looked like a heart attack waiting to happen.

Both sisters wore round trifocals that covered half their faces and made their eyes appear larger than their noses. If Betty's hair hadn't been died flat black and Martha's allowed to stay almost white, they could have been hard to tell apart at a distance.

"Well, okay, we spent one night together in a seedy motel"—Charlie's unwanted fifteen minutes of fame—"but it was—"

"Just one of those things?" Martha lifted a dripping blood-drenched bite of prime rib to her mouth and chewed it a little so she could talk around it. "On TV, he looked exhausted, as I remember."

Charlie had met Mitch Hilsten in the Canyonlands of Utah at the wrong time of the month. Poor guy had been a teenage fantasy of hers and didn't stand a chance. But he took their encounter seriously, couldn't seem to understand Charlie's hormonal cycles—which her biologist mother inelegantly termed "estrus."

"Well yeah, they both did." Ben Hanley came to Charlie's defense. "Hell, they'd just been rescued from death on a cliff."

It had been over a year ago. Charlie's writers would have killed for that kind of exposure. Hell, she could have been on *Oprah.* Charlie just wanted to live it down.

She respected and admired the superstar, but, accustomed to years of celibacy at a time, she frankly preferred that blessed state. Life held enough complication. Every now and then, those one or two dangerous days of the month would come along in conjunction with opportunity and a man of easy virtue.

Raising a daughter had always been her excuse to avoid entanglements. What would she do when Libby left home? Much as Charlie longed for that day and some peace at last, she feared it.

She'd even started tracking those one or two days a month on the calendar and, when possible, arranging her schedule so they wouldn't interfere with her emotional independence. If she believed in astrology, she'd have asked Bradone which of the planets to consult.

But she couldn't begin to explain all this to three grandparents from Wisconsin. So she studied the pictures of grandchildren, complete with dogs and ponies and flaxen hair. She exclaimed over their beauty, hoping Libby wasn't out this night making Charlie a grandmother at thirty-three.

These people were so comfortable and safe, she let them a short way into her family. Even admitted to her unmarried state and seventeen-year-old daughter. They clucked and sympathized. "But look what a success you've made of your predicament," Betty said.

Charlie wondered how they would regard her when they got home and the bloody prime rib and buttery lobster, the martinis and the wine, and the sinful glitter of Las Vegas had worn off.

She even blurted out her problems with Edwina and the dreaded hot flashes. Probably because Charlie's response about the fan kept her guilt close to the front of her thoughts.

"Well, stop right there," Martha said. "Because my sister's got the cure for that. Show her, Betty."

Both women carried purses the size of carry-on luggage. Betty proceeded to fish around in hers and bring out a small white jar. Charlie, who'd imbibed more than enough fat and alcohol herself, was about to make a smart remark about sweet potatoes when a smeared contact lens cleared enough for her to make out the words *wild yam* on the label.

Seems the widowed Betty supplemented her Social Security and what remained of her husband's pension by selling the snake oil to hormonally challenged folks in a three-county area.

"She's everyone's dealer," Martha said proudly. "Everyone I know."

"Supplier," Betty corrected, and went on to assure Charlie that the Mexican wild-yam root also cured migraines and PMS, as well as high blood pressure and depression, memory loss, bloating, lack of interest in sex, and weight gain, because all were caused by hormonal imbalance.

When Charlie finally bid them good-bye at the ticket booth for the Hilton's stage show, she felt coddled and mellow, sort of removed from that persistent threat that Mr. Thug or armed guys from Groom Lake lurked around every corner. She decided to laze in the kingsize with TV until she fell asleep.

But when she opened her door, the message light blinked on the telephone. She was tempted to ignore it. But what if Libby needed her?

An urgent message from Richard. She fought the temptation to ignore that too and punched his room number.

"Jesus, been trying to reach you all afternoon. Big party at Evan Black's. Impromptu screening. He wants you should wear some skirt with a slit up the side. Said you'd know which one. Bradone's invited too. You got ten minutes to get beautiful, babe. Gonna be footage of undisclosed areas to knock your eyes out."

CHAPTER 11

EVAN'S HOME WAS your regular Southern California expatriate stucco and marble—vast in design, limited in imagination. Brand-new, with peeling paint and expensive tile applied with south-of-the border labor, slipping and chipping. Even in home building for the rich, Las Vegas knew how to take the customer.

Half the full-grown desert palms were dead or dying, propped up with two-by-fours. All had come from California tree farms. They were often planted by helicopter.

Charlie had one in Long Beach that would put any of the live ones on Evan's property to shame. But then, the whole first floor of her condo would fit nicely into his foyer.

Bradone wore a long, low-cut cream-colored creation set off by an allover tan, gold chains, and amused blue eyes with color-matching shadow. Richard glowed in proud accompaniment.

Evan Black, obviously taken by her too, tore himself away to tug Charlie into a pantry with a dumbwaiter and announce, "Hilsten's interested in the project. Thank you, thank you."

The producer/writer/director picked up Charlie and her split skirt, whirling around with them at arm's length like a postal employee with an assault rifle, and managed to tip over a tray of crystal too leaded to break. The sound was impressive though.

"Anything you want, just tell me, Charlie love. It's yours."

He was actually wearing a suit, black, of course, and without collar or lapels, but the closest to one she'd ever seen him in. The purple shirt sort of demolished the effect.

"You talked to Mitch?" How was it, when Charlie *did* do something, nobody noticed?

"To his agent and his agent talked to him."

"Evan, put me down. Now."

"Charlie, with Hilsten on board, we've got Ursa Major tied up. I just know it."

"Then why are you thanking me?" But she knew the superstar. "You used my name."

"All I said to his agent was that you were *my* agent. Anything wrong with that?" Evan Black had stopped whirling Charlie, now he hugged her. He had a black belt in something or other and a lot more strength than necessary. "Oh Charlie, the sky's the limit. I owe you one, doll. When you decide what it is, just ask."

"I'm asking—I don't want you getting me in any more trouble like that flight yesterday and Mitch Hilsten in none."

"Babe"—he chucked her under the chin—"you're not in any trouble. Dr. Evan's magic is going to fix everything."

Dr. Evan swept back to his guests, leaving her to face the not-so-dumb waiter who had to pick up all the crystal.

The screening room had couches and love seats, and recliners that vibrated, instead of theater seats. It had floor cushions, a small screen and a huge screen and a medium-sized one, all movable like stage props. It had two bartenders and small movable tables with round marble tops to hold food and beverages.

The screens moved on wheeled mechanisms—a few of which needed oiling. No buffet hors d'oeuvres here. Caterers in faux tuxes—ultrashiny and ill-fitting—maneuvered among the seated and the sprawled with trays of delights that made Charlie's overworked system shudder. She grabbed a recliner so she could be alone and accepted a glass of lemon springwater and two crackers to nibble slowly so the wandering servers would leave her alone.

Soon surrounded by people on floor cushions, she felt like a fat Cleopatra on a barge only slightly above the plebeian waves.

"So, uh, you want this thing to vibrate?" A large hand with manicured nails rested on the left arm of her recliner, the index finger poised above one of the buttons on its tiny console. Charlie didn't want to contemplate what else this chair could do.

"No," and she grabbed the hand with the impending first finger, only to have it flip over to hold hers. Charlie looked into the patient eyes of Mr. Thug.

He used his other hand to press the button and the chair began to gently quake.

"Why are you following me?" You think I saw you help shove Patrick Thompson under a car. You know I described you and your bald buddy to Officer Graden, the bicycle cop. Now that he's dead, I'm to be next, huh?

"You see too many movies." He gave her hand a forceful squeeze and let go of it to lean against the recliner and watch as their host stepped to the front of the room.

Evan grinned, rolled his shoulders up and back repeatedly as if warming up for a workout, his swarthy skin so smooth, it looked greased, his voice pure Teflon. "You"—and his gesture swept them all in—"I am so amazed you could come on such short notice, and so grateful. Me"—and he hugged his shoulders—"I'm so excited about my new project, I couldn't wait to let a few of my closest friends in on it. I'm like a damn kid at Christmas. You know?"

Charlie hadn't noticed any talent in the room, but there must be money. This warm-up act smelled of sales pitch.

"What you are about to see is uncut, unedited, raw. It's the germ of my next creation. It's not even thought out yet. Right now, it is without sound, music, concept. All I've got, my friends, is theme. And a damn good agent."

Whereupon he gestured directly, unmistakably at Charlie. Whereupon everyone swiveled to stare at her as she tried to sink out of sight in her quaking recliner. All agents want to be famous—off-camera, offscreen, off-line. In *Variety*, in *Publishers Weekly*. But not in person.

"Mitch Hilsten is even now on his way here to see what you are about to see first. I think he'll like it. And if he does, he will have the lead in what will come of this germ. I ask you to keep in mind one thing only, a word. That word is"—and he paused as the lights dimmed and sky and cloud filled the mid-sized screen—"*conspiracy*."

"You never told me Hilsten was coming here," her boss rasped in an attempt at a whisper. Yucca Mountain from God's viewpoint appeared at an angle on the screen. A clearly defined, ragged shadow ditch Charlie didn't remember seeing when she flew over it emanated from either side and extended to the horizons. But she'd had her eyes closed a lot.

"Phony fault line," the man at her side complained. "There's no quake activity out there. Damned enviros screw everything around to suit their prejudices."

After several dead frames, the shadow of a small aircraft scudded over rocks and gullies and sagebrush and scratchy-looking bushes, mean sand, and scoured rock.

Richard had crawled through the bodies to her barge. He snarled back at the shushes rising around him, not that there was any sound from the film to be masked. "You gotta stop pissing me off, kid."

"I didn't know, Richard. Remember, you didn't have time to discuss Evan and his project this afternoon at the pool." And somebody with more clout than Charlie Greene should have advised Congdon and Morse's hot new client that this kind of advance, "not even thought out yet" screening was a big mistake. Like her writers killing a story by talking it to death before writing it. But that wasn't what was important right now. "I told you there was trouble."

She stressed the last word of that sentence and tried to gesture with her eyes toward the gray-tinged curls beside her chair.

Either Richard Morse, a man with incessant nervous tics, trembled with anger or her quaking chair caused her to move, which made it seem as if *he* moved. "I got news for you, Greene—"

Charlie never heard the news, because she looked past him to the screen to see a live Patrick Thompson in the pilot's seat of a small, cramped aircraft. The cameraperson sat in a rear seat and the hunk turned with a gorgeous smile, his eyes electric with excitement. She hadn't seen how truly hunky he was when he had exchanged threats with someone at McCarran International on his cell phone. He hadn't been happy and excited then. He hadn't when walking, dazed, out of Loopy Louie's either. Charlie hugged herself so hard, it hurt her elbows, trying to not remember the thing he had become in the gutter.

The next shot showed Charlie in a rear seat, throwing up her Yolie's lunch into a plastic bag.

Richard still whispered from the floor in front of her, but the low voice to the side of her chair cut through her haze of fear, revulsion, and indigestion.

"There any trouble in this town you don't have a piece of, lady?" The Thug rubbed the deep cleft in his chin with his left hand. He wore a turquoise ring similar to that of the floorman at the Hilton.

Why would Evan invite you here? "I came here for a vacation. I just want to play blackjack."

The plane's shadow crawled up and over a low sullen mountain range and dove down the other side.

"And Lazarus keeps hinting you're going to jump ship for ICM. I'll sue your socks off, Greene," her boss threatened, unaware she hadn't been listening. Lazarus Trillion was Mitch Hilsten's agent. "He's also worried Hilsten will switch to you if you do. Then I'll sue more than socks."

"Richard, I don't know what you're talking about—but this guy right here is the one who—" Now, wouldn't you know, her boss wasn't listening to her. He'd turned when everybody else gasped and "whoa"ed and someone even swore at the sight of runways many times wider and longer than those at Denver International Airport. At immense shedlike buildings and a row of unmarked 737s parked at the edge of a runway near huge hangars. A series of rapid-play still shots showed full-sized buses with blackened windows moving in odd jerking paths toward the jets, some already unloading passengers, others driving off presumably empty. All seen through a faint orange haze.

Amid a few jeers of "Area Fifty-one" and "Dreamland," delivered with a mixture of amusement and discomfort from the assembled, Richard said, "Listen, I want to know the minute Hilsten hits town. I mean it. And I'm through with this. Call a taxi, we gotta leave early."

"Where are you going? You can't leave me here."

"Bradone's got a date with the high rollers. Baccarat. I want to watch—what's your problem?"

"Richard, this man wants to kill me—you've got to listen."

"What man?"

Charlie, still seeing orange, could see through it well enough to determine that the floor beside her chair was empty of thugs.

CHAPTER 12

Richard Morse, Bradone McKinley, and Charlie's murderous thug missed the highlight of Evan Black's screening—the casino robbery at the Las Vegas Hilton.

"And now, ladies and gentlemen, for your eyes only, the proof of the pudding," he said, introducing it with relish.

If the audience had been disturbed but dubious earlier, it turned downright hostile now. Yet no one got up and left. No outright jeering, but you could feel the exasperation in the air, hear the grunts of disgust as an infrared camera showed the Hilton's casino in varying shades of sickly luminescent green. It quite clearly caught three figures in identical dark clothing, gloves, and full head masks threading their way through the confusion of people caught in a crowd in total darkness.

These figures wore goggles and could obviously see where no one else could. One mugged for the camera by blowing out a cigarette lighter every time a guy in a Stetson tried to light it. He gestured with what appeared to be a stick, maybe a yard long, but didn't offer to hit anyone with it, more as if to make a point of the thing for the camera.

There had to be four people in the gang. One on the camera, which bobbed between the two making their way into the cage, and the guy snuffing out matches and lighters close by. When a guard with a flashlight searching out possible trouble in front of him began to turn his light back toward the cage, the light-snuffer shoved a disoriented tourist into him. She probably weighed in at over three hundred pounds. She and the guard went down while the light-snuffer took advantage of the guard's guard going down as well to grab the flashlight.

There were other flashlights approaching by now, but the two robbers raced out of the cage with bulging bags and leapt over the downed guard and his heavy oppressor. Charlie knew the casino at the Hilton well enough to detect the fact that the four fleeing robbers did not head toward the hotel's front door. They raced back toward the sport's book area and a back door she'd used today to catch a shuttle to Fremont Street.

This whole robbery and even the clowning for the camera had taken place faster than the time it would take to describe it. The cameraman turned for a shot of security guards armed with flashlights spilling out of a side door Charlie recognized as leading to the restricted area with its warren of security rooms.

It was then that the light-snuffer revealed the purpose of the mysterious stick. With the camera, and presumably the cage robbers behind him, he waved it like a wand across the phalanx of uniformed guards. They stopped. In midstride.

"Oh, come on, Black, not even the government's got that kind of weapon."

"Yeah, man, you faked those shots. We know you."

"Fancy laser, must be a phaser," added someone who felt good enough to joke. "Beam me up, Scotty."

This was a strange crowd for a money party. It had to be three-quarters male. Very few trophy blondes. And half the guys talked like her boss. Even stranger, the less delighted these people seemed with Evan's offering, the more delighted he appeared to be with them.

The wand and the camera panned around to the casino, where the guy in the Stetson stood with his cigarette lighter raised and eyes unblinking. The only moving thing in that confused crowd was the heavy woman who'd landed on the first casino guard. She moved, but as if she was clawing her way through Jell-O.

"Payoff time, cash only," Evan said mysteriously from the back of the screening room when the film suddenly cut to the desert, a burning Mooney 201, and color. Charlie lay spread out on the abrasive sand, shadows of the leaping flames dancing on and around her. A scratchy bush that sat above her head like a tombstone whipped in the wind.

Even to Charlie, she looked dead.

"Vulnerable, not dead," Evan Black insisted after everyone had left. His eyes burned with triumph. He must be on something. This whole screening did not make sense and certainly wasn't a triumph. He hadn't proved he could make a successful project from what he'd shown. He'd proved that he could break the law and fly over restricted government property and that he could rob the Hilton. Why would he reveal the burning Mooney if he'd burned it to get rid of evidence?

"The footage of you is to further entice Mitch Hilsten."

"When's he getting here?"

"Saturday, I hope. His plane from Nairobi was delayed due to nascent rebellion among the downtrodden with access to explosives."

"Mitch is in Nairobi?"

"You didn't even know where he was? He knew you were here." Evan was down to his purple shirt now, sitting on the floor, where servers and barmen picked up plates and glasses while pretending he and Charlie weren't there. He and Charlie pretended the same back.

"I got an E-mail yesterday. Guess I didn't check all the address and routing crap ahead and after it." Damn stuff took up more room on the screen than the message.

Her client's barely contained elation had to mean he was under the mistaken impression his had been a successful screening. Talent is hard to fathom. The more successful, the more deluded they can become, denying the haunting fear they can't do it again. This time, someone will figure out they're faking. They're not sure how they accomplished the success they've become addicted to and fear losing it.

Personally, Charlie was convinced success in the entertainment business had mostly to do with being at the right place at the right time with the right idea. Plus business acumen. Plus a lot of sheer dumb luck. Talent is not that uncommon and few are chosen. When it happens, though, you really need a damn good agent.

This agent thought Congdon and Morse's hot new client was losing it. Or was it just that she was too tired, hadn't really gotten a start on her vacation yet?

"Some of the footage came from satellite, some we swiped off the Net, and a lot of it we'd taken on previous trips. You haven't even seen most of it—the ground stuff. You haven't seen the best yet."

"Why wouldn't you show the best to backers?"

"Backers . . . oh, yeah." He slipped out of his shoes and socks, reached for his toes and lifted them and what followed toward the ceiling, and held the balancing act on his tailbone. "You know the best part about this backing, Charlie? No interest, no taxes, no payback."

"There's no such thing as free money."

"Charlie love, trust me."

"Trust you? This screening involved you, and me by association, in a casino robbery and an illegal flight over Groom Lake. Evan, I have a kid, I don't appreciate your exposing me that way. The mob may not run Vegas anymore, but the corporate-military complex is an incredibly lethal instrument."

" 'Corporate-military complex.' You are such a living, breathing example of my conspiracy theme, you're wonderful." He lowered his legs to pretzel them into a lotus position and did some more deep breathing.

Charlie'd tried that lotus thing once and gotten a cramp in her leg. Her daughter and best friend, Maggie, practically had to sedate her to straighten her out. They were almost crippled themselves with laughter.

By the time he was standing on his head, she bent over almost to the floor to assure Evan Black, "I'm not leaving until you tell me about Mr. Thug. And I don't want to hear any magic shit either."

Charlie rode back to the Hilton with Toby, the second-unit gofer, fuming about Evan's denial of any knowledge of the curly-haired goon. "We didn't check names at the door," he'd said. "Anybody could have come in. People brought friends, you know. It was a party."

When she'd insisted the man was one of the two who had walked his pilot, Pat, to the curb and shoved him under traffic on Las Vegas Boulevard, her client insisted that since he hadn't seen any of it happen, he wouldn't have recognized him tonight.

They were on the Maryland Parkway and Charlie looked up at the lighted billboard with Barry and Terry through that orange smear again. This was the time of night you decide such manifestations mean you've got a brain tumor—she'd probably picked it up by being irradiated over Area 51. Barry's face had been repaired and the restored side looked more like one too many lifts than the other side even. The orange sheen overlay made Terry's bright red Realtor's jacket look anemic.

"So, I suppose you were in on the great Hilton heist," Charlie fished.

Toby wasn't biting. "Like to get my hands on one of those magic phasers. I do magic sometimes, you know."

"What's this magic thing Evan keeps promising is going to make everything just fine?"

"If it works, it's going to be awesome. And funny as hell."

"If it works—"

"Magic's like that." An unusual young man with black floppy curls and a wiry energy, Toby seemed eternally happy, but then the expression in his wide-set eyes would turn abruptly sharp and serious. Maybe it was the magician in him.

Charlie blinked. "Why did I start seeing orange light again with the Groom Lake shots? I'm still getting fragments of it. And that's just from the film."

"Evan's always said you got a great imagination for an agent."

Her only comeback, the soap-opera cliché, "What's that supposed to mean?"

"Hey, nobody else sees this orange."

"So where was Caryl Thompson tonight?" And her tits.

"Her folks are in town for the funeral. To hear her tell it, the two of them together are worse than a dead brother."

"Do you know the big man sitting beside my chair tonight?"

They swirled into the palm-lined drive of the Las Vegas Hilton and pulled to a stop under the lights of the huge marquee and he surprised her with an answer for once. "Yeah. Name's Art Sleem."

"There was money in that room tonight, but Sleem's boss, Loopy Louie, wasn't there?"

"Sleem works for a lot of people." Toby's expression had gone serious on her. "He the man who shoved Pat under traffic?"

"Yeah. Does that mean Loopy Louie ordered the execution?"

"Means Art Sleem works for too many people." Toby nodded at some inner thought and stopped grinning. "Only in Vegas."

"But the party was about money."

"That's what everything's about. That and magic."

"So what was Art Sleem doing at the party uninvited?"

"Looked to me like he was trying to put the make on you."

✣

Too tired for blackjack but too wired to sleep, Charlie stopped at a bank of slots near the Dodge Stealth in the lobby before going upstairs. *Starlight Express* was just letting out and lines of people paraded toward the front entryway or wandered into the casino, drawn by strategically located slots suddenly heaving up heavy metal into their made-to-be-noisy trays.

Unfortunately, Charlie's was not one of them. The squeals of delight, sound effects, and flashing red lights were random, but not on her row. The Hanleys and Betty showed up at a rigged triumph nearby and Charlie called out to them. Illogically happy to see them one more time, she almost wished they weren't getting on a morning plane for Wisconsin.

"Oh Charlie, that was a great show. Can't believe people can dance like that on roller skates." Betty gave Charlie a hug. "You should be in bed. You're too young to look that tired."

Martha Hanley snagged a passing cart and bought a round of dollar tokens for everybody. "Hell, *we* should be in bed. But I still have a little change to lose, and I can sleep in Kenosha."

She plugged a slot two down from Charlie, Ben the one next to Charlie, and Betty sat on the other side of her—ordering Bloody Marys all around from a passing waitress.

God, these people were refreshingly real. Charlie felt so threatened by Art Sleem and even Evan Black, she had half a mind to take a morning plane out tomorrow herself. Leave all the shit to pompous Richard Morse. That way, she could also avoid Mitch Hilsten. What a deal.

Charlie'd never had a slot go off on her. She didn't play them that often, but she'd sat next to a jackpot once. So when the clanking racket began in the tray in front of her and the red light energized on top of her machine, she sat in dumb surprise. This is what's supposed to happen. This is why I came to Vegas. She still didn't believe it.

But Betty was on her feet, screaming, literally lifting Charlie off her stool, when they both went down. Because Ben Hanley's battle with his own body knocked them down.

Everybody but Ben Hanley got up eventually. He couldn't, because he was dead.

CHAPTER 13

"THEY" TRIED TO tell Charlie that Ben Hanley had had a heart attack. Even she'd dubbed him one waiting to happen.

She had also noticed him drinking her Bloody Mary. He'd downed his and absently picked up hers the next time he reached, his mind more on the arrangement of the fruit lining up in front of him.

She hadn't thought much about it and couldn't have touched even a glass of water by this time in her unvacation. Besides, these free drinks weren't called "well drinks" for nothing. They were pretty well watered. You were supposed to get loose, not comatose.

Amazing how quickly and smoothly she and the Hanleys and Betty had ended up behind that forbidden door. That very door the guards had rushed blindly out of with their blazing flashlights on Evan's film.

Ben Hanley wasn't pronounced dead until a good half hour after that door closed Charlie and his family in with him. But Charlie Greene, who had been running into a lot of this lately, knew he was dead before she and Betty managed to get out from under his inert form on the casino floor.

She'd glimpsed banks of TV monitors lining the walls of a room off the hall as they passed to this office. Charlie sat on a couch between Betty and Martha, unable to believe she'd met these people only this afternoon, while a couple of uniformed guards and then a battalion of EMTs tried to resuscitate Ben Hanley.

When they heard the distinct sound of a bone cracking in Ben's chest, the three women grabbed one another's hands in an involuntary motion.

"Why do they keep doing that?" Martha whispered, her glasses steaming over at the top, her hand hot and sweaty. "My Benny's dead."

"Remember when they resuscitated Pop?" Betty's hand felt cold and sweaty. "Lived—what?—ten, eleven years in a lot of pain from a cracked sternum. Never did heal."

"Had to put him in a nursing home." Martha blinked enormous eyes behind enormous glasses. "Betty and me weren't about to quit our jobs, neglect our children and husbands to change diapers on somebody bigger than we were. They had to catheterize him every six hours."

"Cost thousands of dollars a month. He didn't know who he was, didn't know who we were either."

"That's when Martha and I made a pact," Betty confided. The sisters promised each other that the first to go would not be forced to linger. But they hadn't made a pact with Ben Hanley. They also hadn't noticed many resuscitated people over a certain age being successfully rehabilitated.

"Ben carried on like a baby when his sisters wouldn't give up their livelihoods to take his mother in when she got Alzheimer's. And I wouldn't either."

"You didn't give in then, Martha."

"I'm not giving in now." Martha squeezed Charlie's hand and leaned across her to look into Betty's glasses. "Benny went like he'd want to—enjoying himself on vacation."

"Yeah. In his favorite place, Las Vegas."

"Favorite place after Kenosha, Wisconsin, you mean."

"Right. And doing what he loved best . . . after fishing. Playing the slots."

"What do you think we should do, Charlie?"

This was so far out of Charlie's league, she could only shrug helplessly, but she stood as both women rose to their feet and, lifting their hands in the air—hers too—called for a stop to the degradation of Ben Hanley's poor carcass.

Charlie didn't linger over breakfast in bed, but grabbed a quick shower, read her E-mail, and hurried down to the coffee shop. She didn't want to be alone in her room this morning either.

People can too die in a casino, and they can be murdered too.

She ordered one egg poached soft, a piece of dry toast, and a cup of hot milk from Ardith, the elderly waitress with the thick ankles who'd served her yesterday.

"You going to do with it what I think you are, sweetie? Because if you are, there's better remedies for hangovers." When Charlie didn't answer she added, "Not even coffee?"

"I'll eat my breakfast first and then see if my stomach wants coffee, okay?" Everybody's a doctor. "Please hurry it."

If someone wanted to murder you, they could have gotten in your room while you slept. Maybe Ben Hanley really did die of a heart attack.

Betty and Martha were sure that's what it was. "Doctor's been warning him to stay away from his favorite foods, but he figured life wasn't worth living if he couldn't eat what he wanted. Only time he drank was on vacation or with his cheese balls during a Packers game."

They wouldn't let her stay with them. "We got each other. And, honey, he was so lucky to go that way and that fast. We'll miss him, but you don't know how awful it can be growing too old. You're exhausted. We'll write to you from Kenosha."

And that had been it. These people who'd been in her life for one day, one of them dead because of her, the other two already making plans to combine households.

I'm beginning to feel not only threatened but dangerous to others. Three dead in four days. And four more days to go.

It's possible Evan's right about your tendency to believe in conspiracies. You could have nothing to do with these deaths. You could be having panic attacks like Reynelda Goff.

I should leave today. Three dead in four days is a little much for coincidence, or panic attacks, either.

But Charlie and her good sense agreed to have a calm, soothing breakfast before making any plans.

"Good idea," Ardith told her. "You and yourself done talking?" And with a flourish, she presented Charlie the poached egg already on top of the toast, served in a soup bowl, and a small pitcher of milk. "See, milk's still steaming. Bone appetite. There're pills now you can take for ulcers. Know that?"

Charlie did know, but they were for the bacterial kind. Hers was more of the raising a kid half her own age and three people dying around her in four days kind.

Charlie poured the steaming milk over the poached egg on toast and added salt and pepper. She ate slowly, testing her system. It was an inexplicably calming meal that turned other people green to see her eat, but it worked for her. Maybe she'd die early like Ben because she ate what worked at the moment.

Just because Patrick Thompson and Officer Timothy Graden were murdered didn't mean somebody like Ben couldn't die mercifully quickly and easily next to her slot machine. Even in a casino.

Nothing like poached egg on milk toast with salt and pepper to bring things into perspective. She used the soup spoon Ardith had brought to finish the last of the milk and looked up to find the older woman standing above her with the coffeepot.

Charlie nodded and her server shook her head as if she'd seen everything. But she poured Charlie a cup of the empowering brew before removing all evidence of the disgusting meal.

Thus fortified, her universe in at least partial balance, Charlie finally confronted the thought of the morning's E-mail, which she'd answered before heading to breakfast. Libby, Mitch, Larry.

Libby's car and Eric, the boyfriend, were apparently still alive, because she didn't mention them. The problem was Perry Mosher. Libby'd been through a series of part-time jobs, usually quitting them in a few months. Charlie had the feeling it was her daughter's looks that overcame her lousy work record and explained her ability to get another job.

But this was the problem Charlie had dreaded. The boss couldn't keep his hands off the kid's butt. What should she do?

When Libby asked her mother for advice, Charlie knew no answer would suffice. It was a trap. The best answer would be for Libby to keep her mouth shut and quit. Warn her friends to stay away from the creep.

Libby, however, had not been raised to give up without a fight. She worked at a pet supply and grooming store, Critter Spa and Deli, in a small shopping center in a not-too-scary neighborhood.

Charlie had sent back the message, "Tell Perry Mosher to knock it off, and if he doesn't, look for another job."

But she knew that was too easy. That kind of harassment can be subtle and excused as a joke, any protest treated like an exaggeration and turned around to belittle and embarrass the protester. Perry didn't seem dangerous, but he was icky, the thought of him touching Libby disgusting.

Mitch's message that he had finally taken off from Nairobi—how could you E-mail from Nairobi if the downtrodden were blowing up stuff? What the hell was he doing in Nairobi? She'd checked all the routing information and, sure enough, he was there or had been. Anyway, he expected to be in Vegas by Friday night, Saturday at the latest, and couldn't thank Charlie enough for suggesting him to Evan Black, whose work he admired to the nth.

Shit, he's going to decide he owes me again.

Then there was Larry Mann, her assistant—whose butt she wasn't even allowed to think about touching—with the weirdest message of all. Jethro Larue at the Fleet Agency in New York had asked for Charlie to turn over all files on Georgette Millrose, as he would be her new agent. He'd had the gall to offer terms, which were spitting insults, on possible future subrights income on properties Charlie had sold for Georgette.

Georgette had moved fast. Granted, Charlie hadn't read her recent books because the speedily displaced editors at Bland and Ripstop had offered to take each opus as it came. Georgette's historicals were thinly veiled romances without the raw sex.

But the real shocker was that Jethro Larue wanted to represent Georgette Millrose. Charlie's life was so unexpected, even when she wasn't dealing with murder.

An incredibly thick wad of bills landed on the table where her poached egg on milk toast had sat a short while before and Art Sleem said, "You won the jackpot last night."

CHAPTER 14

THOUGHT YOU WORKED for Louie . . . at Loopy's," Charlie heard her confusion say.

"I get around. Not nearly as good as you." His curls were not really shoulder-length. They were collar-length, and then only in back. It's just that he didn't have a neck. "Me, I'm not lucky like you." His lips were full and sensuous, a small spacing between his two front teeth, a Roman—no, an Arab hook to the nose. "But you? You been very lucky lately." A wry, intelligent, aware smile. "Very lucky."

Red alert. What time of the month is this?

Don't be silly. Not even you can forget he kills people.

"It's like wherever you go, people die."

"Wherever *I* go?" Charlie took a slug of coffee and sucked air. The cup was empty.

"Let me get you some serious coffee." Art the thug took a hundred-dollar bill off the top of the roll and handed it to Ardith. "Keep the change."

There was a serious coffee bar out in the lobby by the sleek black Dodge Stealth. Art Sleem ordered them each a skinny latte. He selected a shaker off the counter. "Nutmeg, right?"

"How did you know?"

"Simple, you look like a nutmeg type." He sprinkled it on the foamy milk atop her drink. "What about me?"

"Sugar."

"Right." And he dumped in enough to kill the foam. "Told you it was simple." He led her down a couple of carpeted stairs to the very bank of slots where Ben Hanley died the night before. "Sometimes things are simple. Sometimes they're sheer dumb luck."

He sounded like an agent. "So you're not just a bouncer at Loopy Louie's?"

"Like you, I wear many hats."

"What's that supposed to mean?" There I am doing it again. Next thing, I'll be asking him how he feels.

"Well, look at you. Young, beautiful, apparently gifted, a Hollywood agent, girlfriend to superstars. An adventuress who thinks nothing of flying over restricted areas."

Ben Hanley's eyes had glassed over by the time she and Betty looked down at him. His mouth open and tongue distended as if he'd choked.

"A woman who plays the dollar slots after winning big at blackjack at two casinos in just two days, instead of the five-dollar slots. We don't have a profile on your type. We need a profile on your type."

"Who's we? And what's my type?"

"A woman so above money, she forgets a jackpot."

Charlie had seen death before, and when large men had appeared almost instantly to pick up Ben and escort the rest of his little group away from curious eyes, she'd noticed the wet spot on that carpet. And on Ben's plaid shorts. He had died in a casino. She should have made known her concern last night that the lethal drink had been meant for her, but she hadn't wanted to spoil the man's death for his widow and sister-in-law. They were so pleased at how clean and fast it was. Do people as needy as their parents really linger that long?

"A woman who hobnobs with the high rollers and the hicks of this world, as if they were no different. A woman of great tolerance."

Charlie repressed the brief memory of her distaste at having to care for her own mother after a mastectomy. If the gods expected Charlie to give up her only life and her sanity to nurse Edwina if she got old and "lingered," the gods were in for a shock.

"You surprise me, know that?" Art Sleem said. "Why'd you go off and leave your jackpot?"

"We had a little emergency. Somebody died, remember? Right about here." You must have been here too, to know I'd won and to collect the money. And to maybe lace my drink with a lethal dose of something.

"Nobody dies in a casino."

"What is it you want, Mr. Sleem?" Another great line.

"I want to help you."

"Translation, you want to warn me."

"No, I want to help you *understand* things."

"Things like nobody dies in a casino."

"And things like, nobody's luck holds forever. Stay away from dangerous places." They were sitting on stools and he pushed at the carpet with the toe of a hand-polished shoe. "Things like always watch your back, if you don't. Things like, we don't like counters here."

"I'm not a counter. I can't remember lunch."

"Things like friends in high places can't be counted on to save your ass. Like, you and your friends are not free to go wherever you want."

"Who do you work for anyway?"

"I'm freelance."

"Freelance killer?"

"Educator. Casinos are private property. You aren't free to do whatever you want in one."

"I can't count cards. I didn't expect to win all this money. I came here for a vacation and to play blackjack."

"Restricted areas are off-limits too. You aren't free to ignore the rules."

"Know what? I think you're the one with a problem. I think

you're trying to make me the answer to a question only you know." If there's anything to be learned from modern communication techniques, it's, when in doubt—babble. "Lousy problem solving, Art. You need an educator yourself. And another thing—"

"How is it you know my name?"

"Your reputation precedes you."

Whoa, that's your third cliché in the last two minutes.

Oh, knock it off.

"Well, you tell your high-roller friend she better be careful." Art Sleem was about to say more, but the pit boss with all the turquoise jewelry and the excess hair on the back of his hands came to stand over them. "Hey, Eddie, how's it going?"

"Just great, Art. This woman bothering you?"

"Nah, just good friends. Good seeing you again, Charlie."

Charlie was trying to digest this strange interchange when Sleem headed for the revolving door to the real world.

"You're good friends with Art Sleem?" Eddie was still standing and Charlie still sitting on her stool. She watched his hand flexing.

"No, I don't know anything about him, but he seems to know everything about me. Does he work here?" Charlie explained how he had delivered her lost jackpot winnings to her table in the coffee shop. "And I saw him in the spa by the pool the other day."

"You're a guest here? You lost a jackpot . . . oh yeah, the guy who got sick in the casino last night. I heard about that—not my shift."

Actually, Eddie, he checked out, rolled his last dice, threw in the towel, gave up the ghost, and drank his last drink—the one meant for me.

Charlie thought she was talking to herself until he said, "Nobody dies in a casino."

"Oh. Right. So if he doesn't work here, how did he get my jackpot? Sleem, I mean."

"I'll look into it." Eddie headed straight for that door to this casino's secure area that Charlie had been shepherded into with the corpse from Kenosha.

She had never seen Eddie out on the floor here except when Charlie's high-roller friend had been playing blackjack.

You haven't been looking for him either.

That's true. But I will be now.

Does that mean we're staying in Vegas?

For a little longer. I mean, if Art and his buddies want to kill me, they can certainly find me in Long Beach. Don't you want to know how much money I've got in my purse?

Charlie's purse was too small to carry that much money comfortably, but before she could count it, Eddie was back. "Charlie Greene, comped to room twenty–one fifteen, Congdon and Morse Representation, Inc." He read off a sheet of paper, "Residence, Long Beach, California."

Eddie had another man with him. This one didn't carry the beef most of these guys did. Tall, skinny, stooped.

"Comped? Richard got these rooms comped? How did he do that?" And here she'd thought he was being generous for a change.

Eddie shrugged. "Not my department. This is Mr. Tooney. He'd like to have a word with you."

Mr. Tooney was with the IRS. Charlie had heard tell there were more IRS agents in Las Vegas than any other city in the country. Made sense.

She asked for identification, he showed her a card. She had no idea if it was real or faked. "I hope you are who you say you are, Mr. Tooney, because I have a problem."

"Yes, you do, Mrs. Greene," he said quietly. He led her down a wide hallway that led to the auditorium where Ben and family had enjoyed *Starlight Express* last night, then to a quiet corner of a bar not open until evening.

"What did you mean, 'Yes you do'?"

"You first." He brought out a notebook and pencil instead of an electronic notepad.

Charlie told him how and why Ben Hanley had been murdered, told of witnessing Patrick Thompson's murder and trying to convince Officer Timothy Graden. "Art Sleem probably killed him too. I can prove he did Ben though, Mr. Tooney," she said when he stopped writing and started doodling, "because if he hadn't been here, how could he have known about the jackpot?"

She put the pile of bills on the table in front of him as evidence. She hadn't even had time to count them, but the bills she'd seen were all hundreds.

Mr. Tooney, Matt Tooney, according to the card he'd showed her, counted it swiftly. "Your story is very inventive," he said. "You should take up writing. But murder is really not my specialty, Mrs. Greene."

"Miss Greene. Well, what do we do? That man is dangerous."

"My bailiwick is money. And we have here just short of two hundred thousand dollars."

"Art Sleem took back a bill to pay the waitress for my breakfast and told her to keep the change." But then it hit her. "I won two hundred thousand dollars playing the dollar slots? Come on. They don't pay a jackpot like that with cash anyway." They present you with a check and an IRS form.

"Actually"—and he brought a check out of his wallet and handed it to her—"you won ten thousand. And here it is, and here's your tax form."

"So what's all this?" She gestured to the piles of bills he'd lined up carefully, with Ben Franklin's picture facing up and toward him.

"That's exactly what I and the management of the Las Vegas Hilton's casino would like to know. Apparently, Mr. Sleem was paying you for something else."

"Listen, Matt Tooney, that jerk is trying to kill me. He followed me to the pool. He followed me to Fremont Street and to a screening last night. He never stopped threatening me."

"Screening?"

"At Evan Black's house. He makes movies, you know." Charlie didn't mention the content of the film. Somehow, invading secret government airspace and watching a successful robbery of this very casino didn't seem like the thing to bring up. Like they say, when dealing with the bureaucracy, don't offer more than is asked, and she'd already broken that rule. "Maybe Sleem figured once I was dead, he could get his money back. But if you're going to kill somebody, why give them money? This whole thing doesn't make sense."

"Exactly," said the man from the IRS.

CHAPTER 15

MATT TOONEY SUGGESTED that Charlie go to the police with her story and refused to take the $200,000 off her hands.

Charlie explained she'd been to the police and hadn't heard back and that she didn't want the money.

"Everybody wants money," said the tax man. He ought to know.

"Yeah, right, and nobody dies in a casino. Don't you care that this poor guy was murdered? That his death was a mistake? That I was supposed to die? That I could be next? I mean, I know you're specialized, but jeez. And the police can't do anything until after I'm dead. Probably write it off as pedestrian error or 'Stupid tourist takes dive off the Stratosphere Tower, sources say she was depressed.' "

"This screening. What was its purpose?"

"It wasn't a screening so much as a sales pitch for money, far as I could tell. Project was still an idea waiting funding."

"Money, funding." Mr. IRS looked at the cash on the table.

"You think Sleem was giving me money for Evan Black's next project? But why wouldn't he say so? Why all the threats? Why not just give it to Evan?"

"You're his agent."

"I just handle his writing contracts and his dealings with other writers for the agency. I mean, I don't do finance stuff.

In fact, I don't do most of his stuff." Truth be known, most of the contract work is done by the lawyers anyway.

Charlie didn't know where to start, but, fed up with a helpless situation and fortified by anger, a poached egg on milk toast, and a skinny latte with nutmeg, start she would.

But first she ran upstairs to change into shorts and sandals and check out the voice mail message from the office. Ursa Major was dropping the option on *Letters to Morticia.* Another disappointment. She called Larry to discuss how he would break the news to the author—gently. "Poor guy was counting on that money."

Her little purse stuffed with enough money to pay off her mortgage twice, she had the doorman hail her a cab for Evan Black's house. Charlie was so charged by the time she got there, she sent the cab on its way before she realized no one was home. This was a gated community, with a live guard at the gate, but Charlie was on the list of people to be admitted, and the guard must not have noticed Evan leaving.

She stood next to a propped-up dead palm tree and saw something she hadn't last night in the dark. Evan's house was on a lake. A lake in the desert.

Unable to raise anybody by pushing the buzzer on the gate to the courtyard, she walked around the high pretend-adobe wall until she came to the lake and stepped easily around the wall's end. A sleek cabin cruiser sat almost completely still on the glassy dun-colored water. Evan's backyard consisted largely of pool and fancy tiles. The clear blue of the water in the pool dazzled.

The front might be gated at the road into the development and at Evan's courtyard, but the back of the house, mostly window, was wide open. Charlie could see many houses similar to this along the lakefront—stucco, tile roofs, impossibly stilled boats tethered at most of them.

Traffic was not that far away, yet it was quiet here. The unrippled water made no sound, even the incessant air traffic from McCarran seemed muted. Eerie, like walking around in a void. Only the sound of Charlie's shoes as she crossed the gorgeous blue-and-white figured tiles that cracked and buckled and just plain came loose at irregular intervals.

Charlie had little patience with female-in-jeopardy novels. But every now and again, that primordial fear men needed women to feel, so it was worth their valor to go out and kill mastodons, overtook even Charlemagne Catherine Greene.

Losing some of her determination, she decided to see if she could get into the house to use a phone to call another cab. If not, she'd hike back to the gatehouse and ask the guard there to call her one.

All these houses, set close together along the lakefront, were two and three stories high but long and narrow—allowing access to both street and lake for the maximum number.

She walked along the windows, one panel of them after another. Here is where the living took place in this house. The whole first floor was one great room with kitchen, dining room, lounge, and office space sharing the sunlight and lake view. Comfortable, beautifully thought out and coordinated, this was a different house from the one she'd seen last night. There were two sides to this house, as there appeared to be to Evan Black.

Among the panels of windows were doors with glass panels of their own and doorknobs. She tried one, expecting it to be locked. It was. But at the other end of the length of windows between pool tile and house, a door stood ajar on the kitchen end, where she'd started. Why hadn't she noticed it?

Because in this direction you can see it better and you were too busy ogling somebody else's private space. That's where you began snooping and your concentration was off.

I'm not snooping. And it could have been opened just slightly behind my back while I walked this way. To lure me in.

But a barely visible wire along the bottom of the window line, which was about knee level on Charlie, made her retrace her steps to the suspicious door. Even less perceptible were tiny round sensors attached to the framework between windows.

A fairly quaint alarm system. I could deactivate that with scissors.

It must be deactivated already if the opened door didn't set it off.

It could signal the guardhouse at the main entrance instead of making lots of noise here.

What do you really know about these things?

Nothing but what I read in scripts and manuscripts. You can pick up a lot that way. Like recognizing that somebody else already deactivated it—it's cut right here.

Two ends of the wire drooped in defeat at one edge of a window frame.

That's stupid. Cutting it should send that signal to police or the guardhouse.

Not until she was inside did Charlie realize the front of this great room was open to three stories. A balcony with a staircase at each end connected the second story to this one. A second balcony extended out over the first. All three floors sharing the sun and view. Blank digital clocks on oven and microwave told her the electricity had been cut before the alarm system.

A cordless phone sat upended on a cluttered desk on the back wall under the balconies. A photograph of an enormous building, literally dwarfing the cars and trucks parked around it, caught her attention as she picked up the cordless. And found it dead.

It needs electricity too, stupid. Maybe we should sort of ooze on out of here?

This is the scene in amateurish mystery novels where the female sleuth, instead of listening to her good sense, climbs the stairs and finds a body. Knowing better, Charlie Greene headed straight for the door she'd entered.

And found three.

Charlie's head pounded in rhythm with her shoes pounding the pavement back to the gatehouse. She'd tried ringing bells at the locked gates of several courtyards along the way but was answered only by barking dogs who fell silent the minute she retreated.

"This fries it. I've had it. I'm out of here." She knew she was talking out loud and didn't care. "Six bodies in five days. Gotta be a message there somewhere."

Walking in this direction, she could see that, though Evan was on a lake, most of the homes backed on canals where they could run their boats out to the lake.

One thing for sure, Art Sleem would never demand his two hundred grand back. He hadn't been dead long, but dead he was. Charlie hadn't needed to check to see if he'd wet his pants to know that.

She'd wandered farther into her mysterious client's home than she'd realized to pick up the phone, absently snooping along the way.

When she turned back toward the getaway door, the bodies lay lined up behind two couches and a long chest with its lid open and what looked to be jumbled rolls of paper inside. Art Sleem lay along the chest. He was hidden from the windows, but if she'd been looking in the other direction instead of at the posters of Evan Black's films on the rear wall on her way to the phone, he would have been visible to her. The other two had the privacy of the couches to be dead behind.

It was hot and still with all the pavement and decorative rock and white stucco reflecting back the sun. And a long way to the guardhouse.

She could still smell the bitter scent of gunfire she'd curiously overlooked until she saw all the dead.

But it had been the crack of an upstairs floorboard that sent Charlie Greene out that kitchen door on the run.

CHAPTER 16

CHARLIE RETURNED TO the murder scene in a squad car with Officer Leach. The guard at the gatehouse swore he'd let only one unauthorized man into the subdivision and that because the man had official government identification. That would have been Tooney flashing his IRS card for the last time.

"How'd the other two get in here?" she asked the officer when she'd demonstrated how she gained entrance and explained the squeaky floorboard upstairs.

"Probably rented a boat. Tied it up behind some other house. Takes more than a little water and a gate to keep out the bad guys."

After determining the bodies were all indeed dead ones, Officer Leach ordered her out of the house and around the wall, drew his sidearm, and crept up the stairs before she'd even reached the pool. He didn't look old enough to be a cop. She was back in the kitchen the minute he disappeared.

Art Sleem wasn't wearing his turquoise ring. And the other man who wasn't Matt Tooney had an indentation on his ring finger.

Officer Leach was up there for what seemed an inordinately long time. Charlie grew more curious about up there and less enthused about down here with the dead men.

Careful not to touch the banister, she climbed the stairs,

knowing she was still shedding skin scales and hair dust or something to confuse the crime scene. But Charlie figured she'd already done the damage when discovering the bodies to begin with.

The next floor was the main level from the street side. Here were the foyer and the butler's pantry, where she and Evan had dispersed the crystal last night. A small formal living room and dining room dominated one side of the house, the other taken up by the two-story screening room and elegant his and her bathrooms.

The bedrooms must be off the balcony above. Funny how brave she felt up here now with one cop, young but armed. And there were reinforcements on the way. Floorboards do creak on their own. Houses settle. Probably a lot when at the edge of a lake.

This house seemed to hold its breath as Charlie ascended to the third and final floor.

Two small bedrooms with a connecting bath. A master suite with a huge bath/dressing/exercise room combined. All thoroughly searched and left undone.

The young cop stood next to the Jacuzzi in the master bath, talking to Dispatch on his cellular. He gave Charlie a hard look but went back to his conversation.

"Looks like a burglary as well as murder. Bedrooms torn up. Downstairs put back together, but in a hurry. Up here, it appears the perpetrators had no time to return rooms to normal. May have been surprised by Miss Charlie Greene, Evan Black's agent, or so she says, entering from below. Could have easily made their way out the front from the second story when she entered on the first. Yeah, she's here," and he mouthed to Charlie, "Don't touch a thing."

She nodded and looked around instead.

Despite his reputation for thrift on his projects, Evan lived well. His Malibu home was grander than this. The last she knew, he was planning to build a third home in either Sun

Valley or Telluride. And she knew of a condo on Kauai.

Even with the king-sized mattress pulled off the innerspring, there was something about the care with which the bedding had been stripped but not quite removed. It appeared to be placed in folds on the floor, suggesting the searchers had intended to return things to normal.

And the young officer was right about the first floor too. Charlie wouldn't have noticed, but, now that he'd suggested it, she could see how the rolls of paper, maps maybe, had been put back in the chest, but not neatly enough to allow the lid to close.

And she could see the desk down there with the dead cordless and the picture of the improbable building. The normal clutter of a working desktop was strangely organized. Your regular shuffling of overwhelming paperwork, but the stacking was weird.

Odd-shaped piles . . . wrong somehow . . . the stacks too even heightwise and too quickly arranged. Photos, drawings, scripts, diagrams, and junk mail stacked more by size than subject, but the stacks still oddly shaped. What was she looking for?

And the photo of the gigantic building, surely some Hollywood prop engineered with photography instead of actual construction, appeared to have toppled from a pile of what looked like household bills mixed with restaurant flyers and prostitute handbills available on the Strip. Organized by haste and stack height rather than by subject—that was it.

Anyone living in the house would know something was wrong immediately. But at first glance, strangers like police and literary agents might not. Charlie looked back at young Officer Leach with respect.

Charlie learned something about her enigmatic client too. It took a bit of looking beyond the search destruction to know what it was though. One, he was tidy. Two, he was not celibate. Interesting objects had been pulled off closet shelves and dresser drawers, the very least damning of which were condoms, K-Y jelly, scented aerosols, and flavored creams. Various cruel-looking mechanisms. A puzzling array of chains, hooks, ropes, and pulleys. Rotating hooks in the ceiling. All suggested an athletic sex life. Not surprising. But again, he was tidy, or maybe realistic—no mirrors.

Which doesn't mean there aren't hidden cameras and snuff videos.

Well no, but Evan *is* tidy. He wouldn't leave three dead men in his great room. And where the hell is he?

Evan Black returned shortly after the reinforcements arrived. He'd been at the funeral of Patrick Thompson and helped to disperse the poor pilot's ashes from an airplane over the landscape of his family's request. Charlie didn't want to know.

She sat in a canvas deck chair pulled up to a glass-topped table on Evan's pool patio. The white tile had blue Aztec-type markings. So did the table's umbrella, unfurled now to shield them from the sun. She, Evan, Detective Jerome Battista, and an undisclosed person of authority, who would have worn an overcoat on the Fox Network even in this weather, lunched on turkey subs, bottled water, and crinkled potato chips from some take-out.

Charlie finished off her water before unwrapping her submarine, and Mr. Undisclosed, in shirtsleeves instead of an overcoat, pulled another out of a bag at his feet. He wasn't wearing a ring on his wedding finger. But had one recently left an indentation? He handed her the water with a purposeful look, presumably to make a lasting impression.

He probably hadn't witnessed six dead bodies in five days. Now, *that* makes an impression.

All the water took care of her headache and she bit into the sub with more interest than she'd expected to. Moist roasted-tasting turkey slices—not the slimy cold-cut type—smeared with mayonnaise and cranberry sauce, topped with onions, black olives, shredded lettuce, and sprouts.

The men watched her, almost fondly. Men did that. She would not think about it.

Evan patted the elbow she'd bent to allow her hand to feed her mouth. "My lovely agent here is a fast-food connoisseur."

"Oh, that reminds me." Charlie grabbed one of the hundreds of napkins that always accompanied these meals to wipe the mayonnaise off her fingers and reached into her purse. She handed him the $200,000 minus the hundred-dollar tip. "Compliments of Art Sleem, body number four."

Boy, did she have everybody's attention.

Evan looked especially astounded, but he'd earned any worry it might cause him. Charlie figured the more open she was in front of the authorities, the less trouble he could get her into.

She answered her client's look with a wink. Don't ask me for sympathy, guy. Too many bodies under the bridge, and half-assed nonexplanations of things you are intent upon involving me in. Just handing you back a little bit of the grief, my friend. Enjoy.

She popped the air out of her bag of crinkled chips, feeling more in control than she had since Art Sleem and company presented her with matching bullet holes in their foreheads. No sign of struggle, as if they'd lined up for execution. All laid out in a row. And all that blood in their eyeballs and spreading into the carpet. Recent kills. Somebody had caught them searching this house. She was lucky that somebody hadn't caught her.

Detective Battista held out a hand still smeared with mayo and wearing a wedding band. Evan handed over the money. But Battista, who looked more like a male model than a cop, asked Charlie the obvious question instead of Evan Black. "One of the dead men gave you this money for Mr. Black? When?"

"Well, that's what Matt Tooney thought the money was for, anyway. He's body number six. As well as IRS." And Charlie described her morning.

Evan waited for the half of her sandwich he knew she wouldn't eat and she gave it to him. The other two stared at her, baffled.

"There's only three bodies in there—not enough for you?" Mr. Undisclosed asked. Baggy eyes and jowls, beer belly, gray hair clipped to within an inch of its life. "Oh yeah, the one in the casino. I'm still missing two bodies."

"She's very imaginative for an agent." Evan hugged her.

Detective Battista cut through the crap. "So, why did you come out here, Miss Greene?"

"To give Evan the money. Even the IRS wouldn't take it off my hands. I don't like wads of unexplained cash and thought I'd dump it and all the trouble it might bring on Evan."

"Don't listen to her," the writer/director/producer said with his beguiling grin. "She loves me. Honest. Best agent I ever had."

"So, the other two bodies," the fed insisted.

"Patrick Thompson—the native Las Vegan and pilot for the nonexistent airline that flies workers in unmarked planes to Groom Lake and who did not die by pedestrian error on the Strip—he's number one, and number two was Officer Timothy Graden."

"You were at the scene of the hit-and-run that killed Tim Graden?" Battista's sleek face tensed, dark eyes focused to a squint.

"No, but I did witness Thompson's murder and explained it to Officer Graden, the only one in authority there who would listen to me. And look where it got him."

"Do I detect a certain leap in reasoning here?" the fed asked. "The bicycle cop was a victim of a hit-and-run because you told him about what you imagined happened to Thompson? And as I'm counting, we suddenly went from not enough bodies to too many. There's still one unexplained."

"I told you, didn't I, that there were two goons who walked Pat Thompson out of Loopy Louie's?"

"Oh yeah, and shoved him under traffic that wasn't moving." The fed—what else could he be?—started in on the guy method of handling problems with those lower in the food chain. His condescending smile directed around the table showed the overbite of preorthodontist days.

"Same kind of traffic it would be tough to get killed in jaywalking," Charlie countered. "Anyway, the bald corpse, number five, was Sleem's accomplice in this."

Undisclosed went for the gold. "And what would you say, little lady, if I told you that Mr. Arthur Sleem worked for the government of the United States?"

"Then I'd say the government's in a whole lot of trouble."

"Told you—conspiracy. Right?" Evan beamed at the two other men and would have hugged Charlie again if he hadn't caught the look in her eye in the very nick.

CHAPTER 17

A TRIPLE MURDER at the Las Vegas home of producer-writer, Evan Black, the young genius behind such award-winning films as *All the King's Women,* a fictional exposé of presidential fornication throughout history, and the hilarious docudrama of attempts to hide bungling at the highest levels of corporate America—*The Accountant in the Wardrobe*—starring Mel Gibson and Tom Hanks, has left the Lakes neighborhood and Las Vegas police stunned." This was Barry on the local evening news. He couldn't have gotten through that whole sentence if not for the fact that he spoke even slower than Frank Sinatra used to sing and so could breathe after every three words and you didn't notice.

Did he and Terry work morning, noon, *and* evening broadcasts? Charlie sprawled in an enveloping chair in front of a mammoth TV that lowered from the ceiling on command in Bradone McKinley's really swell accommodations high atop the Vegas Hilton. She accepted a chilled gin martini from Reed the butler. It might be poison, but it had to be a hundred flights up from yak crud. And this had been *one long* afternoon, baby.

Evan Black, "the young genius," spread out on a floor pillow at her feet, using her chair for a headrest. "Hey, what about *Waiter, There's a Government in My Soup*?"

"Never got released." Richard Morse cuddled with their

hostess on a couch so puffy, all Charlie could see was his head.

"Still the best film I ever made."

"How come," Charlie asked, "we're the same age, but you're a young genius and I'm not young anymore?"

"Because you're not a genius. Geniuses are supposed to be old, so, if they're not creaky yet, they're young."

Since Evan's house was a crime scene under investigation, they let him pack an overnight bag and told him he'd have to spend the night elsewhere. He was going to spend it in Richard's room since Richard would be up here.

"Last night," Terry took over, "Black reportedly held an advance screening of an as-yet-unmade film, using raw footage of various scenic wonders of our area, including Area Fifty-one and Yucca Mountain, amazing special effects, and even, get this, footage of the robbery at the Vegas Hilton's casino."

"That Black's always out ahead of the crowd, isn't he?"

"Yes, Barry, and it sounds like Vegas will be in the movies once again. Sources say that none other than Mitch Hilsten will star in Black's latest flick."

Except for a helicopter video of the Lakes subdivision, busy with emergency vehicles, and another of Detective Jerome Battista refusing to talk to reporters as he entered a building, the only visuals the broadcast had for this segment were stills. Stills of Evan, Mel, Tom, and Mitch. And then one of Charlie.

"You gotta have a new picture taken," Richard remarked. "Haven't looked like that since Libby caught puberty."

"Black was reportedly attending a friend's funeral today and the bodies of three men, as yet unidentified—"

"I can identify them," Charlie said.

"Shut up," Evan said.

". . . discovered by Black's Hollywood agent, Charlie Greene," Barry said.

"If this gets picked up by the networks, you couldn't get better publicity," Bradone the astrologer told Evan the genius and predicted, "People will be throwing money at you to get in on the ground floor."

"They already are," Charlie said.

"Shut up," Evan repeated, and asked Bradone, "How much you in for?"

"Don't listen to him," Charlie's boss warned his new girlfriend. "That's not how funding goes."

"Life's not legal without the middleman, huh, Morse?"

"Georgette Millrose," Terry began, and a pub photo flashed on the screen.

"Talk about needing a new photo." Charlie could hear the sour grapes in her voice. "She hasn't looked like that since World War Two."

". . . local celebrity and author of twenty-some romance-filled thrillers, announced today that she would be signing on with Jethro Larue at the Fleet Agency in New York."

"What, she hired a publicist?" Everybody knew midlist writers were not news, especially in their hometowns. "How'd she get that kind of press release on TV?" Charlie waved away Reed and another martini, as did Bradone. The guys accepted.

"No dead grass under that Jethro Larue," Richard Morse pronounced. "Face it, you were just coasting with her."

"But you're the one who told me not to—"

"Shut up," Richard said.

Charlie and Evan had spent the afternoon answering questions both separately and together and were still on the pool patio when the bodies were carried out. They'd offered up skin cells, hair and blood samples, and mouth swabs. Evan looked patiently through the mess of the upstairs and could find nothing missing, nor in the rest of the house either. Charlie did, but kept her mouth shut.

When Battista and Mr. Undisclosed grew intimidating over what the murdered men might be doing in the house, what the burglars might have been after, and whether he or Charlie thought the dead men might be the ones who'd searched it,

Evan refused to say more without his lawyer. Charlie continued to keep her mouth shut.

Over a simple supper of baked potatoes, leafy salad, and hot crusty rolls, whipped up on a moment's notice by Brent the chef, Charlie asked Evan about the picture of the exaggerated building. The simple baked potatoes were topped with a creamy wine sauce creation—thick with hunks of real crab-meat, button mushrooms, pearl onions, raw asparagus tips, and every kind of tasty tiny herby thing. So it took him awhile to answer.

"That's not fake. It's the DAF. Starwars Device Assembly Facility. That was a real picture we took, from very high up. Been building it since Reagan to assemble weapons we don't need anymore. It's over by the little town of Mercury." He turned down Brent's wine choice and ordered another of Reed's martinis. Not to be outdone by the younger man, so did Richard. Bradone McKinley's amusement threatened to make a breakout.

Charlie also turned down the wine. One, it was white. Two, she had enough of a buzz on one martini.

"I read about that building." Bradone allowed a chuckle. "Cost something like a hundred million to build and eight million a year just for maintenance and security."

"It's actually a group of buildings inside a concrete fortress with security sensors, razor wire, and those famous 'armed response personnel,' " Evan told her.

"I've heard of those ARP guys," Richard said. "There's private companies that hire them out to government installations just like commercial security services do to businesses. Only these ARPs are ex–military security instead of ex-cops."

"There's a lot of ex-ARPs on the market now too," Evan added—not to be outdone by the older man. Men compete on everything. "Especially in Vegas, with all the loose cash. There's lots to secure and not enough mob presence to see that it's done quietly and neatly. And they're becoming more political, patriotic. Organizing and going out in groups to take care of people who do antigovernment things. They're like the reverse of the antigovernment militia movement but better armed and trained and with friends in high places. How does that tickle your little conspiracy phobia, Charlie?"

"Seems like you might be asking yourself that question, since you're continually baiting the keepers of the secrets out at Groom Lake. Maybe they'll come after you."

"Maybe they already have."

"A picture of the DAF was on the desk when I found the dead men. But it disappeared before we left."

"Maybe that's what whoever searched the house was looking for." Evan snapped his fingers. "We've got a real detailed plan of that state-of-the-art security system."

"Where'd you get something like that?" Richard wanted to know.

"Off the state-of-the-art Internet."

Charlie actually finished almost all of her baked potato and the men had seconds. They retired to the ploopy couch to argue over how a great project really gets funded and why agents and bankers and brokers are important to the process. Their speech was slurred. They ordered coffee and brandy and didn't seem to notice when Bradone lured Charlie out onto the roof patio.

Charlie wanted to stop and enjoy the amazing light show that was Vegas, the shadow mountains ringing the horizon, and the steam rising off the Jacuzzi next to the pool. But Bradone tugged her through the glass doors of an elegant bedroom and tossed a couple of pieces of cloth at her. "I bought this for my niece, but you can have it." She was already pulling off her own slacks and blouse.

"But I haven't shaved my you-know. I mean—"

"Hell, I don't care. And those guys will be passed out by the time we get wet. Brent and Reed are gay and not easily impressed. Now hurry, dessert is in the Jacuzzi."

Yes, Charlie had a thought or two about whether or not

lovely Bradone was bi. And what this dessert might be. But she put on the bikini and ignored the pubics—it had been that bad a day. Now that Sleem and his bald buddy were dead, all she had to worry about were the ARPs from Groom.

"Finally, I have you all to myself." Bradone laughed low. "You've been so busy finding dead bodies and Richard's been so . . . very attentive."

"I was a little surprised"—*stunned* was more like it, but Charlie too was choosing her words carefully—"at your interest in him."

"Yes, well, he's something of a novelty. I've always liked novelty."

"Nothing stays a novelty for long."

"No, nothing does."

Dessert was a chocolate mint and coffee. And if the guys weren't asleep already, they were certainly quiet in there.

The water bubbled warm against her mostly nakedness. The air blew chill against her face. The rich coffee went down hot. Charlie sighed. "Here I am, a mother, and I can see all these people murdered and feel this good afterwards. Do you suppose Hollywood has hardened me?"

"There's a lot to be said for the survivor syndrome."

"Don't forget good old guilt. I seem to get nourishment from it." Charlie could feel tight muscles relaxing. Even her bones seemed to be readjusting more comfortably in their ligaments and sinews, or whatever kept her together.

"You're not worried that the police think you killed those three men today?" An edge of concern crept into the modulated voice.

"I don't know. But I have had a connection with six murders in five days, and the cops don't think three of them are murders even. Well, maybe the hit-and-run. Driving me nuts."

"Six?" Now Bradone McKinley sounded incredulous but listened without interrupting as Charlie described once again the deaths of Patrick the pilot, Timothy the bicycle cop, and

Ben Hanley who drank from Charlie's glass. She went on to describe what little she knew or suspected of Art Sleem, Tooney, and the bald thug, whose murders in Evan Black's great room nobody denied.

"So what's the connection?"

"The only one I can see," Charlie said helplessly, "is me."

"Why not Evan? He would seem to have more of a connection."

"Not with Ben Hanley from Kenosha, Wisconsin, he doesn't. Bradone, would you believe I feel worse about that death than all the others combined?"

Subdued lighting aimed downward highlighted curving stone pathways among shrubs in pots, flowering plants, small fountains and statuary, concrete gargoyles, and the bottom of the kidney-shaped swimming pool in the penthouse garden. The hot tub sat on a raised platform, so that even the mostly submerged could view the dazzling display of Las Vegas at night, the city streetlights blazing in lines radiating in all directions, the airliners blinking overhead.

All around, the mountain ranges hunkering on the horizon, forming a circular frame to keep reality at bay.

Steam made Bradone McKinley and the arm she raised toward the heavens appear to waver and warp as she pointed out the constellations either by direction or by distinguishing stars that managed to stab through the light refraction from the gaudiest city in the world.

Charlie had begun to tense up again with all the talk about dead bodies, and the astrologer's soothing, melodic voice calmed her. She caught herself yawning as Bradone carried on about planets and houses and moons rising.

"Charlie, what if even one of those planets has some life-form? What if that life-form is even now on its way here? Or already here?"

"What if that life-form has its own system of astrology? What if it reads some significance in the position of our solar system, Earth even?"

The older woman lowered her arm and her head suddenly to ask Charlie the date and time and place of her birth. Charlie answered the best she could remember from what Edwina had told her and then Bradone grew far too quiet for far too long.

"So what's the prognosis, stargazer? Is the body count over for the week? Am I going to salvage some vacation here or what?"

"We should meet for breakfast," Bradone said instead of answering. "Somewhere away from here and Richard and the police. There are so many things I want to ask you, Charlie. About Mitch Hilsten and Georgette Millrose. About Evan and that strange film we saw at his house last night."

Charlie noticed she didn't mention learning more about Richard Morse. "Bradone?"

"Look, I'm going to run your chart tonight." She steamed all over when she stood and reached for a towel. She didn't look real. "I'll pick you up at your door, call you first, think of a place we could go."

"Bradone, talk to me."

Bradone stood on the tub deck with the towel wrapped around her, head cocked to one side, the edges of her hairdo dripping, honest-to-God shooting stars zipping above her. It was creepy. "You're really very perceptive, aren't you, Charlie Greene?"

"No, I'm really very scared." And I don't even believe in astrology. The gambling blimp's tacky advertising board flashed PLAY KENO! over the stargazer's left shoulder. "Are the murders over with for what's left of the ruins of my vacation or not?"

For the first time since they'd met, Charlie heard uncertainty in the woman's tone. "Somehow, I don't think so."

CHAPTER 18

THE NEXT MORNING, a limo drove Charlie and Bradone to a secluded restaurant on the edge of a golf course, far from the glitz of the Strip and Fremont. They sat at an outside table in the sun, grape-arbor decor separating the tables from one another but opening onto the view of bright green greens and distant golfers.

Bradone pulled a cell phone and a paper notebook like Matt Tooney's from her purse. Dressed to kill in a wide-brimmed straw hat and country-club dress, Bradone looked great in black too. But that choice in color didn't make Charlie feel any easier.

"What did the charts and planets and stuff have to say?"

"May I suggest the creamed eggs on croissant?"

"You said if I came here, we'd talk. You're not talking."

"Let's do talk. But not about dead bodies until we've had some coffee and food." Sun drilled through the holes in the straw brim of her hat to pinprick her face and throat. "Have you heard from your mother since last we talked?"

"Well, no, but that's not the problem right now, is it?" And Jesus, why are you in black and hardly any makeup?

Was the shading on her lids charcoal color instead of blue because she'd been up all night running charts about Charlie's future and didn't like what the stars were saying?

Don't forget you don't believe in astrology.

"Charlie, remember when I told you I had a secret about Richard? At the big pool on the recreation deck?"

"Not really, but what were you doing down there anyway when you had your own pool at the penthouse?"

"It was important to Richard. Men need to feel less vulnerable now and then. You know that."

The arrival of coffee and orange juice helped settle Charlie's nervousness. Bradone McKinley's voice was not so soothing and melodic this morning.

"What I found funny about your mention of wild-yam cream and your mother's menopausal problems was this." Bradone drew a small white jar out of her black straw purse. It looked a lot like the one Ben Hanley's sister-in-law, Betty, had shown Charlie at dinner at the Baronshire. "Read the label."

WATER-DEIONIZED, WILD YAM EXTRACT, GLYCERYL STEARATE, PEG-100 STEARATE, ALOE VERA GEL, GLYCERINE, STEARIC ACID, SAFFLOWER OIL, PROGESTERONE, JOJOBA OIL, CHAMOMILE EXTRACT, BURDOCK ROOT EXTRACT, SIBERIAN GINSENG, PROPYLPARABEN.

"Bradone, people are dying like flies all around me. I could be next."

"I swiped this from Richard's shaving kit. Read the directions."

Apply to soft skin regions such as neck, chest, buttocks, inner thighs, inner arms after showering for symptoms of advancing maturity such as incontinence, impotence, memory lapse, stiff joints, and insomnia.

Despite her growing anxiety, Charlie couldn't stop the smile spreading across her face. "You mean my boss rubs sweet potatoes on himself? How come he made so much fun of my mom?"

"Because he'd never read the ingredients on *his* snake oil. Just the name."

The stuff was called Bubba's Youth Enhancer for Men.

"Tell me about Mitch Hilsten," Bradone demanded when a muffin and fruit plate arrived for her, creamed hard-boiled eggs over a croissant with pineapple hunks for Charlie.

"He's divorced with two grown daughters—"

"Everybody knows that. I mean, what's he like in bed?"

"Like, does he snore or what?"

"Richard says you're smitten with your secretary, who's gay."

"How's Richard in bed?"

"Not bad for his age."

"Must be the sweet potatoes."

Bradone tried again. "Is Mitch Hilsten as owly and pouty and reclusive as he appears in interviews?"

"Actually, he's very sensitive and thoughtful and pretty cheerful. He just doesn't like the press."

"That's not smart."

"Seems to be working for him." Mitch's career was skyrocketing after a scary decline. He'd always been a household word with the public but was too good-looking for Hollywood's recent infatuation with scuzzy everyman heroes.

"Does he have a lot of moles or anything?"

"Not really. His teeth are capped. Did you know his smile was insured through Lloyd's of London when Lloyd's was the place to be insured? One time, I was in the Utah dessert with him and that smile nearly blinded me."

"Charlie, can't you throw me a crumb?"

Charlie pretended to consider the request while enjoying her food instead. "Okay," she relented. "Mitch has the most wonderful—" She caught the waiter's eye and raised her cup. "The most beautiful—"

"What? The most beautiful what?"

Charlie shook more pepper onto her creamed eggs and

picked out a big hunk of hard-boiled egg to savor. "Back."

"Back of what?"

"Back of his back."

"You slept with Mitch Hilsten and you looked at his back?"

Once. One night. And I'll never live it down. "Look, he's threatening to be here tomorrow. You can see for yourself."

"His back?"

"It's very nice." Charlie wondered how much Bradone was paying for that limo and driver waiting out front.

"Okay, you win round one." The astrologer put her hands up, palms outward. "How about Georgette Millrose?"

"She fired me and signed on with Jethro Larue. It happens. She got tired of being midlist. I don't know an author who isn't tired of it. Maybe Jethro knows something I don't."

Bradone's phone mewled faintly and she opened her notebook as she picked it up. She listened carefully to somebody named Harry, turning pages in her notebook that were scrawled with diagrams and iconlike sketches. She studied one at the very back that had a plastic-coated table of figures and signs and dates.

"Sell Singer and buy Stryker and double the number of shares we discussed yesterday. . . . Harry, you know I don't care about your little insider tips. Do what I say, like a good boy." She punched him off and closed the notebook. "My broker. He's not very clever, but I never take his advice."

"You play the stock market too? I thought you just gambled at the tables."

"Charlie, I have to invest my winnings so they'll grow. You have to lose big-time to be allowed in the high-stakes games."

"I'd think just paying to stay in that penthouse would make the Hilton happy enough."

"Those penthouses are comped to a select few who are expected to lose heavily. Trick is to lose a few million one time, win it back, say, the next two times you visit a resort."

"A few million?" Charlie searched for words that weren't

there. "I suppose you have DRIPs too."

"Of course. The secret to the stock market is not playing it, but in compounding."

Did everybody know about this but Charlie? "Okay, we're even. You win round two. He whistles."

"Who whistles?"

"Mitch Hilsten. Instead of snoring."

"Were you really flying over Yucca and Area Fifty-one or was that trick photography?" They were in the limo. The driver had been ordered to drive around for a while. "Tell me, Charlie."

"Not till you tell me why you're dressed in black and why you are avoiding talking about the one thing I want to know."

"Black seemed the proper mood for what I wanted to do with you today."

"What, bury me?"

"If I'm to help you, we'll have to do some detecting. But first, I have to know about Area Fifty-one and that robbery at the Hilton's casino."

So Charlie, who hated detecting, described her experience with the illegal flyover of undisclosed areas on the vast government reservation of the Nevada desert. "When I got back to the Hilton after that sickening flight with Evan and his motley crew, the lights went out. I didn't know about the robbery until the next day."

And why am I trusting you with all this?

"Trust your instincts, Charlie, they're good ones."

Tell that to Georgette Millrose and Jethro Larue.

Charlie's impulse to trust this woman made her skeptical, but she felt drawn to Bradone as she might a female mentor or even a mother. Charlie, who was adopted, wondered fleetingly if her birth mother was more like Bradone than Edwina Greene. And then felt immediately guilty. But she also felt an unconditional acceptance here she never had with her mother or daughter.

Bradone doesn't know you as well as your mother and daughter.

"This is all so peculiar." The stargazer who earned her living gambling and compounding removed the oversized sunglasses to chew on an earpiece. Vertical worry lines formed at the corners of her mouth and between her eyebrows. "This plane you and Caryl Thompson, Evan, and his cameraman flew in was the burning plane out by Rachel on the news, wasn't it? The Mooney."

"They torched it themselves. I suppose so they couldn't be traced to it. But then why did Evan show it burning at his little titillating screening? I think he's gotten us all in a lot of trouble."

"I'm afraid I do too. He's acting like a little boy, thumbing his nose at the authorities."

"He says it's all going to be fine because of some magic he's intending to pull off. Somehow I don't find that reassuring. You've got to watch out for these geniuses."

"This morning's paper claims all aboard that plane were incinerated." The astrologer's worry lines deepened. "The story used it as a warning to people trying to invade that airspace, hinting that it was shot down by keepers of the secrets out there. Evan's armed response personnel? They must know you all got away."

"They could sift through the ashes and notice there are no charred bones, and now, after the screening, they have to know who we are." They'd also be able to tell the Mooney landed instead of crashing. Why was the truth being covered up here? Force of habit? Were military authorities playing along with Evan's amateurish stage setting for a reason? Maybe they were getting ready to spring a surprise of their own. What if that wand thing, that fancy laser-phaser in the casino-heist clip—wasn't special effects?

"So the young pilot was murdered because he angered somebody by flying Evan and crew over restricted areas when he himself was a pilot for this airline ferrying workers out to those same areas. And Timothy Graden died because you told him the pilot's death was murder and not jaywalking, and he may or may not have suggested same to someone or left a note or two around the police station declaring such—that one's pretty weak, Charlie."

"What if he did some investigating of his own?"

"And Ben Hanley from Kenosha, Wisconsin, died because he drank a poisoned drink meant for you. A tiny mention of that in this morning's paper claimed he died of a stroke in his room at the Hilton."

"They were staying at Circus, Circus."

"Okay, but that means your life is in danger."

"Not if Art Sleem poisoned the drink. He's dead."

"But you think he was working for someone else. That someone isn't dead."

"Art said he freelanced. He was a bouncer for Loopy Louie's. The government guy investigating the murders at Evan's said Art worked for the government."

"Sounds like he was for hire by anyone. We need a motive for three easily documented murders. Sleem, Tooney from the IRS, and the other bouncer from Loopy's."

"I thought astrologers read the stars for answers. You sound more like a cop." Much as Charlie hated detecting, she enjoyed this woman. Must be fun to live life as one big adventure.

"We need the deductive methods of the police and have at our disposal added insight. But who could walk up to three grown men and have time to shoot each squarely in the forehead without at least the last one lunging forward and getting shot less than squarely? They were most likely at Evan Black's house for nefarious reasons, but what would two bouncers have in common with an IRS man? And how did Tooney get there before you if you'd just left him at the Hilton?"

"Stolen money? And they might not all have been shot at the same time, but in different parts of the house and moved to the great room. And I changed clothes and made a phone call before I left. Maybe Matt Tooney got a faster cab than I did, surprised Sleem and the bald bouncer searching the place. Maybe they shot him." Or were they looking for the wand-phaser?

"Who shot them?"

Charlie leaned toward her friend's hat brim and whispered, "Can we trust this guy?" She gestured toward the driver and the glass panel between them. There was something about the back of the guy's head under the improbable cap . . . or was it the neck? "Do we know it's really soundproof back here?"

A touch of the familiar playfulness returned to Bradone's expression as she picked up the speaker phone and rapped on the window. "The Janet Terminal, please."

CHAPTER 19

CHARLIE AND THE stargazer gazed through a chain-link fence at an unmarked building on a far corner of McCarran International Airport. An eight-foot chain link with barbed wire in a Y formation on top, as if intended to keep people in and out at the same time. According to legend, this is where Patrick the hunk and his fellow pilots would have picked up and returned the workers they transported between Groom Lake and Vegas.

Behind them, their smirking driver leaned against the limo, and every time Charlie glanced over her shoulder, he raised thick black eyebrows above small round sunglasses. He wore a dark suit but with a tam-o'-shanter pulled low over his forehead.

Between them and the driver stretched an unnecessarily wide drainage ditch of hardscrabble graded sand/dirt. Charlie had painful pieces of it in her sandals still and dreaded the return trip. It was more like a dry moat that extended around the front of this little corner of the airport, as well.

Across the side road, along which the limo was parked, a concrete block wall formed the back of a row of hangars for the private jets of the elite, according to Bob, the smirking driver. Charlie had an irrational problem believing in men named Bob. The eyebrows alone made him highly suspicious.

"How do we know this is the Janet Terminal?" Bradone

asked. "There's no sign on the building."

"If there was, it wouldn't be undisclosed," Bob said.

"But it could be a warehouse, a repair shop. Anything."

A small nondescript concrete building in tiered levels and two-tone gray. Its windows either heavily tinted in bright green or covered with inside shades of that color. No markings, no flags, just a plethora of tall light poles among the cars in the lot and surveillance cameras on the corners of the building. The tails of two white airliners with no insignia were poised over the roof, one on each side.

"So now what?" Charlie asked.

"Let's try another tack"—Bradone lowered her voice and turned away from their driver—"now that we're not in the car. Let's start with murder number one. The pilot was connected with Area Fifty-one through this airline, with Evan through flying him over it, and with Art Sleem, a freelance enforcer who could well have had more than one employer."

"I can't believe Sleem really worked for the government."

"Governments hire temporary help just like everybody else. And a lot of it undercover so they can't be held accountable. No reason why Sleem couldn't be working for Loopy Louie and one small sliver of the government. Maybe himself too. But what, Charlie, if all this was connected to the robbery at the Hilton casino, as well?" A jet screamed low overhead and a whirly little wind tunnel, which may or may not have been caused by it, lifted Bradone's hat high in the air, flipped it a couple of times, and dropped it on the other side of the fence.

"Looks like you blew your cover," Bob said behind them, and guffawed.

They dumped Bob and the limo back at the Hilton, slipped into their rooms, and, ignoring telephone message lights, donned blue jeans and shirts for the Jane Doe tourist look. Charlie felt pretty silly by the time she met her accomplice outside a corner door by the glass elevator on the outside of the building.

Bradone looked mysterious behind her Jackie Onassis sunglasses. Avoiding all ears, they walked to the Strip. "I have the feeling the police are going to be looking for you with further questions. We'll just keep moving and thinking and sorting this out. You may be safer away from the hotel."

Charlie would rather be playing blackjack. "Art Sleem never seemed to have much of a problem finding me."

"Good thought." Bradone pulled her into an alley behind the old Debbie Reynolds theater and museum, the pictures of the stars—Marilyn Monroe, Gary Cooper, Joan Crawford, John Wayne, Judy Garland—still gracing its front. All beautiful then. All dead now.

They watched for passing foot traffic. There wasn't any. The heat coming off Debbie's white stucco met that of the white-painted concrete block of the Bank of America, where they stood about midalley.

"See, what you have to understand about astrology, Charlie," Bradone started off again, "is that it doesn't give answers. It gives clues. Its study can recommend paths to follow and those not to take. Think of it as more like a road map than a manual."

"Sounds more like new software." Like, not a lotta help. "You must have had some opinion last night when you suddenly went all serious and then stayed up running charts."

"All I really know at this point is that it's not a good time for you to be in the position you're in."

"What position *am* I in?"

"The position of being in great danger."

"There's a good time for that?"

"Charlie, Mars is squaring your sun." Just the way her modulated tone deepened, that hint of breathiness that crept into it, the dread when she made that ridiculous statement—she could have been a doctor informing Charlie her cancer was inoperable.

Charlie couldn't swear that the sinking feeling was her stomach, but something somewhere was sinking. "God, that reminds me—Art Sleem, while loading me down with threats he called 'warnings' yesterday, said to warn my high-roller friend she better watch out."

"You're making that up to get even with me for being so obtuse. He didn't even know me."

"No, honest. Maybe he was working for the Hilton too. Maybe they're onto your scheme. He kept talking about nobody liking counters and casinos are not public property—they're private. Which, I suppose, means they can make their own rules."

"I hate to tell you this, but it's even worse for me to be in a dangerous position about now."

"What are we going to do? We can't just keep walking."

"I can think of three things right off the bat and I'm sure there are more. But we have to make a game plan first. We need to talk to Officer Graden's widow and to that pilot's sister, and I think we should visit Loopy Louie's."

They turned left onto Las Vegas Boulevard.

"But take heart. Venus is on your part of fortune in your first house. Otherwise"—Bradone shook her head as if in disbelief—"I've never seen a chart like yours."

They sat at the bar at Loopy Louie's, Charlie looking longingly at the blackjack tables across the room.

"Don't even think about it." Bradone studied a small calendarlike chart that fit in her billfold. "This is no day for you to chance anything. I expect you've been on a winning streak the last few of them though."

"I thought it was all a setup having to do with Art Sleem, after the hot shoe I shared with you, that is. But it was really the planets and the houses and moons rising and stuff, huh?"

"You were in Venus trine." Bradone took a long swig of cold beer.

Charlie stuck with a diet Coke. "I don't get you. You serve your guests yak crud and then you drink martinis and beer. What's the deal?"

Bradone peered over her reading glasses and billfold star chart. "Yak crud?"

"Breakfast on Tuesday, remember?"

"Oh, I thought you knew." Her laugh, out loud for once, turned heads for some distance, even considering the noise in the place. Trying to hide with this woman around was fruitless. "You seem so intuitive."

Loopy Louie's was literally indescribable, and this was Charlie's first time here. It had still been under construction on her last trip to Vegas and she'd never made it inside the night Pat Thompson died. "Tasted like chalk ground into goat's milk. Left a coating on your tongue like a hangover gone postal."

"It was a test of Richard Morse. Your opinion of him was obvious. I had to form my own."

He apparently passed.

The bartender was dressed like a eunuch, the dealers like sinister bedouins, and the floormen like even more threatening Arab oil guys—black suits with fezzes (red upside-down flowerpots with tassels). The bar girls were draped like belly dancers in gossamer veils and transparent harem pajamas over G-strings.

Even the noise was different. The calliope bleeps of slots elsewhere were cymbals, gongs, tambourines, camel calls, and weird pipe music here. The racing, blinking colored lights meant to stir up excitement in other casinos were muted colors seen though gossamer scarves blown about by ceiling fans and revealing huge lighted scimitars when they parted.

Charlie wasn't sure whether to be on the lookout for Bogart, Lawrence of Arabia, or the Ayatollah. The more she saw of this place, the more mundane and reassuring Bradone-the-astrologer became.

Charlie plugged a quarter into the video poker monitor embedded in the bar top to calm her nerves and get her drink free. And lost four dollars in quarters as fast as she could plug them in. Expensive Coke.

Bradone McKinley drew a computer printout from her bottomless purse and grew so agitated over it and her calculations, she ordered another Heineken.

"Maybe you shouldn't have sold the Singer and bought the Stryker," Charlie said with little sympathy. "Do you run your charts on a computer?"

"I've got a notebook in the penthouse loaded with special software. I don't know how we managed without them."

The eunuch leaned over the bar to look at Charlie's monitor. "I never seen anything like that. Must be something wrong with the machine."

"Nah, it's just the stars and the houses and the moons falling. You know, trines and stuff. Don't worry about it."

The clamor of a gong startled Charlie into dropping the quarter she was about to play and lose.

Shift change.

Blondes replaced red-haired Arab potentates with freckles and steely eyes. Sweating bedouins in full headgear and robes were replaced by already-sweating new ones. Their eunuch pulled off his rubber baldness to scratch a full head of matted hair as his bald replacement stepped into the bar pit.

And a man, even shorter and older and less impressive than Richard Morse, stepped up to the bar between Bradone and Charlie. "I am Louie Deloese. And you, I understand," he said, leaning down to pick up Charlie's quarter and handing it to her, "discovered the body of my good friend Arthur Sleem."

CHAPTER 20

LOOPY LOUIE DID not look Middle Eastern, Mediterranean, Arabian, French, or even loopy. He looked inconsequential, small graying mustache and piercing blue eyes notwithstanding. His little office looked even less consequential. "I understand my friend Arthur gave you some money."

"Two hundred thousand in cash," Charlie answered. "Did he work for you?"

"Arthur Sleem worked for whoever paid him, Mrs. Greene. As I have learned, to my dismay."

"Even the government?"

Louie shrugged narrow shoulders. He didn't look Las Vegas either, in a tweed jacket over a pale blue shirt and frayed collar. "Who has more money than the government?"

There had been no real overt threat as yet, but Charlie didn't feel safe. It must have showed.

"Mrs. Greene—"

"Miss."

"Miss Greene, I just want to know what happened to the money and the details of Arthur Sleem's death. You are in no danger—not from me anyway."

"I'm just concerned about my friend," Charlie lied.

"That is no problem." He opened a side door of his desk, clicked some buttons, and the wood paneling on one wall parted to reveal a bank of monitors like those in the security area of the Hilton. One of them showed Bradone still engrossed in her billfold chart and scribbling things in her notebook.

Is that why she wanted to come here? Couldn't she have done that anywhere?

Well, she could have been showing more worry over me.

Why? She can tell what will happen to you by her charts.

"You see? Your friend is fine." But Louie Deloese left the panel open and that monitor on.

"Art Sleem delivered a whole lot of threats, threats that he called 'warnings,' along with the two hundred thousand in cash, Mr. Deloese. One of them was that my friend should be careful. What does she have to do with any of this?"

"Where is the money?" he countered.

"I went over to Evan Black's yesterday to give it to him because I didn't know what to do with it, and I found the three murder victims instead. The last I saw of your money, it was in the hands of Detective Jerome Battista of Metro Police."

He nodded and turned to the monitor, chewed on a fingernail. "Miss McKinley is a well-known high roller. She beats the odds more often than is comfortable, but she does not fit the profile of a counter. Arthur might have been asked to let her know subtly, say through a friend, that she shouldn't push her luck. This is, of course, only conjecture."

"By the gaming commission?"

Louie gave the eye roll and sigh that signified he was dealing with a doofus—which he was. "Someone at the Hilton casino? Or the Mirage? She frequented both. Or Bally's? They see her often." He watched Bradone scribble and drink beer. "Intriguing woman. But high rollers usually pay out better. Now, about Arthur's demise."

Charlie, still feeling honesty would be more likely to get her out of this and still feeling intimidated, described how she found Sleem and the others all lined up behind the furniture in Evan Black's great room, with identical bullet wounds in the center of their foreheads. She wanted to ask him about the third man on the floor of the great room, but she didn't know how to word it. Like, Who was that balding friend of Art's who helped him shove Patrick Thompson under the wheels of a car in front of your casino last Sunday night? Instead, she described how Evan Black's house had been searched.

"Was the two hundred thousand meant for Evan's new project? Why in cash?"

"This, after all, is Las Vegas, Miss Greene."

"A bet? You were paying off a bet? You gave it to Art Sleem to give to me to give to Evan?"

He did the eye roll for doofuses again. "I was honest with you. Do not pretend you know nothing of Mr. Black's wager of the century, Miss Greene. He has become a very wealthy gentleman."

"Free money for his project. Even Evan Black can't get away with stealing money."

Deloese shrugged, gestured with both palms upward. "The odds that it would be the Vegas Hilton were minuscule—it has the best security in town. Most, including me, thought it *would* be here. It was brilliant. So I am assuming your client would know better than to keep his winnings in his home."

"Stolen money is hardly winnings."

"I'm a little confused as to whose side you are on, Miss Greene. But I assure you the money taken from the Hilton is minuscule compared to those winnings. Everybody in town wanted in on this bizarre wager."

"But why did Sleem say it was the money from a jackpot I'd won at the Hilton casino?"

"In a way, it was. But for the lights going out at the casino, which won Mr. Black and, I assume, those connected to him a true jackpot. I saw to it that my relatively small debt to Mr. Black was paid. And then I think my friend Art Sleem decided to become greedy."

"Why are you telling me all this?" Nobody else will tell me anything.

"Because I think you, as a representative of Mr. Black, are not as confused as you pretend. Because those lights went out at the Hilton as you entered it. And because I can help Mr. Black with another problem. Tell him there is a channel, most secure, by which he can move tangible assets. I know he will have other offers, but I think my charges will undercut them. If he'd like to discuss this, my nephew will set up a meeting."

He stood and reached across the desk to shake her hand in dismissal. "I think I would be very careful if I were you, Miss Greene. There are those who will tie you to the robbery, but even more dangerous are those outraged by the method used so casually to achieve it. And she"—he looked back at the monitor, where Bradone started on yet another Heineken—"she should be careful too, your friend. Arthur was right about one thing. I do not believe the stars will be of much help."

Emily Graden lived in a white stucco duplex with a red-tiled roof. Inside, all was white except for yellow furniture, blinds, and carpet. Charlie felt like she'd walked into a daisy.

Emily Graden was packing boxes of dishes on the kitchen table. Emily and her children would move in with her parents until she could find less expensive rent. They were down to a teacher's salary. The little boys were already with Grandpa, and Grandpa wasn't well. All this, Charlie and Bradone learned from Emily's mother before they reached the kitchen. A collection of framed movie posters lined the entry hall, one of them for *All the King's Women.*

Graden's women looked hollowed out and empty, in shock over the abrupt change their lives had taken.

Charlie'd called ahead to explain she had witnessed the accident Timothy Graden was probably investigating at the time of his murder. What she didn't say was that if she hadn't insisted he look further into the young pilot's death, Emily's husband might still be alive.

Charlie felt awful. She looked to Bradone for guidance. But the astrologer'd had one too many Heinekens or trines in the wrong house—whatever.

Charlie tried to ignore the high chair in the corner, gunk still smeared across the tray and caked on the armrests that held it in place. Libby used to do that. When she wasn't hurling the whole food dish at the wall.

Emily Graden leaned against the counter in front of the sink, hugging her ribs. She would be a pretty woman when her face wasn't bloated with grief. She wore the same kind of faded denim jeans as Bradone and Charlie. So did her mother. The great homogenizer, like aprons and hats were once.

"Did you see your husband after I did? Did he say anything about Pat Thompson's murder or my reporting it?"

"He called. Said he had to look into an accident and might be later than usual, see if I could get Mom to take the kids for a few hours the next morning." He worked nights, she worked days. "Said he was on his way to the Janet Terminal."

Emily Graden's mom made a hissing sound.

Bradone finally came back on-line. "The papers and broadcast-news services gave no details about where the hit-and-run occurred or who found your husband. What happened to his bicycle?"

Grandma banged two skillets and a saucepan into a box and threw in a can opener to enhance the racket. Grandma was about to kick them out. You didn't have to be intuitive to know that. "You don't have no right to come in here and ask questions of a grieving widow. Shouldn't have let you in. But she said to."

"It's okay, Mom. I assume the bike is back at the station. He took his own car to work. He told me he was going to check something out on his own before involving the department."

Grandma opened a drawer, took out a cleaver, and studied it.

"But they found him out on the road to the Cherry Patch. Said I shouldn't want everybody to know about that." Emily looked at Bradone as if she might consider trusting her. What secret powers did the stargazer have? Besides a compelling personality and a tankful of Heineken.

"The pedestrian killed on Las Vegas Boulevard that night was a pilot who flew workers out of the Janet Terminal, and for producer Evan Black on his off-hours," Charlie said.

"I know. His sister phoned. Wanted to know if the department had found the vehicle that ran Tim down."

"Have they, Emily?" Charlie just wanted to get this over with and get out of there.

"Apparently it was a limo like the ones used by several services that ferry men out that way. They're looking for the driver."

Brothels were illegal in the city but existed less formally than the legal whorehouses in the county that advertised in the city (even on top of taxicabs). Limo services made a good business transporting vacationing johns out to the flesh and back.

"Was his car damaged?" Bradone insisted. "Was he in it when he was hit?"

"It was in the ditch, out on One Sixty." Tears came then, without sobs. Emily reached for the Kleenex box next to her.

"Emily, you got two kids, *and* a daddy with one foot in the grave. What's the matter with you?"

"Tim wasn't going to any whorehouse, Mom. He was dumped out there after he was run over. And these women look like they believe me."

CHAPTER 21

CARYL THOMPSON'S CONDO was white stucco on the outside with, a red-tiled roof too. It was attached to three other condos on a street of similar combinations, all with tiny front yards and gated patios at the four corners.

Inside, Caryl's home was largely beige. Beige furniture, carpet, and blinds. Tall dried wheat grass in a floor vase. Three-story, with a drive-in basement garage. Two humongous cats moved over on the sofa to make room for Bradone and Charlie.

At Bradone's insistence, they'd dropped in without calling first this time, giving Caryl less time to fabricate answers to questions she'd expect to be asked. The astrologer reasoned that since Charlie was Evan Black's agent and Caryl worked for him, they'd gain admittance.

Dressed in sweats, sweat, and stringy hair, still gasping after her run, Patrick Thompson's sister sprawled on a recliner. A concrete gargoyle leered from the hearthstone of a gas-log fireplace.

The feline who chose Charlie to torture began kneading her thighs through the denim of her jeans, hard enough to make her squirm.

"Why did you call Timothy Graden's wife?" Charlie wedged an index finger under each of the offending paws to pry the pricking nails loose. "If you didn't think your brother's death was murder?" The fat cat hissed and bit Charlie's thumb before crawling off her and onto as much of Bradone's lap as its obese partner had left vacant. "I mean, you wouldn't go to the police, so you must not have thought it was. Or is it that you are just as involved in whatever Patrick was that you're afraid to?"

"Look, my brother is dead. My parents just left, hallelujah, and I must have run ten miles to get those two disasters out of my system. And now you turn up. I have to shower and get to work." The bones in Caryl's face looked larger without makeup, her eyes smaller. "How did you know I called Emily Graden?"

"We just came from there." Charlie sucked her thumb and tasted blood. "Was your brother run over by a limo too? The kind that takes johns out to the Patch? Did you think it might be the same one?"

"Having them both run over the same night—of course I wondered. And, yes, I'm just as involved as he was." Caryl pulled the stringy hair up off her face and neck and knotted it behind her head. "And now you are too, Charlie Greene," she said, and shrugged. "Involved, I mean. These people don't take prisoners."

That's exactly what Charlie was afraid of. A roomful of people had seen her flying over Groom Lake with Evan and company. It was documented on film. "You mean the government?"

"Might as well be. You're Evan's agent, ask him."

"Where did Pat live?" Bradone asked.

"Here. He had too many girlfriends to move in with one. But a sister—what the hell."

Bradone reached across seventy-five pounds of cat fur to right a picture frame lying facedown on the end table next to the couch. She held it up for Charlie to see and then for Caryl Thompson.

"That's him. Patrick," Charlie said.

Patrick's sister just looked away.

"He was beautiful." Bradone laid the picture frame down

as she'd found it. "I'm sorry for your loss. But why would he risk so much for Evan Black? What did he want out of life?"

"His own plane. That's all he ever wanted."

"Evan was going to buy him a plane?" Charlie thought that sounded too generous for a low-budget producer. "Why?"

"Pat would share in the profits and buy a plane. Eventually, he hoped to own a charter service."

"To produce something of this size, Evan will have to go to a studio. There won't be any profits. Not after production costs and wages and once Evan Black and Mitch Hilsten take a percentage. There're never profits."

"Is that really true?" Bradone asked, "or just Hollywood paranoia?"

"Well, if there are, they get absorbed in the grease that's cooking the books." That's why damn good agents demand every cent they can squeeze out of a project up front for their clients and why the guilds make all the salaries so expensive.

"Pat was to be paid up front," Caryl said, as if reading Charlie's thoughts. Then she stood, so they also had to. "And now I will be paid instead."

"Paid for what?"

"For goods delivered." She walked to the door and opened it.

"Just one more thing," Charlie pleaded. "That fancy phaser-wand thing one of the robbers waved around in the film—that was special effects? Or some real doohickey from, say, Groom Lake? That and the gizmo that turned off the lights at the Hilton? And what else, Caryl? Was your brother killed for smuggling secret stuff out of Area Fifty-one?" What kind of trouble had Evan gotten Charlie into?

Caryl Thompson ushered them out onto the patio without answering and even opened the gate for them.

"Pat wanted a plane. What do *you* want out of life, Caryl?" Bradone insisted.

"I want to help Evan get even with the people who ordered

my brother's death." And she closed the gate and then the door as she went back into the house.

Charlie whispered an explanation of the wand-phaser to Bradone in the cab that had waited outside for them and the effect it supposedly had on those caught in the dark at the casino robbery. "I'd bet it was Evan waving it, and I just assumed he was showing off, that maybe it had some connection to the Star Trek Experience at the Hilton. If it was real, it was awesome."

"If only the heavy woman could move, it might mean that the phaser couldn't affect her as much because she had more mass to penetrate."

"That could be faked. There's little Evan can't do with film—although there wasn't time to work up computer animation. But if Patrick persuaded one of the workers to spirit some secret weapons off the Groom Lake base for Evan's conspiracy project . . ."

"For the price of an airplane of his own," Bradone said thoughtfully. " 'Goods delivered.' Wonder what all those goods were?"

"The infrared camera and goggles can be bought on the open market. Could be just copies of important papers or plans that Evan could use in the project."

"Whatever it was, its theft explains why Caryl's brother had to die." Bradone tapped a tooth with her sunglasses, nodding sagely. "The keepers of the secrets out there might have wanted to make an example of him among workers and those who fly them to work. And why Emily Graden's husband was going out to the Janet Terminal."

"The question, Detective McKinley, is Evan Black's role in all this. I'm not sure I'd trust him as far as Caryl Thompson does. And Loopy Louie's offering Evan some kind of way to get, I thought, all his winnings out of the country. Sounds like he's bidding against others for the job. I wonder if it's also to get some secret doohickys out."

"Wish we could talk to Evan while avoiding the police, the murder or murderers, and—"

"Richard Morse?"

"And Richard Morse. Don't underestimate the man's usefulness to you, Charlie. He has great admiration for your abilities. In his way, I think he's very proud of you."

And you're getting tired of him. And I'm tired of small favors Richard's pride lets him drop, "in his way."

They left the cab on a street corner and walked a few blocks to a deli with outdoor seating in an inner courtyard. Bradone made a discrete phone call to her butler before their salads arrived. She made another after they'd been served and spoke to Evan Black himself, giving directions to their location.

"Someone named Mel will pick us up in about forty-five minutes. So we can relax and enjoy our meal."

"Mel is Evan's cinematographer. What are they up to?"

"Same thing we are, trying to avoid the police. Evan left word with Reed so we could get hold of him. It seems Metro has taken Richard Morse in for questioning."

"Richard doesn't know anything. He's been so smitten with you, he won't listen to what I've been trying to tell him about all this." Charlie put down a fork full of radicchio, sprouts, arugula, and godknows. "What? That's not all. I'm not being intuitive. You look funny."

Bradone speared a cucumber slice and took an eternity to chew it. "Looks like we're going to get our chance to talk to Evan."

"God, are there more bodies?"

The unreadable expression on the stargazer's face grew even stranger. "Evan doesn't want to spend time with the police because of an important meeting. And he wants you there too. I guess I get to come along by default."

"What meeting? Will you stop this?"

"Charlie, Mitch Hilsten is in town."

CHAPTER 22

DO YOU KNOW parents drive kids to schools two blocks from home in neighborhoods so safe no kid has been molested by anybody but relatives and family friends for decades?" Evan Black, the young genius, swung his legs from side to side over the edge of an upper bunk and gazed down on them all. The hanging light fixture over the table, a gas lantern with a lightbulb in it, swung in rhythm with his legs across his little round glasses. "Kids are safer out on the streets than in the house."

He was making Charlie seasick. She and Bradone sat on the bench on one side of the galley table, Mel Goodall and Mitch Hilsten on the other. Mitch leaned against the bulkhead of the boat Evan had borrowed for the meet, tied up at a marina somewhere on Lake Mead.

"All because the media makes big on false statistics and rare but memorable occurrences in a small portion of the population."

Mitch had one elbow on the table and one on the sink counter. He was in his denim mode—clothes faded to powder blue, like his eyes, like Charlie and Bradone's pants. He faced Evan, hands clasped in front of his mouth, biting one knuckle, watching the writer/producer with skepticism.

Charlie blinked. Skepticism? Mitch Hilsten, who believed in every kooky thing that came down the Ventura Freeway?

Maybe he was acting. Hard to tell with this guy.

"And then the rest of the entertainment industry picks up on the latest fear—books, movies, documentaries of odd events make us feel they're common. Somebody figures out how to train police and psychologists and publishing houses on how to handle the fear, discover it, treat it, prosecute it, recognize it. Hell, a whole new industry or three are invented right there, job descriptions and new college studies—not to mention pulp genres. It's beautiful, man."

Mel Goodall pretended sleepiness but watched Charlie through slits.

"People are even afraid of the fucking sun. Kids get fat and turn into listless couch potatoes because nobody wants to smear sunscreen on them every time they want to go out and play. Old people suffer from vitamin D deficiencies because the sun will give them cancer. Hell, life will give you cancer. Everything's gotten out of hand. One baby is swiped out of a nursery in one city and every hospital in the country's got to have surveillance cameras and security checks on the obstetric wards," said the man, responsible for stealing government secrets, joyfully. And he'd already involved Mitch in that theft by announcing his probable participation in the project.

And Charlie, caught in a quandary, watched Evan. Hard to square this boyish, excited, earnest, creative creature with the man who showed no emotion other than impatience with Charlie when she insisted on discussing with Officer Graden his personal pilot's death on the street in front of Loopy Louie's. The man who promised Patrick's sister he would get even with the people who ordered that death and yet told Charlie he wasn't sure that it hadn't been an accident. Who were the people who hired Sleem and the bald bouncer to walk Patrick into the traffic? How did Loopy Louie fit into all this?

Again, she looked to Bradone for guidance, but the astrologer had zoned out the minute Mitch Hilsten came into view. She squirmed every time he inhaled.

The boat, sort of a motorized sailboat, rocked with the lantern light crisscrossing Evan's glasses, nudging the dock gently. Nobody but Charlie seemed to suffer from indigestion.

"So, what's all this got to do with Groom Lake?" Mitch slid a studied glance at Charlie.

"It's the ultimate in conspiracy. Okay, maybe along with Roswell."

"But what's the purpose? To poke fun at people's beliefs? Eccentricities? What?"

Charlie gave Evan an "I told you so" smirk.

"No, man, to poke fun at their fears. We're talking concept here. Theme. Groom Lake is the epitome, but only symbolic, of the way conspiracy has taken over our lives. We don't trust anybody in a position of authority because the press and entertainment industry, one and the same, blow mistakes and corruption out of all proportion. And you know what, man? They're . . . we're going to make our fears happen. And that is the theme behind *Conspiracy.* We'll start with the small stuff—like perfectly healthy kids in bad need of exercise being driven to school two blocks away, never allowed outside without sunscreen, women in grocery stores scared to death the food's unsafe in the cleanest country in history—all the way to the billions spent on things that aren't needed, like Star Wars, all because of fear."

"Is there any script here?" asked Mitch, still skeptical but now showing some interest.

"Script it as we go. You know me, or you've read how I work. But see? The conspiracy is us, Mitch, living our lives out of fear of things that mostly don't happen or don't happen to most. The cause of the fear is not the dangers real or imagined in this world, but the media hyping them out of proportion to their impact in the name of news-entertainment. Fiction that becomes fact because we believe it so strongly. We could be missing the best days of our lives, Mitch, the best days of our country, the best days of our planet."

There were smears on both of Charlie's contact lenses—she could be missing something too. How do you finance without a script? And why hadn't he pitched this way to the moneymen at the screening? He'd have had them pulling out checkbooks in droves instead of groaning.

Hell, because they were groaning and pulling out cash instead. To pay off the stupid bets that Evan couldn't pull off a casino heist or which casino it would be. Did he really have enough money from that wager to produce the film himself?

Even given her mistrust of him, there was no mistaking this producer's energy and enthusiasm now. Charlie could feel it in the small space.

"What do you think, Mitch? It's okay, tell me."

"Well . . . it's kind of murky."

Charlie took another look at the superstar. Was this a new Mitch Hilsten? She thought he ate murky for breakfast.

"I know this is long for a pitch, but you're a deep mind."

"Where do I fit into this?" the deep mind asked.

People will flock to see you do anything. Even if it's stupid. That's how you fit in.

"You, Mitch, are a pilot for Janet. You know what that is?"

"Call name for a certain airline flying workers out to Groom."

Charlie was not surprised he knew that. Mitch probably knew all about compounding and DRIPs too. Even with smeared lenses, she was seeing all kinds of holes in this theory, but wouldn't think of interrupting a young genius and a superstar. AIDS, for instance. Cigarettes, for another. Or were they not part of the conspiracy theory because they were very real dangers?

"Your wife is the one taking your young children to school, panicking at the fresh-vegetable bins at the local grocery because of a TV newscast reporting one child dying a mysterious death after eating an avocado or something. This is all short background playing behind the front credits."

"Hope my wife isn't Cyndi Seagal. She drives me nuts."

Evan had him and knew it. His smile said it all. As his agent, Charlie should be happy.

"Nah, she's too old. We'll come up with somebody."

Cyndi Seagal, younger than Charlie by several years, was a client of Congdon and Morse Representation, Inc., on Wilshire Boulevard in Beverly Hills. And a favorite of Richard's. She was also a hell of a lot younger than Mitch Hilsten. She and Mitch had starred together in the hit that had rejuvenated his career. Didn't seem to be doing as much for hers.

"But the point here is Groom Lake—Area Fifty-one is the ultimate showcase of what happens when people feel victimized by what they perceive to be a conspiracy. Their fears come true. Their belief in those fears, instigated by a callous media, make them so. And nowhere more than on the vast military-owned desert spaces of Nevada. This is no big Spielberg extravaganza, Mitch. It's a quiet, low-toned, 'creep up on you and you'll never forget it' film."

"*Psycho* meets *The Player,*" Charlie interjected.

"Exactly." Evan's approval was discouraging. She'd thought she was being funny.

"Where are you going to get footage to pull that off, Black? Fake it in a studio? Computer animation?"

"Don't have to," Evan said.

"Already in the can," Mel said. "Right, Charlie?"

"You'd have seen it by now, if I could get in my house. There's a lot of it Charlie hasn't seen either. Most of it, in fact. Some great satellite stuff."

Mitch turned his full attention to Charlie now. "Hear you found the bodies. Rough. I'm sorry. Tell me you're not going to do any investigating."

"I'm not going to do any investigating."

"Charlie?" Bradone came out of her trance.

"I'm just helping Bradone. Tagging along, you know."

"No, I don't know." Mitch turned around to face Charlie

and thus Bradone across the table. The astrologer sunk back into her trance. "But Maggie says you're in bad need of a vacation, and this doesn't sound like one."

Oh really? "You talked to Maggie Stutzman?"

"Well, you wouldn't answer my E-mail."

"Everybody's ganging up on me. Jeesh."

"See? Conspiracy." Evan rubbed his hands in obvious glee. "Charlie's indicative of the national mood. Everybody who sees this film is going to relate. And they'll never forget it was Mitch Hilsten who was flying for Janet. How did you know it was called the Janet Terminal, Mitch?"

"The Internet." But Mitch was still glaring at Charlie.

"Well, okay, enough. Maybe we better go topside and let you two have a big fight and then kiss and make up or whatever you kids do." Evan jumped down from the bunk and held an arm out to Bradone. "Come on up and tell me about your investigations, Detective McKinley."

"Wait, how do you know that nameless government guy with Battista hasn't confiscated this footage you're so proud of?" Charlie called up after him. And all that cash Loopy hoped you weren't keeping at home?

Mel Goodall rose and stretched, chuckling. "Because the can wasn't in the house."

"Was it there yesterday when those three men were murdered?"

"Nope."

"Maybe that's what they were looking for."

But Mel and his long, lean Dockers disappeared above deck, leaving Charlie and Mitch to stare at each other across the table.

"Sounds like you're going to deal."

"Certainly going to think about it, and seriously. Evan Black is becoming an icon in the industry. I keep thinking I should pay you instead of Lazarus. You've done more for my career."

"Mitch, I admire Evan's work as much as you do. But this

project is being financed illegally, and I think you should walk away from it. And I didn't do anything to get you this part."

"You suggested me to your client for it."

"He wanted me to ask you because he thinks I'm your girlfriend. He thought he was using me. But I didn't ask you. He merely mentioned my name to your agent, hoping that you'd think I lined this up. I didn't do anything, Mitch. I've been too busy with all the dead men."

"And you didn't get Richard Morse to suggest me for the role in *Phantom of the Alpine Tunnel* when Eric Ashton walked at the last minute, I suppose. The role that turned my sliding career around."

"I've told you a million times, Richard called me to approach you for the part the morning after our one infamous night together in that rat-infested motel in Moab. He thought he was using me too, but I didn't do anything that time either."

"What do you mean, you didn't do anything? Most exhausting night of my life."

"I mean I didn't ask you about the part for Richard. He suggested I sleep with you to get you to play it. The pig."

"But you already had."

"Not to get you to take the part—it was just—"

"Estrus. I know," he said fondly. "Know what?"

"No, what?"

"I've had my astrologer charting this estrus thing."

"What?"

"Guess where the moon is tonight, Charlie? It's in your eighth house."

CHAPTER 23

"TERRY, DID YOU know that Mitch Hilsten is in town?"

"Yes, Barry, he's shacking up with that Hollywood agent Charlie Greene. She represents Evan Black, the young genius."

"Yeah, well, did you know this Charlie Greene is an unwed mother and that she told her own poor old brokenhearted mom to sit in front of a fan when she complained of hot flashes?"

"Really? She's shacking up with Mitch Hilsten at Loopy Louie's. We better get a camera crew over there right away."

"And Terry, that's not all—this Charlie Greene is responsible for the murder of Ben Hanley from Kenosha, Wisconsin, as well as Officer Timothy Graden, who left two small sons, one still in a high chair, and she's been stealing secret weapons from our government."

But the combination of the words *camera crew* and the fact her eyes burned brought Charlie upright, heart trying to pound its way up her throat. She should have discarded her contact lenses and let her eyes rest overnight, replacing the lenses with fresh ones in the morning.

There was no camera crew and it *was* morning. She didn't have any new lenses with her because she was at Loopy Louie's, just like the news team said.

But the TV screen was black, the set silent. It sat huge and square and out of place in the center of the room on a round table that revolved to face any direction ordered. Instead of exhibiting the ugly bulges of most TVs, the back of this one had a pictured cover depicting a view of sand dunes and desert palms rippling in a wind that blew at the flaps of the tent door framing the scene. Like the old animated beer signs.

Another table surrounded the square TV's rotating table, this one narrow and itself encircled by a continuous round divan. The narrow table contained the remains of a sensuous dinner eaten and drunk in installments, interspersed with business utilizing other sensations.

The round bed had gauzy curtains looped back with menacing curved scimitars. A scimitar hung above the bed too, just below the mirror in the ceiling. Charlie looked away fast. Not the time of day to be looking in a mirror.

With the bed round, the bedside amenities sat along a shelf at the top, and of course the only remote within reach was on the other end of the shelf. Actually, there were four remotes in the room, and one made things rotate, including the bed itself, but Charlie wasn't up to that either.

So she had to reach across the superstar for the one on the shelf. Round beds, even as large as this, force people to sleep pretty much in the center, unless they are curling up in fetal positions.

Mitch stretched out right alongside her, facedown, back bare.

Charlie smelled like canned tuna fish.

Mitch was not as tall as he looked in his films, but his back was state-of-the-art. It had heavy muscle and some moles and a patch of fine blond hairs where it tapered toward the buttocks, a scattering of freckles across the shoulder blades. Muscle and bone were well defined, any love handles exercised off.

Mitch was basically a granola, yogurt, pasta, fish, fruit, and vegetable guy unless he felt amorous. Then it was red wine and red meat.

Remote in hand, Charlie paused to measure. The entire length of her arm and hand with remote extended could not reach across the width of his shoulders. In the attempt, she brushed the marvelous flip side and he groaned.

"Guys with smiles insured by Lloyd's of London shouldn't sleep on their faces."

"Protecting myself." He lifted his face off the pillow to shake his head. "Jesus. Gotta up my insurance to cover more parts." He lifted to his elbows and reached above them for the phone. "I need coffee."

"I need eggs."

"What I really need is oysters, raw."

"Do they work?"

"I doubt it. How do you want your eggs?"

"Over easy, toast, orange juice. Coffee." Charlie punched the remote to Barry and Terry. "No potatoes."

"I'll eat your potatoes." He ordered and then added, "Just leave it at the door."

"Raw oysters and camel fries?" Charlie wasn't shocked to find Barry and Terry on the screen—they seemed to live at the station. But she was surprised to find it the noon broadcast.

"You must have a bladder to match your libido," Mitch said when he came out of the bathroom to find her immersed in the noon news. Their clothes were still scattered across the divan.

How come he didn't smell like canned tuna? Wasn't fair. There'd been no time to talk to Evan last night, and Mitch didn't want to discuss business, like why he should turn down this project.

He gathered the congealed and bloody remains of their prime-rib dinner, placed them on the wheeled table on which they'd arrived, and rolled them toward the door.

"Mitch, do not open that door until you put on a robe. There could be a camera crew out there."

"Why would there be a camera crew out there?" He looked down at himself, which was everywhere apparent. He was blond of hair and tan of skin wherever the sun got to him. If only he could see his back, where she had left not one scratch anywhere. A work of art is to be respected.

"I don't know. I just sense that it might be."

Mitch disappeared immediately and reappeared looking like Lawrence of Arabia without the headdress. His powder blues damn near shimmered. Problem was, Mitch Hilsten believed in Charlie's nonexistent powers of being able to "sense" things.

It drove her nuts.

". . . last night at Rachel. In other news—"

"Rachel?" Lawrence whirled his robe and all back into the room. "What news about Rachel?"

"I don't know, it's over."

"Four young men are dead and five wounded after the shoot-outs yesterday afternoon in front of Loopy Louie's and a second outside the Golden Nugget. Mayor Jan Jones has requested law enforcement be beefed up on the Strip and on Fremont Street. Authorities believe the incidents are drug-related and have videotape of them in progress at both places."

"Yes, Barry, since the private security guards at the two casinos in question were armed only with nightsticks, they had to wait until the shooting stopped before entering the fray. The killers escaped, but the security guards—and the Metro officers who arrived shortly thereafter—chased fleeing tourists with camcorders instead of armed killers. Witnesses say that the acts, the murderers, and the victims are captured on film from every angle and at every moment because so many vacationers use video cameras."

"Modern technology has certainly changed the world and the way we do things," Barry concurred. "The debate now seems to be—should private security guards at the casinos be armed?"

"And should they be allowed to tackle fleeing tourists with camcorders?"

A taped interview with one of the fleeing tourists followed.

The tourist's face and voice were disguised, but his fear was not. "Hey, man, I just filmed it because it would be fun to show family and friends at home, okay? I don't want to be no witness at no murder trial, man, you know? On *Good Cops, Bad Guys,* the cops catch the bad guys. On the real-life channel, the bad guys' friends catch the witnesses, man. You know?"

"But your identity is kept a secret from the bad guy," the interviewer insisted.

"Yeah, man, but not from his lawyer. Makes the witness a sitting pigeon. Lawyer tells his client—moral obligation. Client tells his friends—witness meets unexpected death. Works for everybody but the victim and the witness. Hey, man, don't start in on witness-protection stuff. All depends on who is greasing whose what. You know?"

After commercials for Coca-Cola, Chrysler, IBM, Sustacal, and Depends, Terry came back on a sad note. "Services were held this morning for Officer Timothy Graden of the Metro Police, the young father of two small sons."

Emily Graden and one small son walked between rows of somber police officers standing at attention. Her husband's casket carried before her, Grandma carrying the other small son behind her. Emily wore the expression of the widow—anger and helplessness seeping through shock. "Authorities are still tight-lipped about their investigations into the hit-and-run that led to the officer's death and the motive behind it."

Charlie looked away.

After commercials by Coca-Cola, Chrysler, IBM, Sustacal, and Depends that played through twice this time, Barry came on with the news of another upheaval on yesterday's stock market, which had sent food stocks broadly higher and technology stocks plummeting.

"Mitch, do you know what a DRIP is?"

"Guy who doesn't eat raw oysters."

✣

"Jeeze, babe, you look great." Charlie's boss stuck his nose in her face. "Nice to know somebody's getting a rest out of this vacation." He nodded spastically and lowered an eyelid halfway, somehow making it stay that way.

"Richard, why did the police call you in for questioning? You don't know anything."

"I mean, your skin glows, dewylike. And your cheeks are rosy. Your eyes aren't even red."

"That's because I'm not wearing any contacts and I can't see across the room. Now—"

"And your voice is softer and those anger lines between your eyebrows are gone. Your color's terrific. I should make you take a vacation more often, kid. You win a pile of money, get laid, or what?"

Bradone was cracking up. She was the lump rolling on the couch next to Mel Goodall, whom Charlie identified by his length.

They were in Evan's great room. In the kitchen part of this room, he busied himself cooking pasta-something. It did smell good, but Charlie was so ravenous, she could eat the pan.

"So," her boss said, "when is Hilsten getting into town?"

Evan howled. Mel hooted. Bradone's laughter broke into choking sounds.

"What the hell's the matter with you guys?" Richard Morse finally tuned in. "Charlie, what's going on?"

"Mitch'll be here in time for dinner, Morse," their host intervened. "Pour everybody some more wine, will you? Especially Charlie."

"Richard, what did they question you about?"

"About you, Charlie."

CHAPTER 24

INTERESTING THAT THEY all ate Evan's marvelous pasta-something by candlelight in a room where three men had died and it didn't smell of death. It smelled of garlic and onion and basil.

And Charlie.

She'd showered before leaving Loopy's but wore the same clothes she had the day before. It was embarrassing. Everyone else in the room pretended not to notice.

Everything so softened by candlelight and myopia and wine. Everyone blissful, tired, content. Three men lay dead the day before yesterday on the other side of that furniture there.

The only sounds—the chomping of mixed lettuces, the slurping of fine Chianti, the crunch of crusty bread, an occasional soft sigh.

Mitch sat across from Charlie and next to Bradone, who was struck dumb again by his august presence. She should have seen him eating raw oysters and camel fries for brunch.

The superstar had dropped Charlie off here and then sneaked into her room at the Hilton to get her some fresh contacts. Hard to imagine Mitch sneaking anywhere, but he'd worn sunglasses to hide the powder blues and promised he wouldn't smile and expose the famous flashing teeth.

He waited until they'd settled over dark roasted coffee, French-pressed, and sliced pears with cheese and chocolate truffles to explain what had taken him so long.

"Charlie's room at the Hilton's been tossed. Hard," he announced virilely. "Found her box of contact lenses under the bed. What the fuck's been going on around here, Black?"

"I've been trying to tell you, but you won't listen," Charlie snapped. Evan had put off her questions too. When she'd told him about Loopy Louie's strange offer, he'd said that Toby'd already mentioned it.

Now, Evan belched with pleasure. "Bring your coffee. Somebody grab the wine and the dessert trays. Come on up to the screening room. And we'll show you, Hilsten." He laughed and swung his ponytail back over his shoulder. Right now, he reminded Charlie of a pirate, but then, she wasn't seeing clearly. "Charlie, you put your eyes in. I want you to see this too. Maybe it'll answer some of your questions."

"Tell me they didn't take my laptop," Charlie whispered to Mitch when they stretched out on floor cushions in the screening room.

"I didn't see one, but the place is a mess. I reported it to hotel security and promised to bring you back there tonight to see if anything had been taken. Where'd you keep your computer?"

"In the safe in the closet. Though I don't think that safe's very safe. I saw a security man operate the combination from memory." Charlie took a sip of coffee and a slug of wine.

Why me, Lord? It's like I'm marked.

"Does what happened to your room have anything to do with those concerns over the conspiracy project you keep going on about?"

"The financing is not legal."

"Wouldn't be the first time. They searching your room for money?"

"I suspect for what turned the lights out at the Hilton."

"Anyway, it's going to be okay, Charlie." He gave her shoulders a proprietary squeeze. "I'll help you clean up the mess at the Hilton."

"Yeah, right. And we'll spend tonight in my room, I suppose."

"Well, I'm not leaving you there alone. Besides, my astrologer's calculations say you're not done yet." The bastard chortled. "And that this should be your best month of the year. Venus is transiting your sign."

"You want to know why I'll never really get in a relationship? I hate the smell of tuna."

"You do not smell like canned tuna. I told you."

"What do you know? Men have no sense of smell." And Charlie crawled over to Bradone's cushion.

"Quiet on the set," their host joked. "Roll it, Mel. And somebody pour Charlie some more wine."

This time, the footage started with security guards wrestling a camcorder away from Evan Black while their cohort bopped Evan with a nightstick.

"That's right, Black. I forgot you always do a cameo in your films." Mitch sounded appreciative.

"Is that guy really hitting you, Evan?" Bradone sat up.

"Put it on pause, Mel." Evan rose to stand in front of the stilled frame of himself being beaten and pulled his shirt down at the neck like a teasing stripper to reveal a black-and-blue shoulder, turned around to lift the shirt from the waist to reveal a bruised back.

"Don't look, Charlie," Mitch advised.

"I hate you."

"I know."

"How'd you know when to be there?" Richard raised up on one elbow to stare at the stilled screen with his bug eyes. "You didn't set this up, I hope."

"Nah, Mel and I were out in the van, had the radio on. We got there just in time to get attacked by the law. It was beautiful. Never say I don't do my own research." A self-satisfied

Evan walked away from the screen. "Okay, Mel."

The cameraman shooting Evan's beating, probably Mel, turned away from the scene, camera still running. He was running himself, as were all kinds of people with him. Their race down the Strip was a study in control, the man behind the camera holding it in front of him, the world leaping and jostling around him in a frantic but oddly rhythmic step. Like the rescued film of a dead reporter caught in war-torn wherever.

"Holy moly, Superman," Richard Morse said.

"That's Batman, I think." Gullible Mitch fell for it.

But even then Bradone sighed and turned her head to Charlie. "If you don't get back over there, I will."

"Be my guest." Charlie took a slug of Chianti.

"You want to cuddle up to Richard?"

Charlie took another slug and thought it over. She crawled back to the cushion next to Mitch but asked Richard, "What did Metro want to know about me? You never said."

"Just a background check. I'm your employer, remember? Wanted to know how long you'd been with the agency, what you do there."

The next scene showed the same security guards jumping over wounded and dead victims of the shoot-outs, probably borrowed from someone else's camera. A shot obviously out of sequence in real time, but Evan often used that technique to startle audiences. Critics called it a "conceit," disciples, a "trademark." Charlie had always liked Evan's films in spite of herself and had to admit that with careful editing, it worked.

"They especially wanted to know what you do for Evan, here. If you're sexually involved—"

"Richard—"

"They're cops, Charlie, they're supposed to ask things like that."

And then came the footage of Charlie laid out in the desert night with shadow flames for lighting and that gross bush at her head like a tombstone.

Mitch tensed beside her, put an arm around her, drew her into his warmth.

That made Charlie tense. She loathed heroes.

"Besides, I told them you were not sexually involved with Evan and that it's a damn shame. You could use a little."

Mitch put a hand over Charlie's mouth and held her down until she calmed. But Bradone and Evan howled in unison. Which made for a seriously strange sound.

The next sequence brought them all back to the matter at hand. Charlie and Mitch sat up. Richard raised himself on an elbow again to see better. Evan gave a satisfied sigh.

It was the "ground stuff" he'd kept baiting Charlie with.

This was all shot without sound, which made it spooky. Knowing Evan, who loved to play in the Foley studio, there would be lots of silence in the finished product and real or natural sounds mixed with the score, or sounds from another film even. Charlie could imagine him mixing war sounds with the shoot-out in front of Loopy's. Instead of police sirens, there might be air-raid sirens from the bombing of London during World War II. Just enough to throw you off.

Sometimes he'd begin a scene with sounds from the last sequence. He liked to call this technique "transition." Again, it would be labeled conceit—distracting and unnecessary—by some, brilliance by admirers. You either liked or hated an Evan Black film. They were as controversial as their maker. And more than once he'd been termed *mad*—as in nuts. Charlie had always wondered how, in Hollywood, you could tell.

But when his projects worked—and probably three-fourths did—they grossed bucks, big bucks on the cheap. Because he did so much of it himself. No second unit on his films, despite Toby's title. No power struggles between egos on the set that drove costs up on most projects. Talent or production crew, they were free to walk, because he wasn't paying squat anyway and there were people lined up to take their places. People worked on a Black film as a way to become better known in their specialty, not for guild or union scales. Studio brass got intimidating, interfering, Evan would walk the project to another studio, never shooting anything in L.A. While endless lawsuits were being filed, threatened, some scheduled in court, he was garnering awards. If this guy was nuts, he was like the Einstein of nuts.

The question was, Was he capable of murder? And treason?

✣

The raw oysters and camel fries seemed to have worked, but Mitch ordered up a deluxe hamburger and french fries sometime in the wee hours. And a bottle of red.

Charlie'd had enough of everything but sex. Well, she did eat one fry. Okay, five, but that was it.

Between bouts of lust that had little to do with the lustee—he could have been anybody that night—in her savaged room at the Hilton, which she and the lustee had no time to put right or to inform security of what might be missing from the obvious search, Charlie dreamed. And when awake, she relived that ground stuff.

It was awesome. In her head, she mixed the sound herself.

Groom Lake even in wide angle from a nearby mountaintop stood well disclosed, impossible to hide on open desert. The massive runways looked able to launch a fleet of ocean liners, or aircraft carriers three at a time—side by side. What could possibly require such spaciousness? No stealth bomber needed anywhere near that width or length. And those runways were in excellent condition, not patched up like at most airports.

The vast hangarlike buildings and sheds sprawled low, flat, and again were impossible to hide. Perhaps the only option *was* to deny their existence. Stranger things have happened. The fleet of white 737s, unmarked but for a wide red stripe along the side pocked by the windows, showing white here, lined up as she remembered them from her brief flight over that ridge with Caryl Thompson, Evan, and Mel. Just before the orange light knocked her out.

That orange light, really more of a thing, had more substance than normal light does. Yet Charlie couldn't be sure it was an object. Round, huge, and spinning, it reminded her fleetingly of a sun before it vanished. It didn't go away or dissolve or spin past the little Mooney. It couldn't. It filled the sky. And then it just simply wasn't. Like it had never existed. This was not on the footage in Evan's film—it was in Charlie's head, at the back of her eyeballs, leaving the orange smear that still returned now and then.

Or it was in her dream. Her imagination. Probably induced by the french fries. And a sex and Chianti hangover.

No, on the screen in Evan's screening room, the Groom Lake, or Area 51, sequence had continued with the wide-angle lens turning in a slow circle, panning empty desert and low mountains until it faced an enormous eye. It seemed to be some sort of surveillance or sensor thing on a tripod. The wide angle moved on to people in denim and straw hats sitting on rocks, raising sandwiches and beer cans to the camera, bloated distortions, too large because they were too close to the lens. It continued its circle to come to a stop on what appeared to be barren desert scenery.

Until you noticed the dirt road snaking off to the horizon, the white Jeep parked to the side, and two or three figures bent over the road next to it. About all you could see was their movement, not its purpose. Spreading tacks? And in the distance where the road dropped over into a gully, was that a tow truck?

"I still don't see what all this, as impressive as it is, has to do with Charlie's room being tossed," Mitch had said either at the end of the screening or in her dream, or both.

"They're looking for clues as to how she did it. There are bets still out there." Was it Evan who said that? For real or dream?

"Do you know who searched my room? Was it those good old boy reverse militia guys? Retired ARPs?"

"Wouldn't be a bit surprised, but not to worry, Charlie. A magical event is about to occur that will make them all look so silly, they won't dare get smart with us."

But before Charlie could ask the young genius what this magic was, she was sucked into a giant orange and taken advantage of. Was it a dream, Mitch Hilsten, or an omen?

CHAPTER 25

CHARLIE SHOWERED AND dressed before Mitch Hilsten stirred an eyelash, studied herself in the mirror in the bathroom to see if she really did look different, younger, less stressed, dewy—like her boss had said.

She didn't look bad. She felt great. Her room was still a mess, the search a thorough one, but her computer was safe. Surely "they" had found what they were looking for. She downloaded her E-mail and hurried downstairs to the serious coffee bar in the lobby next to the black Stealth. And next to the bank of slots where she'd won a jackpot and Art Sleem had dumped cash and warnings on her in the morning, before getting himself murdered in the afternoon.

She took her skinny latte with nutmeg to the café and looked for Ardith. There was something reassuring about Ardith and her attempts to mother Charlie's eating habits.

But it was a harried Bobby Sue—the name badges gave only first names—who stopped by Charlie's table with the menu, masticating gum as if holding her face together depended on it.

"First time in fifty years Ardith Miller's missed work, except once when the union struck and another time she got the flu. I'm working her section too."

"Fifty years?" Charlie reconsidered her retirement options.

"Something's happened. I just know it." Maybe not fifty years, but Bobby Sue had been around awhile herself. Her ponytail was snow white and thinning. "Something bad."

Charlie, who'd eaten only five french fries—okay, maybe seven—last night while the granola-boy lustee consumed a huge hamburger, decided it was time for two eggs. Over easy so she could cut up and scramble them on her plate, making the whites all yokey, and then dip her toast in the yoke that remained. Well? This was a rough vacation.

She sipped her latte, felt the caffeine booting her up in that marvelous way it did only first thing in the day, booted up the Toshiba notebook on its battery power, and read her E-mail while breakfast cooked.

The news from Larry—three out of five really important deals she had going were toast. The industry was like that—string you along with awesome fantasizing material for months and then kick you in the stomach with rejection in one afternoon. The worst part—Charlie got to break the news to the writers, and she'd better do it before they read it in the trades.

Nebula had decided not to renew the option on Parnell Davidson's legal thriller. Universal had rejected Jerry and Leo's final script revisions for *Thelma & Louise: The Early Years,* and Mega Studios had scrapped the *Trojan Hearse* project. Charlie represented three of the writers on that baby.

The new office witch, Ruby Dillon, threatened to quit if Richard didn't call her immediately, which was yesterday. Lovely Libby had decided she was going to college to learn to become a veterinarian and Tuxedo the Dreaded had gained forbidden access to Charlie's closet and peed on all her shoes.

"It really stinks in there," the kid reassured Charlie. No word about the groping boss, the retarded boyfriend, or the secondhand car that defied all emission standards known but which Libby managed to get passed anyway. All together, a worrisome communication.

But even more worrisome—a message from an address she'd never seen before and unsigned, the server something obscure she'd never heard of. "Good thing I know where you live. Too bad you don't know where I do. Will they call it murder or suicide, do you think?"

She'd already consumed her meal before it occurred to her that just because Art Sleem was dead didn't mean "they" had given up trying to poison her.

Charlie hoped the unidentified message was just one more threat from Sleem, powerless now that he was dead, and not some "they" who took no prisoners. Could somebody be threatening Libby, still back in Long Beach, where Charlie lived? She got on a pay phone in the lobby to leave messages with her neighbors Maggie Stutzman and Jeremy Fiedler to keep an eye out for Libby and any strangers hanging around the compound, explaining the E-mail letter.

Then more calls to commiserate with six writers. They'd every last one already heard the bad news. Trying not to, they blamed Charlie. She was the middleman-woman. The shield and the target for both sides.

Charlie peeled a couple of hundreds off her roll and threw them on the blackjack table. One thing, the tossing of her room hadn't been your ordinary robbery, not that she'd ever suspected it was. Her cash winnings were still in the safe with her computer.

Please tell me we're not going to investigate.

Why, you think I'm not up to it?

Charlie, we are staggering under a load of problems now. We can't take on any more.

We are being threatened by E-mail, stumbling over dead bodies by the truckload, involved in scary, maybe antigovernment, stuff, and I am worried about Ardith Miller.

Ardith Miller—the waitress we barely know—

Did not show up for work today after fifty years, minus a union strike and sick leave from the flu. And she knew me.

Lots of people know you.

Doesn't keep them from going to work.

Your problem is not conspiracy. It's guilt. You take on responsibility for a waitperson not showing up for work when you've seen her maybe two, three times.

What are you today, my conscience or my good sense? Charlie did wave away the cocktail person. No more drinks in this casino.

I'm the you you don't want to listen to. Call me what you want.

So now what do we do?

"Decide whether to stand or hit would be nice." This dealer was a woman and as unfeeling, unemotional, and unimpressed a robot as you could imagine.

Until Charlie scratched for a hit and asked, "Do you know Ardith Miller?"

The dealer squeezed the card she'd slipped from the shoe. It hit Charlie in the face.

Eddie, the pit boss with the hairy, flinching hands and turquoise jewelry, appeared from nowhere. "You gonna make it, Zelda?"

Zelda nodded, blinked a lot, took in a raspy breath, and retrieved the errant card. It mated with Charlie's hand to produce twenty-one.

There might be something to this idea of not concentrating on what you're doing while playing blackjack. Made more sense to Charlie than moons, planets, stars, houses, and trines.

"It's you again," Eddie said from behind the stoic Zelda.

"She knows." With what looked like a rapid waving of her hand, Zelda clicked cards from the shoe to begin a new game.

"You know?" Eddie watched every move at the table and Charlie at the same time.

"I know," Charlie said, and she did. "Ardith Miller is dead for no good reason." She beat the house on the next hand too.

What she didn't bring up was the fact she hadn't a clue why

or how. Hell, at her age, Ardith could have dropped dead of a heart attack. Charlie didn't like knowing things. It was depressing. I am *not* psychic.

The game played out, Charlie doing well, if not as well as the house. The two men at her table were losing heavily, keeping a balance to this game of chance. A new dealer appeared to replace Zelda, who apparently was not stoic enough, and Eddie escorted Charlie to the very room in which a zealous staff had broken Ben Hanley's sternum while he was dead.

The world was a fun, exciting, dangerous place. And totally screwy.

"I just meet somebody and they die," Charlie explained to Eddie and a couple of suits in the secure area. "When I heard Ardith hadn't shown up for work today after fifty years, I just figured it had happened to her too."

"After fifty years of what?" The suit with reams of paper on his lap and a ballpoint pen poised above the top page looked up at her. He had to be a lawyer or a super-number-cruncher. Charlie met this type all the time in showbiz. They financed things or worked for those who did. They were seriously powerful dudes, whether they worked for banking interests or Pepsi or gaming.

"Being on time to work."

"Do you always become so involved with resort staff when you travel?" He lifted eyebrows carefully trimmed. Older guys often make money but no sense—they go bald and then grow long hair in their noses and eyebrows.

"You don't look very sad." The other suit leaned forward—no paper or pens on his lap. He must be even higher on the honcho ladder. "About the waitperson's death."

She noticed these suits didn't feel the need to introduce themselves. Like the shorthaired fed with Detective Battista.

"I'm just numb. She's what, number seven in a week?"

Both suits wore shiny gray and sported tailored gray hair and spa suntans. And very expensive eyeglasses. This was obviously big money sitting here. Why? For the death of a wait-person? Charlie didn't think so. Both wore plain silver bands on their wedding fingers.

"Seven what in a week?" Eddie was trying to keep things rational for his bosses.

"Seven murders. Might not be that big a deal in Vegas, with all the loose change around, but that's one for every day of my vacation, if you can call it that."

"You've been involved in seven murders in a week?" This was the guy with no paper on his lap.

"I've just been involved with the victims, which does not make me feel comfortable. My Las Vegas experience has been ruined by death, violence, and destruction."

The lawyer/accountant type leaned over the paper on his lap and raised his chin to study Charlie without sympathy through the magnification at the lower end of his eyewear. "Why do you suppose your room here at the Hilton was so methodically searched? And have you found anything missing?"

Charlie remembered her dream. "They,"—the ones who probably work for you—"wanted to know how I did it."

"How you did what?" one suit asked, but all the men wore identical expectant expressions.

"Someone thinks I had something to do with the power outage the night the casino was robbed. Maybe that I had some kind of device that could make it happen. I think they were looking for it. They didn't touch my cash or a valuable computer. If they took anything, I haven't missed it yet."

But Evan Black knew what they were looking for. Charlie was sure these men were not to be tarried with, even by Evan Black. Why would he risk such a thing? And involve Charlie too? And now old gullible Mitch?

Charlie needed to talk to Bradone. But when finally released from the inner sanctum, she found that Bradone McKinley had checked out of the hotel.

CHAPTER 26

WHY WOULD SHE check out and not say good-bye? What if she's number eight?" Charlie asked Mitch, who was back to coffee and granola—granola he glopped up with yogurt instead of milk. Tickled Charlie's gag reflex just to look at it.

"Number eight what?" He sat on the foot of the bed with the room-service table on wheels in front of him. He didn't even have the TV on. "God, how do you do it?"

"Eighth dead body in seven days. Good thing I'm leaving tomorrow." She began tossing the stuff strewn on the floor into drawers. "And you're the one who had to have a deluxe hamburger, fries, and a bottle of red zin at two in the morning."

"Who's the seventh dead body?" He did look some worse for wear. "And you ate half the fries."

"I only had seven—okay, maybe nine. There must have been fifty on that plate anyway. Ardith Miller, a waitperson down at the café, didn't show for work this morning after fifty years."

"You know, Charlie? We sound married. Here we are talking away, making no sense at all. And we understand each other."

"Now don't start on that." Charlie found another pair of panties under a pile of sofa cushions, and couldn't believe how many she'd brought along. What could the people who searched this room think Charlie possessed that turned out the lights in the casino and a good part of the hotel?

"Haven't you ever wondered what it would be like to be—"

"To a man who eats raw oysters with camel fries? I don't think so."

"See, there we did it again. We're a natural."

"Mitch—"

"Okay, so what happened to Ardith Miller?"

"I don't know. I just know she's dead."

"What's that got to do with you? It's not like you don't have an alibi for last night. Boy, do you have an alibi."

"I just know that if I hadn't come to Vegas, she'd still be alive. Because people I've been meeting are dropping like flies." She was really tossing stuff now, just to get it out of sight and out of mind. The fact someone she didn't know had touched it was almost worse than Tuxedo peeing on her shoes. "She was murdered like the rest of them, I'm sure of it. You just might start looking over your shoulder yourself, guy."

"Know something else? We've had two very full nights together and you're not even talking guilt. We're making progress. Our relationship."

"It's just Vegas. Even *I* can't feel guilty in Vegas."

"When you say you're sure of these things, do you mean your special sensing ability has kicked in?"

"Besides, dead bodies are distracting. And I do not have a *special* sensing ability. But I can see with my *commonsense* ability. Mitch, if in one week you came in contact with seven—and I hope to God Bradone won't make an eighth here—people who later turned up dead, you would see a pattern too. And if I were psychic, maybe I'd know the reason."

"But they don't have anything in common, at least most of them don't."

"Yes they do. One thing. Me."

"What about Vegas itself? What about Evan Black?"

"He didn't know Ben Hanley or Ardith Miller. But he sure

had connections to the rest. Mitch, we've got to talk about Evan—"

"I really think you're making something out of this that isn't there. You're always blaming yourself for stuff that isn't your fault."

"Good, fine. You believe what you want. That's your right. Just listen to me about—"

"Wanna see my back?" He had the nerve to look smug.

She reached for a table lamp to lob at him, and the only thing that saved the superstar was the phone. Charlie always threw a fit when her writers used that ploy.

Bradone McKinley's relief that Charlie and not Mitch picked up came in an exhaled grunt. "Don't say my name. Act normal. I'm on a cellular in a rental car outside the Hilton. Come down as fast as you can. Don't tell anyone where you're going and don't use the lobby door. The paparazzi and TV crews are setting up shop. They probably discovered that you and Mitch are a hot item upstairs. Remember the side door we used the other day, by the glass elevator? See if you can get there unnoticed. And Charlie, put on some jeans and walking shoes. Bring a jacket. We got work to do."

Charlie almost walked around the white Jeep Cherokee with heavily tinted windows standing directly in her path, until it beeped at her.

"What are you doing in this? And why all the clothes? It's hot out here."

The astrologer was in a safari outfit—Banana Republic right down to the weird khaki hat. What role was she playing today? Much as she was drawn to this woman, Charlie had her doubts.

The Cherokee blasted out onto Paradise. Bradone switched on the air-conditioning and headed south. "Check to see if we're being followed."

"I thought you'd left without saying good-bye." Charlie

checked, to see them being followed by your normal three lanes full of cars.

"I was comped in the penthouse longer than most people. I've just moved to another hotel. I would have gone home, but I feel I must stay and help you."

"Why were you comped longer than most?" They took Flamingo east to the 515 and headed north.

"Because I was smart enough not to lose my shirt fast enough. When are you leaving Vegas?"

"Tomorrow. Bradone, what is going on—where are we headed?" They were headed out of town.

"Charlie, you can't leave tomorrow," Bradone said fifty miles or so later. "You can move in with me. We have to get to the bottom of all this."

"All this what?" They'd picked up I-15 until they came to State 93 and turned north. No one was following. The landscape looked like it always did when you left Vegas in any direction—bleak.

"All this murder. Don't doubt me now. You need me."

Charlie told Bradone about Ardith Miller and the unknown threatener on her E-mail and about getting called into the security room at the Hilton. "Zelda, the dealer, told Eddie, the floorman, that I knew—I'm assuming about Ardith. And that was it. I was behind closed doors with threatening suits. I know she's dead."

"Charlie, I realize it sounds unlikely, but it is possible that all these deaths are not connected. Most of them surely, but not all. Was Ardith's death what they questioned you about? These threatening suits?"

"They seemed even more interested in what might have been missing from my room after the search."

"And was there? Anything—"

"Not that I could see. My computer and cash were still there." Not to mention two zillion pairs of panties. Better I should have packed all my shoes so the cat couldn't have fixed them. "I figure someone was looking for a device of some kind I could have used to turn off the lights at the Hilton that night, so somebody could rob the casino."

"Anybody could cut wires or pull switches, couldn't they?"

"Not that selectively, I wouldn't think. Given that the lobby and casino clear through the sports-book area are on one electrical system, that outage followed me that night. From the marquee outside right up to my room. Most of the building and attached convention center weren't affected at all."

"The penthouse wasn't and the Star Trek addition—that's true. But Charlie, the Hilton has made no statement as to the amount of money stolen. Metro does not appear to be searching for the robbers. It's all being quietly ignored. Why isn't the press hounding them about it?"

"Yeah, why isn't the Hilton heist page-one news?"

"Precisely. There's something going on here far stranger than your happening to pick this week to come here on vacation. It's bigger than you. And it's not your fault. But you are liable to be swept up in it anyway."

Like, I already am. "What's going on?"

"I'm hoping you can tell me, Charlie. That's why we're heading for Area Fifty-two—"

"Fifty-one."

"Oh, right. Groom Lake, whatever." The floppy hat and huge sunglasses hid too much of Bradone's face.

Not only was there nobody following, they didn't meet anybody. "How is it you know the way so well? Bradone, have you been here before?"

"Actually, I have—but I wasn't driving. You're going to have to help me watch for a town named Alamo."

"On this road, you could miss a town named anything."

"There's some bottled water in that grocery bag in the backseat and some fruit and sandwiches, when you're ready. I'll have an apple and water, please."

There were pillows and blankets on the backseat too.

"That's why the jackets and comfortable shoes. You're planning to spend the night up there."

"Probably safer for you there than in Vegas."

"Bradone, I really do have to get home and back to work. I appreciate your wanting to help me, but I can't spare the time. I might not be safe in Vegas, but I know I'd be safer in Long Beach than at Groom Lake."

The astrologer leaned into the wheel, as if eager for adventure. "What if that threatening E-mail letter was written on *your* computer by whoever searched your room?"

Any other day, an adventure with Bradone McKinley would be a blast. But not today. Not after seven dead bodies—assuming Ardith *was* dead. Not after watching Emily Graden, holding the small hand of one of her sons, walk in the funeral procession behind her husband's casket. "With my software, there's no way to write a letter to yourself, to the in box. Anything you write on it goes in the out box."

"I imagine some hacker could figure out a way quite quickly, but, disregarding that, someone could bring in another computer and E-mail you."

"I don't see that as a reason for our having to come up here and spend the night."

"If they were looking for something in your room that would turn out the lights at the casino, they must have been looking for some kind of high-tech device. Charlie, you said Evan was one of those masked burglars we saw on his film."

"With Mel shooting it. And probably Caryl and Toby too. Evan had to be the one snuffing out the guy's lighter. Toby picked us up when we left the burning plane on the desert."

"And they dropped you off at the Hilton lobby and the lights went out as you moved through the building."

"It was more like just behind me. But I don't have a device. Maybe they found it."

"Maybe they slipped something in your purse or clothes that shut down the electricity selectively."

Charlie turned out her purse in her lap and fingered everything before putting it back in. "Another of Pat Thompson's goods delivered. Everything seems to come back to him."

Detective Bradone laughed, took a crispy bite of apple, and gunned the Cherokee toward Alamo. "This case is beginning to come together, Charlie."

Charlie had the uneasy thought that no one but the astrologer knew where she was at this moment. Or where she was going.

CHAPTER 27

THERE WASN'T MUCH to Alamo, where they stopped for gas and directions, the latter not adding measurably to Charlie's confidence in this trip. A few miles up the road, they turned off at Ash Springs—a few house trailers. A Texaco station—closed. Not a car or a soul in sight.

"What do people do out here to keep from going nuts?"

"Maybe they eat. Way past time for those sandwiches. Let's have the chicken now and save the roast beef for dinner."

"Bradone, I have to catch that plane tomorrow." But Charlie pulled the bag over into the front seat. Sliced baked chicken breast with some kind of Yuppie sauce instead of mayo, with nut slivers and sprouts, shrooms and black olives. It was delicious, but having anything to eat out in this wasteland would have seemed a luxury.

Scraggly, stunted Joshua trees flew past the Cherokee and sickly cactus topped with bunches of long spikes gathered at the bottom and splayed outward like a bouquet of swords.

"So, Evan and company somehow managed to put something in my purse or on me when I blacked out, and it shut off the lights so they could film themselves robbing the casino, and it came from Groom Lake. Smuggled out by Patrick Thompson." Charlie hadn't found anything in her purse. "Bradone, we can't get anywhere near the place and wouldn't know what to look for if we did. We are not detectives. This trip is just going to involve us further in what you yourself termed 'something bigger than we are.' We're totally out of our league and should leave it to the professionals."

"Which professionals? The ones who ordered Patrick's murder? Or the police, who were so sure he was a silly tourist who jaywalked under that car? The casino suits, who seem more interested in how the lights went out than what happened to the money? This trip gets you out of Vegas."

High-voltage power lines and desolation lined the road. Far away, bumpy rock mountains surrounded them.

"So will that plane tomorrow." A desert's lack of trees was stunningly apparent here. So boring, Charlie wanted to fall asleep.

"When does it leave?"

"Five something."

"No problem. We'll have you back by then."

"Bradone, when were you here before, why, and who with?"

"How do you know I was with someone?"

"You said you weren't driving, and you had to ask directions in Alamo."

"See, you are a detective. I was here with a group of astrologers on a field trip. Aren't these sandwiches good? This is an onion-dill bread that's so hard to find anymore. There's this wonderful deli—"

"We're beginning to sound married." Every mile closer to the dreaded secret installation made Charlie's mouth drier.

"Have some water. You may be dehydrating."

A smoggy haze at the base of the bumpy rock mountains cut them off from the desert floor, appearing to levitate them. There could be a big power plant nearby . . . or something even more suspicious.

Charlie decapped a bottle of lukewarm liquid—springwater, of course. Amazing how many springs had cropped up since bottled water became the rage. "Why do we have to stay all night?"

"Because night's when you can see things in the dark. The lights and everything. And I want you to get close enough to maybe see what made you black out. Like the lights did at the Hilton."

"It wasn't really black."

"It was orange, wasn't it?"

"Did I tell you that?"

Ugly landscape. Worn-down mountains. That ground layer of haze couldn't be moisture. So many dust devils. Maybe it seemed like so many because she could see forever. Charlie didn't feel comfortable in wide-open spaces.

"You didn't have to." Bradone laughed for no reason. This crazy woman could enjoy herself anywhere. "I've been here before, remember."

"It happened to you? You saw the orange light? But I was in a plane."

The vegetation grew relatively lush as they approached the summit of the first mountain range. But the valley on the other side was back to dust devils and hardscrabble.

Their paved road stretched across the valley ahead in a straight line. They met one car leaving the valley as they entered it.

The sides of the road were strangely free of broken beer bottles and trash. But a sign with a litter barrel, signaling there was one coming up, stood riddled with bullets.

More frequent were the yellow signs warning OPEN RANGE and featuring the profile of a feisty black bull, reared back as if he was cocked and ready to go. They came across one huge red bull for real. He gave them a grouchy stare.

Charlie didn't know she'd dozed off until a roaring sound jolted her awake. The car swerved all over the road. "Did we hit a bull?"

"No, but we're lucky we didn't crash into something. I went to sleep at the wheel."

"But that sound—"

Bradone pointed ahead where something rose into the air on a plume of smoke while she fought the Cherokee to a safe landing on the shoulder. "God, I'm sorry. You were having such a good nap, I didn't realize I was too. Whatever that thing was, it may have saved our lives."

"Let me drive for a while and you can sleep," Charlie offered. Let me get behind the wheel and turn this baby back to Vegas.

"Thanks, but I'm fine." Bradone's smile seemed to know that's what Charlie would do. "Rachel's not far, and after that encounter, adrenaline alone will keep me up and running for hours."

"That was no flying saucer. I don't think they smoke."

"Some military aircraft, more likely. He sure came in low. Lucky for us he did." They scanned the skies for others.

But the only things on this road were dust devils and scattered cows watching them with suspicion. Then a gravel road stretched across the valley in a straight line to the next low heap of mountains. A dust plume followed a vehicle many miles off.

"I don't see how you could hide anything out here. Can't even find a private place to pee."

"Hang on, Rachel's just ahead." The Cherokee passed up the graveled road and stuck to the blacktop.

"I can see for a hundred miles and there's no town." Charlie was only partly wrong.

They sat staring through the Cherokee's tinted windows at the Area 51 Research Center across the road. The Area 51 Research Center was a permanent mobile home house trailer with a pickup parked at its contrived wooden porch. Two tall antennas, a satellite dish, three wandering cows, and twisted metal wreckage served as lawn ornaments.

"Oh, come on, Charlie, you're too young to turn off interesting experiences. This whole place is a hoot."

This whole place was a few dusty mobile homes with a couple of clapboard buildings thrown in for good measure, most of them acres apart.

"This is a long way to come for a hoot. Bradone, I don't want to meet up with that orange thing again, okay?"

But Bradone slammed the Cherokee's door and crossed the road, taking the keys with her.

Charlie raised dust when she hit the dirt.

Why do I get involved with people like this? I was sure she was an unusual and interesting woman. Instead, she turns out to be a nut, and here I am at the end of the earth with her.

I want to go home. I don't like this.

Well swell, when you figure out how, be sure and let me know.

By now, Charlie too had crossed the road. The trailer home next to the nut institute advertised alien T-shirts by hanging them outside as lures. A cow ambled over to take a lick at one.

Five cows, Bradone, waiting for her on the research center's wooden porch, and Charlie the gullible were the only living things moving in all of Rachel, Nevada.

Whenever Charlie left the fiction that was Hollywood to reassure herself in the real world, she found the real world stranger than fiction.

Inside the Area 51 Research Center trailer, a little guy dressed like a truck driver sat glued to a computer screen, a phone receiver tucked between a shoulder and an ear. "Be with you in a minute," he mouthed, then said to someone on the phone, "Yes, sir, there's close-ups of the base, aerial and satellite pictures, and topo maps. Yes, sir, Visa and MasterCard."

All the while, his fingers flew over the keyboard doing something else because he had to switch files to key in the guy's order, address, and credit card number.

Maps and photos clung to the ceiling and the walls above bookcases. A table in the middle of the room offered books, pamphlets, and UFO newsletters—stacks of them. No pictures of big orange things.

A normal-appearing woman in a midcalf dress and tennis shoes stepped out of a back room with still more stacks of stuff, and something brushed against Charlie's leg and stepped on her foot.

At her gasp, the truck driver stood to look over his desk to the floor at her feet. "Name's Underfoot 'cause that's where he lives. He's from Mars, isn't he?"

The woman stacking stuff under the table paused to think, then shook her head. "Venus, I'm sure. He's a she."

Meanwhile, Underfoot had fallen madly in love with Charlie's socks. Bradone picked up the black-and-white cat and it fell madly in love with the stargazer's throat.

She bought a booklet and several maps from the guy who dressed like a truck diver. He swiveled in his chair to look out the front windows at the white Jeep Cherokee across the frontage road. "Sure hope you nice ladies aren't planning to take that 'over there.' " He nodded in some vague direction. "Because 'over there,' they know their own."

CHAPTER 28

CHARLIE SAT IN the Cherokee, watching Bradone fight the wind for her floppy safari hat as she leaned against a wooden telephone pole and talked into a pay phone in a black box attached to it. Probably one of the more ridiculous sights in a given lifetime. Indiana Jones's mother meets V. I. Warshawski.

Bradone didn't trust the cellular to work out here and worried that the mysterious technology at Groom Lake would find a conversation on the airwaves easier to pick up than one on wires anyway.

The wind grew chilly as the afternoon wore on and Charlie punched the windows up. A turpentine smell permeated the enclosed space.

Besides the Cherokee, two pickups and a motorcycle parked in front of the Little A'Le'Inn Motel/Restaurant/Bar/RV Hookups. The sign on the side of the shedlike building, and another out at the roadside, pictured an oval bald head with those giant black almond-shaped eyes, sloped upward at the outer edges, so popular in extraterrestrials these days. It assured Charlie EARTHLINGS WELCOME.

A grand, if scruffy, tourist trap with tongue in cheek, out in the middle of nothing. The Little A'Le'Inn, a gas station, the T-shirt trailer, and the Research Center comprised Rachel's commercial district—all located along the frontage road and separated by weed acres. What else did the people around here have to do? It looked like welfare-check city.

Well, this earthling has to pee.

Inside the A'Le'Inn, an older couple with drinks in hand played at the one tiny bank of slots. Four guys in baseball caps, plaid shirts, tight jeans, and cowboy boots leaned on pool cues to watch her. Along one side of the room stretched a saloon bar with bottled libations on the wall behind it and diner stools in front of it. Eight or ten dinette sets, mostly fifties chrome and tape-patched red plastic, helped the pool table fill up the room.

Charlie was about to ask directions when one of the guys pointed a cue at a door opposite the bar. A vertical poster covered it:

WARNING, THIS IS A RESTRICTED AREA. DO NOT ENTER. IT IS UNLAWFUL TO MAKE ANY FILM, PHOTOGRAPH, MAP, SKETCH, PICTURE, DRAWING OF THIS INSTALLATION. TRESPASSERS ARE SUBJECT TO IMMEDIATE ARREST AND CONFISCATION OF ALL PERSONAL ITEMS. USE OF DEADLY FORCE AUTHORIZED. 18, U.S. CODE 795/797 AND EXECUTIVE ORDER 10104.

Having taken time to read the door, Charlie nearly didn't make it on time into a one-commode bathroom with a window that opened to a world of jumbled house trailers. They had to be the motel part of this joint. The only warning inside the room was to please not flush sanitary pads et cetera because of the primitive plumbing and Rachel's earthbound sewage system.

When Charlie stepped out, Bradone, obviously still enjoying an adventure, raised a Coors to her from one of the chrome dinette sets. Two more men sat at the diner bar. A florid guy stood behind it and watched Bradone.

"I've ordered us alien burgers and fries for dinner. We can save the dinner subs for breakfast."

"Bradone—"

"And I've ordered you a glass of red."

"Bradone—"

"I didn't ask. Probably dago, but we'll need—"

"We just had lunch and I am *not*—"

"Here's your dago." A cheerful woman in comforting stone-washed jeans and Reeboks set a glass in front of Charlie. "Actually, it's a not-too-bad merlot."

"You have merlot?"

"See, this seriously finicky extraterrestrial left it behind. I don't figure he's coming back. Probably got shot out of the sky by the government or Steven Spielberg." She set another Coors in front of Bradone and winked at Charlie. "Be back with your aliens minus the secretions in a sec."

"Secretions—"

"Cheese." Bradone drained the first Coors and reached for the next. "I didn't think we needed the extra fat."

The alien burgers differed from earthly burgers in that they came in oblong sesame-seed buns instead of round. Charlie ate half the burger and a fourth of the fries but, unfortunately, drank all of the wine.

Bradone insisted on a doggy box for the rest of their dinner and retrieved two large thermoses from the Jeep to have filled with hot coffee.

"Now you ladies be good girls and drive straight back to Vegas, hear?" the proprietor cautioned with a wink when he took their money.

"Just don't do it too fast," his wife added.

The boys around the pool table leered.

Knowing it was the wine talking, Charlie pointed out two things that should have been of interest as they drove out of town. The first was that she had no intention of sleeping, let alone breakfasting, near some forbidden military installation and, second, the proprietress of the A'Le'Inn had warned Charlie, when Bradone visited the restricted potty, about the real danger in this "neck of the woods."

"What we really need to worry about is cattle mutilation."

"Oh well, that's a relief." Bradone made a shooing motion with one hand. "Tell you what, you worry about it for me. I've got a lot on my mind right now."

Then why did you drink three bottles of Coors? "No, listen to me, the cattle mutilate us. That's why she didn't want us to drive too fast."

"Right, they crawl in the Jeep and cut us up with their horns. No more wine for you, my dear."

"No, they wander onto the road in front of us and we and the Jeep get mutilated. I suppose they do to, but we wouldn't know by then. Just slow down, will you?"

The intrepid adventuress was already slowing down, not because of road cattle, but to turn the Cherokee onto a side road where a large white graffiti-riddled mailbox stood out like a lone sentinel. A wooden sign tacked to its base read STEVE MEDLIN HCR80.

"Is that—"

"The black mailbox." Bradone let the low melodious laugh loose. It was a lot like her voice. "Charlie, cheer up. This is going to be so much fun. Aren't you even a bit curious about Groom Lake?"

"No." Actually, she was a bit, but knew there was no way Bradone McKinley was going to get them into the base or would know what to do next if she did.

Charlie argued all the way to the warning signs. Her astrologer had gone over the edge. They'd left a plume of dust along the washboard gravel, marking a trail that had to be traceable by satellite.

It was nearly dark when they pulled up behind three other vehicles, one a pickup camper. Charlie planned to ask someone in them for a ride back to Vegas. But they were all empty. Her panicky feelings began to interfere with her breathing. She knew Ardith Miller was dead and she *knew* she didn't want to be even this close to that orange light again.

"Were we supposed to meet somebody here?"

"Let's get out and stretch a little. Be noticed."

"By who?"

"Whom." Bradone pointed to tripods on rock inclines on each side of the road. Spikes on top of them sported what appeared to be white-painted coffee cans on their sides and small antennas pointing northwest. "They look fake, don't they? Might well be."

Signs similar to the one on the Little A'Le'Inn's potty door peppered the low hills, as well. USE OF DEADLY FORCE AUTHORIZED seeming to stand out in the decreasing light down here. Up there, the sky began to glitter.

Bradone crawled up a forbidden incline and sat next to an orangish post. "Don't worry, Charlie, I'm not trespassing until I step around this stake. Enjoy the night sky."

"So, what are we waiting for? I demand we get back to Vegas tonight. I'm not kidding."

"This is what we're waiting for."

"This" was the thrashing blades of a helicopter.

Which weren't nearly as noisy as the squealing, swearing, laughing figures who came charging over the incline and past Bradone, shoving Charlie aside. Two women and five men and everyone of them sporting video cameras on straps around their necks.

"Out of here," a guy roared in her ear, and before Charlie could control her surprise, the helicopter blades above threw grit in her contact lenses. Three vehicles almost ran her down in their haste to turn around and head "out of here." The nutty astrologer pushed her back into the white Cherokee.

"Show time," Bradone yelled, and gunned the Jeep to follow the other trespassers.

Charlie, busy trying to find eyedrops in her purse, didn't realize they were not staying on the gravel road that eventually met the paved highway like the vehicles ahead of them until the Cherokee bucked like a tortured rodeo bull and she and her purse and her eyedrops landed on the floor under the dash.

She yelled, pleaded, and swore before Bradone hit the brakes and the bucking stopped. "Get back in your seat," she said patiently, "and this time, put on your seat belt."

Before Charlie could regain her seat and composure, she found herself deserted. The dash and headlights were out. Only a small button stayed lighted on the dash. Suddenly, it went out too. No helicopter hovered above. They were obviously off the road and the keys were not in the ignition.

When Detective McKinley jumped back into the driver's seat, she deposited heavy-duty wire cutters on Charlie's lap. Off they started with neither lights nor logic. Charlie hefted the wire cutters experimentally.

"Don't even think about it," the older woman warned, but with a grin. "Just be a good sport a little longer."

They stopped again when that small light blinked on the dash again. Bradone took the wire cutters with her and came back soon after the small light died. They started off across country for a short but jouncing distance and parked up against a rock outcropping.

"Okay, Charlie, we've got to cover this thing." She pulled a dark tarp out of the back of the Jeep and they spread it over the vehicle and themselves, Charlie still complaining but too afraid of what she didn't know about all this to refuse to hide. The tarp smelled like turpentine.

"What, you think we look like a rock here? You think they don't know exactly where we are? They've been tracking our dust for miles."

Bradone peered out of a crack in the tarp edges and a faint light shown on a face that appeared surprisingly older. The sound of the helicopter drew closer. "Then why are they circling over there, Charlie, and not here?"

Charlie looked out, to see the helicopter hover over tossing

Joshua trees, raise spectral dirt clouds in the searchlight that shone down from it. It wasn't nearly as close as it sounded.

Bradone shoved a water bottle in Charlie's face. "Drink as much as you can now. We can only carry so much once we leave the Cherokee behind."

"I am not leaving the Cherokee behind." But Charlie took a swig or two or five, mostly because fear and wine had dried out her mouth. "I'm going to give myself up before we get inside the restricted area and come face-to-face with that authorized deadly force. And I strongly suggest you do too."

"Charlie, I think there's something you should know first."

"I'm not listening to you anymore. You're crazy."

Charlie threw back a corner of the tarp, but before she could rush out and flag down the authorities, Bradone said, "We're already inside the restricted area."

CHAPTER 29

THE MINUTE THE helicopter disappeared, they took off in the Cherokee again. "We won't be going far this time. Hang on."

"Did you ask the stars about this?" Charlie could not believe they were out from under the tarp, moving across country, with no headlights. Behind enemy lines. The enemy was armed and they weren't. "They'll follow our tracks."

"Charlie, will you stop whining? The helicopter stirs up so much dirt, it destroys the tracks."

"What if the white Cherokees come after us?"

"There aren't any motion detectors on this side of the boundary. At least there didn't used to be. They can't mine the whole damn place with them. This restricted area is humongous."

"You mean there were motion detectors on the outside of the boundary?"

"That's why the wire cutters. That's what the helicopter was investigating. It must have triggered a signal to somebody that they'd been disabled. Least we know they work. I always wondered if they were just there to intimidate curious tourists."

"I thought Evan was bad about getting me into trouble."

"I have to tell you about the last time I was here." The outrageous woman laughed again.

"Stop that. They can hear your laugh clear back to the Pentagon."

"The last time I was here, we almost stumbled over a bunch of ground troops slithering around on their bellies, loaded down with fantastic equipment. Oh Charlie, it was so funny—wait a minute, I think this is it."

"What? The edge of a cliff? How can you see anything?"

"I almost can't." She stopped and studied a sketch with a penlight. Looked up at the sky and back at the terrain around them. "Pretty sure this is it. Be back in a minute."

"Don't leave me here alone." Charlie'd gone from half-considering knocking the woman out with the wire cutters in order to get control of the Jeep to wanting to cling to her for safety.

But Bradone returned as suddenly as she'd disappeared to drive the Jeep Cherokee into the deeper darkness of a cave.

"What if they have land mines around here?"

"Then we're in big trouble." Bradone turned on the dome light to parcel out food and water between two backpacks—even the cold, greasy leftovers from the Little A'Le'Inn. "We can snack on these tonight. It'll be like a slumber party."

"Why can't we stay here in the cave?"

"Because we can't see anything in here, silly. And this isn't really a cave. It's a mine tunnel, long abandoned. Probably full of bears and lions farther in, so you better stay with me."

Charlie followed her over hill and dale and across rocks and rubble, carrying rolled-up blankets and pillows tied across the top of the pack. Not because she thought there were bears and lions in the mine shaft, but because right now getting into terrible trouble with the air force and the armed response personnel didn't seem as terrifying as being left alone out here at night with no idea how to get back out.

The crunch of their shoes, the brushing sound of scurrying night creatures when Charlie stopped whining and Bradone stopped to get direction from the stars. Was she looking at the position of the constellations to chart their course? Or searching for UFOs?

There are no such things as UFOs.

Without a trail, the going was risky. Sometimes a shadowed rock looked like a depression. And vice versa. Charlie followed as precisely in Bradone's footsteps as possible in the surreal lighting, hoping for a warning of cliff drop-off or rattlesnake or alien presence. Or more likely armed response personnel guys with big rifles. It was just her imagination that the smell of oranges was in the air. That's all it was.

Her guide and tormentor went on and on about her last visit here and the ground troops. Charlie was sure pursuers could hear the chatter, but the woman would not lower her voice.

"We could see them. They couldn't see us. They wore goggles like you say were in Evan's film, but we could see without flashlights because of the starlight, like we can now. They couldn't see anything. They were crawling around and into each other with these imposing guns—more boy toys, swearing and sweating. And it was chilly."

"Why were they crawling around on the ground? This is air force, isn't it?"

"Oh, who knows? Some silly war game, but these goggles didn't work as well as the ones on the robbers in the now-famous Hilton heist. The packs on their backs, Charlie, they were computers, and these guys could not only not see, their computers were taking forever to boot up and were so heavy the men under them could barely get to their feet."

"You're making this up."

"No. They were testing this new technology and the computer was supposed to tell this sweating kid where the enemy was and everything. You should have heard them. It was also telling them the weather, which was inaccurate."

"Boy-toy stuff like Pat the pilot smuggled out of Groom Lake for Evan. Bradone, we didn't have to come out here to figure that out. We already had, and we're both too old for slumber parties. Wait, that light on the dash that told you where the ground sensors were. Where did you get that?"

"Same place I got the Cherokee—from Merlin. That's nothing extraordinary. But maybe that wand-phaser thing—think of it—small enough to hold in your hand, but it can freeze an entire crowd in their tracks without harming them. Can you imagine what a weapon that could be? All kinds of things are tested out here."

"Merlin who? And that's all the more reason why we shouldn't be out here."

Bradone turned unexpectedly. Charlie bumped into her, lost her balance, and she and the pack and the bedding came down on her tailbone. This place made the surface of the moon seem cushy. And it smelled like orange juice. No, it didn't.

The astrologer stood above her with arms crossed and stars shooting every which way over her stupid hat. Her face in shadow. "Charlie, Richard says you don't like to admit to your psychic powers, so—"

"I don't have psychic powers. But you get labeled with that condition just once and every time your plain old garden-variety common sense comes up with a logical explanation for anything, it's hailed as psychic phenomenon. Total pain in the keister."

"But you know Ardith Miller is dead." She reached a hand down to help Charlie up. The starlight was so bright, it made shadows.

"I don't *know* know it—but she hasn't missed work in fifty years—"

"She could be too ill to call in sick."

"That wouldn't account for the horrified look on Zelda the dealer's face this morning." Charlie dusted grit off the seat of her pants and whined, "What does that have to do with anything? So we're out here because we have to see some lights in the dark, find out why I blacked out on the Mooney, have an adventure, and a lot of fun, and—"

"Get you out of Vegas, where I don't think you are safe—"

"I'm 'safe' on a forbidden and undisclosed military installation where probably even the cleaning ladies have permission to shoot me on sight? If the snakes don't get me first."

"But mostly, we're out here to give your exceptional garden-variety common sense a chance to study some uncommon phenomena and hopefully come up with some logical explanations."

"Is that all? Why didn't you just say so?"

Tucked in their blankets and munching cold fries, they watched the amazing heavens. Charlie raised up on an elbow occasionally to look down on a supersecret air base that didn't exist. It looked more like an oversized, well-lighted factory complex with runways.

Charlie, convinced her companion was suicidal and intent upon taking Libby Abigail Greene's mother with her, consoled herself that at least Libby was seventeen. She'd inherit Charlie's winnings in Vegas and the equity in the Long Beach condo and the college fund. And a trust would dole it out until the kid was twenty-one, in case a jerk boyfriend decided he should spend it for her.

She had her grandmother. And Maggie Stutzman, Jeremy Fiedler, and Betty Beesom, who all lived in their little gated compound. Larry Mann would keep an eye out for Libby too. And someday Libby would get her grandmother's money as well, not that there was much of that. The kid would not be without resources just because she would be without Charlie.

But who would take on Edwina Greene and her hot flashes?

The stars so very clear, the heavens so full. "This is probably the last night sky I'll ever see."

Bradone laughed aloud again. Why couldn't she go back to

that safe silent laughter? "You are so melodramatic and droll. I thought you'd be happy to solve some of the mysteries that surely lie out here where Patrick Thompson flew workers who come and go from the Janet Terminal, where the bicycle cop felt he had to go before alerting the whole department, and got himself killed. It's not Patrick we keep coming back to in our investigations, Charlie, it's here. I maintain that Ben Hanley was a natural death. So we've taken care of almost half the dead bodies already, and we just got here."

"We don't know who ordered any of the murders, Bradone, and we only know who performed the first one. But not to worry, I'm peaceful, composed. My stomach isn't even hurting." Charlie stuffed another cold, greasy A'Le'Inn fry in her mouth. "I'm resigned to my own death."

"No dear, the stars are with us tonight, trust me. That is, if you were accurate about the date and time of your birth. Were you, Charlie? Many people don't know."

"Well, I am one of them. I'm adopted. Edwina has that information somewhere."

Bradone was silent for so long, you could almost hear her holding her breath. But when she spoke, the melody was gone. "You fool. You crashing imbecile. You fucking cretin. You slathering cunt. You—"

"Well, the day is right, and the place. But the time—I think I was remembering Libby's birth." It felt kind of nice to be upsetting Bradone the detective for a change. "I mean, what's the big deal?"

"*What's the big deal?*" The woman's invective continued and grew even coarser. That generation really knew how to swear. But it was interesting that after all Charlie's pleading before, *now* Bradone whispered.

She ranted on until even her whisper grew hoarse, then sat up, letting the covers puddle around her waist. Her arms flung gestures at the sky and Charlie and the creepy earth around them.

"Do you realize what you've done, Charlie Greene? You've added two more bodies to your death count. Ours."

CHAPTER 30

THE A'LE'INN fries felt better to Charlie's ulcer than the ground did to her butt. "Okay, so now what?"

"Shut up."

Charlie lay back in her bedding, awaiting death by murder. "You sound like my mother."

"Then I'm elated that I never had children. Charlie, why do you hate me so?"

"Because your presentation sucks. You come on like a spy novel. 'Trust me, Charlie. Follow me behind enemy lines. With full unquestioning cooperation. Because I am your friend. I know all and you are stupid.' And then it's, 'Oh my, it's your fault, Charlie. You've put us in dire and deadly danger.' Hell, I'm the one with a kid and a crazy mother—all you're responsible for is a fun life, two cats, and a houseboy."

"You're right. I've been stupid."

"No, babe, you've been manipulative. I've been stupid to let you get me this far. And you know what we're going to do about it? You are going to tell me in plain language your full agenda here."

"Or you will do what?"

"I will walk down to that nonexistent base and turn myself, my blankets, my pillow, and my backpack in to the authorities. And I'll turn you in too. Your story better be good. You got yourself ten minutes, max."

"How do you know they won't shoot first? Before you can say a word? Deadly force is authorized, don't forget."

Charlie sat up and began rolling her blankets.

"Okay, but you're such a skeptic, I didn't think you'd understand." Bradone's phone call from the naked telephone pole in Rachel had been to the guru astrologer who led her field trip here just a month ago. He had confirmed her reading of the charts by doing his own and helped her remember how to get to the mine tunnel. "His name is Merlin."

"The guy who rented you the Cherokee and told you to cut the wires on the ground sensors." Charlie rolled up the other blanket. It was cold out here. "Cut to the chase, McKinley."

"He's Merlin Johnson."

"You are so squirrelly, I don't know how I could have thought you fascinating."

"Keep your voice down." Bradone pulled the puddled blanket up over her shoulders.

"Why? We're dead anyway."

"Not necessarily, but our chances of being in that condition are better than they'll probably ever be in our lives."

Oh yeah? You never hung from a cliff in the Canyonlands of Utah with Mitch Hilsten. But Charlie sat on one blanket and wrapped the other around her shoulders for warmth. This place was weird. The air even smelled sweet.

Bradone, Merlin, and the rest of the group had come here to study the stars. The constellations were so snapping clear behind the astrologer now that it was really dark, Charlie could see why. But there had to be other remote areas away from city lights where they could have done that at less risk. For sure Charlie and her stargazer would have to spend the night if they weren't captured. They'd never be able to find their way back to the mine tunnel in the deep of this night.

"Your coming here before to study stars does not explain why you dragged me out here tonight. Nor what you plan for us now. Bradone, I really liked you. If you'd just been up front with me."

"There's something about this place, Charlie, that clears the mind. Something in the air like no place else. And this place could be related to all of the deaths but Hanley from Kenosha and I don't know about Ardith Miller. The three men who invaded Evan's house and died for it could have been looking for those boy toys and the films of Area Fifty-one Evan showed at his screening, right? And I think either Evan or someone working for him killed them."

"You couldn't have figured that out in Vegas? Tell me something new or I turn us in. I'm not kidding, Bradone."

"You saw the two bouncers kill the pilot. They probably killed the bicycle cop because he went to the Janet Terminal to look into things he wasn't supposed to know about. So we've solved five murders and they're all related to this place. And when we came out here before, we got more than we bargained for."

"Those ground soldiers got their computers together and were out to kick butt."

"No, we saw more than stars and airplanes. And Charlie, one of our members swears he was seeing everything through an orange haze for a week. He'd gone off on his own and disappeared for over an hour, and he too is psychic."

"Give me a break—"

"He'd been abducted, Charlie. You may have been too."

This woman was logical and deductive one moment and totally off-the-wall the next. "Look, give it up. Evan Black may be able to beat a dead horse and make it live again, which I doubt, but you don't stand a chance. Conspiracy theories are dying in video stores even, but alien abduction is out, babe. What's that noise?" But Charlie knew.

"Quick, cover yourself completely with both blankets and curl up around your pack and the pillow. Breathe shallow and don't move a muscle."

"What, they're going to think we're rocks again?" But Charlie did as she was told.

"The blanket ends mustn't flutter in the wind. Try to keep them battened down all around. And keep your smart mouth shut."

This helicopter was but a whisper of the one trying to flush them from the boundary line. This one whished, where the other slashed the air. Charlie was torn between wanting to hold the blanket down and throwing it aside to see this stealthy machine. This might be a more controlled chopper, but the air it heaved around tugged at her hiding place. The earth under her vibrated.

Fine, so the military was developing new weapons with which to defend Charlie and her livelihood. It made sense to do it in secret. She had no business being here. This was not a conspiracy. It was not an other-world experience. It was a senseless intrusion on her country's vital secrets, which she had no need to know and wouldn't have understood if she did.

Maybe they'd give Charlie a chance to say that and not just shoot her first. Maybe she could promise to never talk about being here. Maybe they'd put her behind bars so Libby would not only have an "UM"—her label for unwed mother—but a jailbird for a mom.

Charlie burped Little A'Le'Inn merlot; her stomach had the good sense to start the familiar burn. She loved her country—well, most of it. She wanted to live to see Libby graduate from high school and college. And Charlie wanted Edwina beside her so she could say, "See, I can be successful at motherhood."

"Charlie? You can come out now." Bradone pulled the covers off Charlie's head and appeared as a shadowed silhouette against the star dazzle. "Sounded like you were crying. Human, after all, are we?"

"Go to hell." Charlie pulled the blankets back over her face.

"Okay, but you're missing the best part of the show. It's

even better than—oh no. God, Charlie, don't—"

Charlie was trying to pull her cover aside to see what brought on the sudden panic. But the covers fought back. Damn near smothered her. "Let me out. I have to throw up."

By the time she'd heaved up everything she'd eaten for the last year, Charlie was tasting blood. But she was seeing orange.

"You do a lot of that, don't you? Keep your eyes closed." Bradone sounded mesmerized instead of mesmerizing. She sat on her blankets in a lotus position, legs pretzeled, forearms resting on knees, hands cupped with thumbs and forefingers pressed together. The stars either gone or diluted in the brightness of the light around them.

"Ulcer. Why should I keep my eyes closed?" Charlie moved her bedding away from the stench of vomit and sat on the other side of her companion. No point trying to hide in this brightness anyway.

A yellow-orange globe thing rose slowly into the sky. When it stopped, it hung over the base like an artificial moon. It was not the orange thing that made her pass out the night the Mooney burned, the thing that Charlie dreaded from somewhere deep and hidden.

"There's medication for ulcers." Bradone had her eyes closed, like she was in a trance. "If you look at it, it will get you."

"That's for the bacterial kind." The scene reminded Charlie of sitting on the edge of a volcano. At least the lighting did, not the temperature. Or the smell. It was a heavy citrus now. "My ulcer is caused by stress."

Every building on the base was lighted. The runway lights streaked along in front of the buildings and out until they were hidden behind a peak on another ridge. A higher set of ridges behind the base stopped the stars from reaching the ground. The lights of the giant complex twinkled back at the stars as the orange cleared from her vision.

"They can be cauterized now, you know," Dr. McKinley

proclaimed. Why did older people think they knew everything?

"Been there, done that. My ulcer is 'persistent' as well as nonbacterial."

The blinking lights of a plane approached, circled, and landed—tiny on the vast runway.

"I am sorry, Charlie. I should never have brought you out here." Her hat gone, her hair tousled, bathed in the odd light, Bradone made Charlie think of a high priestess in an old Stewart Granger movie.

"Exactly what I've been saying all day and half the night." They were not on the first ridge next to the nonexistent base, but on the second one back. It was higher and angled differently. She couldn't see the entire base, but a good deal of it.

"Be sure and keep your eyes closed, Charlie. Concentrate on keeping your mind your own."

"Right." Like, you drag me all the way here to see something and then I shouldn't look at it.

The helicopter hovered out over the base now and Charlie couldn't hear it at all. It began to bob up and down before the orange globe as if inviting it to dance. This orange globe was solid.

Nothing more than a black shadow in front of the lighted globe, the helicopter had a triangular shape, no tail or tail propeller. The only propeller sat atop the point of the triangle and rotated so fast, it looked solid. The machine under it reminded Charlie of a flying pyramid with four stubby legs, one at each corner of its base.

A flat, elongated triangular craft flew circles around both the globe and the bobbing pyramid. It flew on its side at dizzying speed.

"As soon as we can open our eyes, Charlie, I'll get you some bread for your stomach from one of the breakfast subs and some water. Hang on."

Another more conventional helicopter joined in the dance. It hovered and zigged and zagged instead of bobbing. The three smaller craft looked like dancing shadow moons around a planet.

"Doesn't your doctor offer dietary advice?"

"Last time, it was 'Stay away from raw vegetables and stress.' Changes every time he reads about a new study in the health section of the *L.A. Times.* Hey, if I carried some doohickey into the Hilton that shut off power, why did it *stop* shutting off the power?"

Something, somewhere, throbbed. More an air-pressure thing than a sound.

"It could be remote-controlled, or like the little bug that warned us of the ground sensors—only built to last for a short time after being activated," Bradone said, actually making a little sense. Maybe there was something in the air here.

The one thing they couldn't have found when searching her room was her purse, because she'd had it with her. Now she pulled it from her pack and felt the linings inside the compartments. Nothing. She felt along the strap and the metal things that connected it to the purse. But when she felt along the bottom of the outside, one side had two studs and the other three. And that third was about twice as big as the rest.

"Maybe you could marry Mitch and not have to work. Yours is a stressful job."

"My work is the one part of my stress I enjoy." Unlike dead bodies, menopausal mothers, hormonally overdosed daughters, and the prospect of dying right here. Or going to jail because I am right here. Could Charlie offer the stud to the armed response personnel?

At least her government appeared to have a handle on cool new technology. That yellow-orange globe wasn't suspended from anything visible, sitting on anything, moving in any way, not even floating. That ought to keep aggressors restrained until they could be tranquilized with McDonald's, Coca-Cola, Pizza Hut, theme parks, and shock/schlock movies.

The stationary sphere seemed too far away to be responsible

for the glow from below their ridge that had reminded her of sitting on the edge of an active volcano.

Charlie was sure of that when the thing that had made her see orange the night the Mooney burned, the thing she'd dreaded asleep and awake since, the thing that *was* responsible for tonight's volcano glow, rose up out of the valley between their ridge and the one bordering Groom Lake on the throbbing pressure in the air.

The throbbing filled Charlie's head. The orange thing filled the world.

CHAPTER 31

BRADONE STOOD ON the edge of the ridge, perilously close to the sickly orange mist. She screamed with her hands over her ears, as if she didn't want to hear herself either.

Charlie would never say so if captured, but she thought her government was beginning to overdo this. Sure the woman was about to topple into the mist, Charlie squirmed across jagged earth on a sore belly to grab her by the ankles and yank her feet out from under her.

Bradone fell forward and would have gone over the precipice if Charlie hadn't hung on and dug the toes of her shoes into the jagged earth.

Duh—why *wouldn't* she fall forward? You pulled her feet out from under her.

Look, it's easy for you to show up whenever you feel like it to be critical, but I live in this body, okay?

Yeah, well, heads up, this body is trying to slide over a cliff again.

The problem was not only Bradone. The problem was also the shoes Charlie had dug in the toes of to stop their slide into oblivion. Keds don't have tough toes. It's not like they were rushing to their doom, more like a slow, inexorable slippage. Bradone, inert and silent, as if she'd been knocked out or killed in her fall, hung about halfway over the side. All Charlie could see was her rump.

Any more of Bradone McKinley over the edge and the weight would increase the speed of their slide toward death. Didn't take a rocket scientist to figure that out.

More of Bradone went over the side. Charlie couldn't see much through the orange fog by now but knew this because her sore belly was scraped of clothing as she followed Bradone.

Any common sense worth its salt would have commanded Charlie to let go of the dead weight of the astrologer, but there wasn't time anyway. She had only two thoughts before death. The first was anger. Charlie was too young to die.

The second was, Oh please, world, give Libby a chance. No time for thoughts of Edwina and Maggie and Larry and Mitch and all the others.

Charlie's hands were still locked around Bradone's ankles as they followed her over. She tried to open them at the last minute, but they'd frozen.

The hair on the back of Charlie's neck did not rise when it too went over. But the entire skin under it did when something grabbed her own ankles.

Sort of a patriotic tingle. The government. Charlie's government. Some ground trooper or foot soldier or some armed response person from a white Cherokee must have seen their plight. Right?

Amazing that her front wasn't scraped off down to the ulcer as she, still locked onto Bradone, was hauled back to level ground. Poor Bradone bumped up over the edge to safety in hideous notches. When only the stargazer's hands and wrists remained hidden in the orange fog, Charlie dared to steal a glance over her shoulder at their rescuer. She even gave half a thought to what she'd do if it were a little bald alien with huge black almond-shaped eyes that slanted up at the outer corners.

She'd hoped for a big strong John Wayne marine type in a camouflage outfit who'd be sternly disapproving—"Listen, little lady"—but would listen to her before shooting.

The caboose on the end of their short train to disaster was

not her government. Instead, Toby, Evan Black's second-unit gofer, with the lopsided grin, lay sprawled on his stomach, the toes of his sensible hiking boots dug into the hard dirt. Beside him a pair of upright, long, lean Dockers.

Head and shoulders enshrouded by clouds of orange, Mel Goodall clasped a camera to his chest.

✣

"So, nobody but me saw orange." Charlie accosted Toby as they tried to revive the prostrate astrologer.

"I never saw that before."

There appeared to be something solid in the orange mist that obliterated the air base, the giant globe with the black aircraft bobbing or zipping around it, the next mountain range, and that side of the sky from horizon to horizon. And still it continued to rise up out of the valley next to them.

"Shouldn't you be shooting that?" Toby asked the main-man cinematographer. Whatever was inside the roiling mist was more unidentifiable than invisible.

"Can you believe that mother?" Mel said. "I'll never eat another orange as long as I live."

The odor did still suggest the fruit but smelled too concentrated now, too . . . chemical-like—like something you'd use to cover an even worse odor. Charlie had finally met up with what she'd feared.

"Do you think it's giving off deadly fumes? Chemical warfare? Why does it have to be that big? Talk about overkill. Like the hydrogen bomb. No wonder our taxes are so high," Charlie babbled and tried rubbing the back of Bradone's hand. It felt warm still. She didn't have the heart to feel for a pulse. Bradone had been the closest to the thing.

"What's that supposed to do?" Toby started on the other hand.

"I don't know—I saw it in a movie. Is Evan here?"

"Too risky. Lose him, we're all out of a job. Which reminds

me," Mel said, sliding the camera into a cloth bag, "I gotta get this contraband out of here. Tobias, ol' boy—"

"I know. Come visit us in prison."

But Mel was off across the Mars-like terrain with strides so long, shadows swallowed him in seconds.

"What do you mean, visit us in prison?"

"We're parked right behind you. Minute ol' Mel takes off out of there, those security boys'll be all over that mine tunnel. Looks like I'll have to carry her. You grab the blankets and packs. I'm for taking my chances with security types—might get shot, but this thing is unhealthy in a way I don't know."

"If we're going to die from orange gas, we've already been infected. How did you know where to find us?"

"We didn't even know you were here. Vegas news is reporting you and Hilsten have eloped or something. He come with you?"

"He doesn't know anything about this little side trip. How did you find the mine tunnel?"

"Guy named Merlin—"

"Now stop that—"

But the megalithic orange thing with all its gases finally cleared the ridge and the pulsating air grew horrendous—palpitating Charlie's eardrums, forcing air into her nose and mouth one second, trying to suck it out the next. Loose dirt spurted in all directions and Charlie closed her eyes to protect her lenses. Imprinted on the back of her eyelids was a silhouette of Toby's shadow standing up against the orange light with the lump of Bradone McKinley hanging over one shoulder.

When Charlie opened her eyes, she was alone.

CHAPTER 32

LIGHTNING AND THUNDER filled the world. Charlie could see the giant air force base now and the self-suspended yellow-orange globe with even more satellite aircraft around it.

Above and behind her, stars once again littered the heavens.

The orange thing might be gone, but everything had an orange hue now—even the darkness. "Toby?"

The bastard had gone off and left her.

Charlie sat on a pillow and chewed soggy mayo and mustard–flavored bread. She sipped bottled water just as cautiously. And jumped every time lightning streaked from the cloudless sky.

If Libby heard Charlie had eloped with Mitch, she'd probably run right out and get pregnant. Libby hated Mitch.

Charlie put all the food and water in one pack, tucked one rolled blanket through the straps meant for a sleeping bag, and waited for dawn.

She didn't like being alone with wilderness and discomfort. What if the orange thing came back? What if it wasn't really gone?

Oh hell. She opened a thermos of Little A'Le'Inn coffee and poured a cup in its lid. Just the smell made her feel better. Well, two years ago it had been "Stay away from caffeine, booze, and soda" with that doctor. This year, it was fresh vegetables and stress. The coffee made her happy—thus alleviating stress, right?

Charlie would simply walk down into the valley in front of her and up over the next mountain range and turn herself in to her outrageously extravagant government. If they shot her, they shot her. No good trying to find that mine tunnel. Toby and Bradone and the Cherokee would probably be long gone already arrested by armed response personnel.

We aren't feeling a tad sorry for ourself, are we?

If you aren't going to be any help, leave me alone.

Do you really think even your extravagant government can make lightning in a cloudless sky?

"Oh." Charlie drained the thermos cup and poured another.

That would take Mother Nature or God or—

Little orange aliens?

Both Charlie and her inner voice knew that simply because something appeared to have no rational explanation did not mean it didn't. But she decided she was too out in the open for all this lightning, no matter who or what was responsible for it.

Maybe it would be safer down there with the government. Charlie didn't have a better idea, so she crawled over to take a peek at the drop. The grade wasn't real steep as far down as she could see, which wasn't very. But, with all the lightning around, her position on this promontory didn't seem like a good plan either.

Well, don't stay here and be a lightning rod.

Maybe go back the way I came and look for the mine tunnel. Maybe find a ground sensor and set it off and the government will come for me.

"Charlie?" Bradone McKinley stood swaying not six feet away, unaware she'd nearly startled a nervous literary agent over the edge of a cliff.

"Where's Toby?"

"Who's Toby?"

"One of Evan Black's entourage. I told you about him."

"After what happened to me, I can't be expected to remember much." The astrologer looked like a tousled, battered doll in the half-light. The impression of command had mutated to defeat.

"Nothing happened to you." Charlie didn't have to be psychic to know where this was heading. "Last I saw Toby, he was walking out of here, leaving me to my fate and carrying your unconscious body over one shoulder."

"Oh, the man laid out half-dead at the entrance to the mine tunnel. . . . I think he may have tripped over a rock. But how did he get here, and why was he carrying me over his shoulder? Charlie, I can't find the words to tell you how disturbing this whole thing has been. Did this Toby rescue me from them?"

"Them who?"

"The aliens. On the huge orange ship. The voices in my head." Bradone grabbed her temples.

"Nobody did anything to you, Bradone. Nothing happened. Got that?"

"Charlie, I was raped."

"I had a solid hold on your ankles and a great view of your crotch the whole time you were hanging over the edge, damn it. You didn't go anywhere. You were not abducted."

The orange globe out over the air base had disappeared while they talked, and all its satellites too. Except for the elongated triangular aircraft. It swooped up the valley toward them now with no warning and very little noise.

They were too buzzed already to hide.

"Must be a smaller craft from the spaceship," Bradone said.

"It's a new test plane you'll be glad to have when Saddam and Muslim fanatics unite to spread nerve gas across the country or poison our water supply."

"Charlie, no aircraft could intercept nerve gas. Some suicidal stooge could bring it in on a United Airlines flight. And our water's already poisoned."

"Yeah, well, there's no spaceship here either and nobody could rape you while I was holding on to your ankles."

Planes lined up behind one another to land on the humongous runways, their lights emerging from the sky full of fading stars and brightening as they approached.

"More spaceships," Bradone said through shallow breathing.

"737s from the Janet Terminal delivering a shift of workers."

"You can't know that."

"I think we should see if Toby has left us the Jeep. Could you find your way back to the mine tunnel before it gets any lighter?"

"The stars are disappearing fast." But Bradone staggered off with considerable confidence for a woman who had just been raped by orange aliens.

Was it possible they could actually get out of here without being arrested or shot by security forces who worked for an installation that didn't exist? Armed response personnel whose nonexistence put them above the law because deadly force was authorized?

Charlie and her common sense didn't even have to discuss that one. Not a chance. But they followed Bradone in better light than they'd had the night before.

"Maybe you were raped too while holding on to my ankles."

"Bradone, let it rest. Toby was holding on to my ankles, or we'd have both gone over the side. Nobody was raped. Not even Toby, because Mel Goodall was standing behind him."

"I know what I saw and what I felt."

"Please don't write a book about it."

✣

"How did you and Mel know about our ridge?" Bradone demanded of a dazed Toby they'd found sitting up in the tunnel.

"Guy named Merlin advertised it on the Internet."

"Damn him. He sold out," the stargazer-turned-detective said, and made a gurgling sound, as if she were choking on the thought.

"You get this Cherokee at Merlin's on I-Fifteen?" Toby was in worse shape than Bradone—a purpling knot on his forehead, dried blood on his cheek and down his neck, one eye swollen nearly shut. And he kept trying to chew on a loosened tooth. He'd wrapped his muscle shirt around his head and his jacket opened on a scraped chest.

"The car rental was named Merlin's, and you are surprised he sold out?" Charlie asked Bradone. Charlie was driving, since she was the least injured.

"I thought it a coincidence."

"How many Merlins do you know?"

"The sign didn't say Merlin Johnson."

Charlie didn't care what the advertising claimed, these Cherokees were not off-road vehicles. Bad-road vehicles, maybe. The damn thing managed to hold its doors on as they bucked over assorted rocks and gullies and rocks *in* gullies. Tanks might be off-road vehicles.

"No kidding? Merlin's last name is Johnson? Cool. So is mine. But there's a lot of us around." Toby leaned forward from the backseat between the two bucket seats in front, trying to help Bradone with directions. He was about all Charlie could see in the rearview mirror. "There, those tracks? We're on course—those are Mel's."

"What was he driving?" Charlie bit her tongue as the front tire on the driver's side ka-chunked down off a boulder.

"One of these from Merlin's. Weren't about to fuck up our own stuff or Evan's. Besides, these babies got special reversible license plates. Little lever there under the dash by your right knee does the front. First helicopter we see, I jump over the seat and switch the one on the rear too."

Bradone turned to Toby. "I've been raped. Have you?"

The second-unit gofer was pretty perky, considering blood matted his black curls to his forehead. But that question stopped him for a while. "Nnnn-ot in this lifetime, I don't believe, no."

There would be gas in Rachel if they ever got out of this rock and cactus warren without killing Merlin's Jeep. Without being shot dead from a dark helicopter above or the government's white Jeep Cherokees down here. But Charlie would try to make it to Alamo for gas and bandages. She didn't want to backtrack. Was it possible she was escaping the orange thing?

"Hey, turn left here. There're the tracks to a real road." Toby gave a lesser second-unit Evan Black victory whoop. "Oh baby." He patted Charlie's shoulder. "You *are* the best agent in the biz."

"So Merlin Johnson gave you a map with the rental." The alien rapee did not sound so pleased at their possibly imminent survival.

"Yeah, to Merlin's Cave and Merlin's Ridge. We paid extra because he had a scout out here cutting the wires on the ground sensors." Toby laughed for no reason. "Said it'd be a breeze."

"Why did you contact him last night? I mean, that is a suspicious coincidence," Charlie said.

"Merlin's Cave and Merlin's Ridge?" Bradone was coming alive again. "That imposter, that motherfucking bastard, that—"

"Man, that generation knows how to swear, huh?" Toby managed to choke off the unwarranted hilarity. "Evan had a deal with Merlin to contact him when the time was right to go out to Mer—uh, the ridge and get footage. How'd you get out here?"

"We followed the stars," Charlie answered dryly, "and cut the wires on the ground sensors for you. And solved five murders in the clear air."

"You solved five murders?" Toby feigned astonishment for the rearview mirror.

Charlie explained their deduction, which didn't seem as logical as it had last night in the orange glow.

"You think Evan killed those guys in his house? He wouldn't kill anybody."

He might ask you or Mel to. Which would be the same thing. Then she remembered where she'd heard of Merlin's Ridge, at McCarran, where she'd first seen the first-to-be body. Patrick the hunk had mentioned it to someone over his cellular. Probably someone at the Janet Terminal.

Charlie barely missed a sickly Joshua tree and did kill the engine as they rounded a hill and saw two dark helicopters above an advancing contingent of white Cherokees sending up dust for the choppers to chop into clouds.

Libby Abigail Greene was about to become an orphan, or worse—the daughter of a jailbird.

CHAPTER 33

"MAN, MOST OF that stuff coming at us is Merlin's Cherokees," Toby Johnson said. "Start your engine, damn it."

"How can you tell?" Through holes in the mushrooming dust, Charlie noticed a pickup camper about third in line and then more of them interspersed among the white Jeeps farther back.

"We have a chance," Bradone said low and more vengeful than melodious, her tone reminding Charlie of Caryl Thompson. "Don't flood the goddamned motor."

"Chance for what? There're two helicopters this time."

"Yeah, but they got all Merlin's friends to baby-sit here." The second-unit gofer grinned around his loosened tooth. It was not a pretty sight. "Go for it big time, agent lady."

Charlie saw one of those motion sensors Bradone had cut, unwittingly abetting Merlin Johnson, before she ran over it to avoid the barrage of pickup campers and Cherokees coming at them. It resembled a big rusty can connected to an oblong box by wires, something like an amateur bomb might look. The helicopters appeared to have help in their attempt to round up the herd of curiosity seekers and nuts from two official white Cherokees with light bars on top.

Charlie almost overshot the gravel road when they came to it because of the dust still in the air. One of the helicopters peeled off to head their way. She gunned her unofficial Jeep onto the road, throwing up a plume of white-gray rock dust herself. That plume couldn't be missed from the sky, probably couldn't be missed from outer space. She'd get them as far as she could.

"Just pray there aren't any cattle on the road this morning." Charlie floored it. "Just get us to Alamo, baby."

Car chases were one of Charlie's least favorite kinds of scene in action movies, ranked right up there with vivisection. Now she knew why.

"Wait, stop a minute," Toby ordered after a few miles. The windows were so covered with dust, he had to step out of the car to use the binoculars commandeered from Bradone's endless supply of expedition provisions.

"Hurry up," Charlie warned, "or I'll leave without you." She'd thought he needed to relieve his bladder. They were off again before he could get the door closed.

"That chopper isn't following us. He's parked behind Merlin's caravan and the other one's in front. God, I wish we could have got some footage of that." His eye was swollen in a permanent wink now. "Maybe somebody back there's getting it on video and can smuggle it out in camper bedding or something."

They didn't turn off the way they'd come on the road to the black mailbox, now white, connected to the paved highway leading into Rachel. Instead, they headed straight on the gravel road until it reached the pavement on its own, putting them much closer to the road to Alamo. Charlie's inner ears tickled unbearably from the vibration of their washboard journey.

"What makes you think we're going to get away with this?" Charlie asked Toby.

"All we got to watch for now is the Lincoln County Sheriff's Department, which Merlin says is getting fed up with having to use manpower to back up a government installation that's not there. That Merlin, he's really something, I tell you."

"Wouldn't it be simply lovely," Bradone said, "if that Merlin were in the captured caravan back there?"

"He's got to be nuts if he thinks they're going to let him continue to run a scam like this. How could he invest in all these Cherokees knowing they'd be half-ruined by going off the road and he'd be closed down in a week or less anyway?"

"Seeing as he's so smart, Mel and me figure he leases the Cherokees from other dealers." Something in the gofer's expression in the mirror reminded Charlie of someone else, but the memory byte was gone before she could nail it. "I mean, hell, he's renting these out of a tent, probably never planned on being around long."

"For what purpose?" Bradone tried to turn around in her seat to look at Toby and groaned. Her ribs had to be bruised from hanging over ledges and Toby's shoulder.

"Who knows? Very mysterious, that Merlin. Did I tell you he's a magician too? Maybe he's just trying to annoy the nice people at Area Fifty-one. Maybe it's a scam we haven't figured out yet."

"That's a lot of effort and money just to annoy someone. How long has he been in business?"

"Couple days. I'd be willing to bet, we get back to Merlin's, there's no Merlin. Checks cashed to a drop somewhere, he and the cash disappeared already. I just hope we won't be turning this sucker in to the police."

"How is it you know so much about Merlin?" Bradone asked.

If Bradone ever caught up with her mentor, Charlie figured he'd be left holding a whole bunch of regret.

"Me and Mel checked him out for Evan." Toby opened the back windows, that almost goofy delight with life everywhere on his battered face, except for the deadly serious look in the one eye remaining open. "He was into astrology, voodoo, and this deal where you could get credit cards good all over the world, no matter your credit rating."

"Why would Evan check out Merlin? Bradone, when you were here before, did you come in white Cherokees?"

"Two of them. I never questioned where Merlin got them."

"Hell, he's probably into all kinds of other stuff too. Reminds me of Mel and Evan, and damn near all of Hollywood, for that matter."

"If you knew this about him, why did you rent from him?"

"Hey, we do fiction, you know? It's all grist, babe."

Bradone seemed to have forgotten her exceptionally personal close encounter of the orange kind. She leaned toward Charlie to watch Toby in the rearview mirror. "Have we met before?"

"Saw you at Evan's the night of the screening. We weren't introduced. I'm just a gofer—Jesus, what's that?"

Charlie, still flooring the poor machine down the road, pumped the brake and the windshield washer to see whatever it was, praying it was not a great huge stupid bull standing on the center line. She just wasn't up to cattle mutilation.

A machine of some kind, an aircraft, flying lower than a crop duster, streaked down the center line toward them. It tipped a nose with a hummingbird proboscis straight into the air at the absolute final moment, soaring over them with a sucking sound instead of a roar.

Charlie and the Cherokee fought each other and her heartbeat all over the road and off it and back onto it and then off it again before coming to a phenomenally abrupt halt.

"Get us out of here," Bradone shouted. The second unit gofer, who had not been belted in, grunted in the backseat and Charlie sat there, stunned to find the engine still running.

Her contacts were dry and gritty, there was grit between her teeth. Buzzy from lack of enough sleep, coffee, water, eggs, and vacation, Charlie wanted a hot shower to quell the itches in the most private of her parts. She wanted to tell the whole world to go to hell, beginning with the inhabitants of this car.

But Charlemagne Catherine sat tall and pulled back onto

the two-lane highway that was in good repair but seemed to have more cattle and airplanes on it than it did cars.

She mashed the pedal. At least she wasn't falling asleep like she had on the way in. "We are going to make it to Alamo."

It couldn't have been ten minutes before her passengers were screaming at her again and Charlie mashed the brake instead. The Cherokee screeched and zagged all over the pavement and shoulders on both sides. This time, they came to a stop up against a poor Joshua tree with a rock behind it.

The rock won.

The lumbering animal that had caused this event stopped lumbering and began to trot toward them, testicles and such swinging in the wind.

"God, that's a lot of beefsteak," Toby murmured.

Merlin's white Jeep Cherokee eeeeked, sputtered, and died.

"Toby, find the eyedrops in my purse. My contacts are killing me." Charlie turned back to her task of restarting the engine, to find eyes much larger than hers and just as bloodshot staring in her open window. The beefsteak snorted, lowered his head, and farted.

"Punch your window up." The stargazer coughed.

The big red bull with the big curved horns pawed the desert floor, lifted his head and then his tail, and, before Charlie could get her wits and the window under control, squirted out two days' graze.

"What purse?" Now the gofer was coughing.

"Mine's up here." Bradone pointed to the floor at her feet with the hand not covering her nose.

The engine eeeked, growled, and purred into being.

"It was in my backpack."

The bull, apparently satisfied with his statement, lumbered off to the middle of the road, where he seemed more at home.

Charlie backed the bruised Cherokee in the same direction, her eyes watering from that portion of the bull's statement that had joined them. Tears floated her artificial lenses. She opened all the windows from her center console to clear the air.

"I got no pack, no purse. I got a big canvas thing. I got a grocery bag with one apple—"

"What do you mean, no pack? There were two." Charlie drove more sedately now. "Keep looking."

"Oh, Charlie." Bradone had tears in her voice, if not in her eyes. "We left the packs and your purse with your identification back at—"

"Merlin's Ridge," Toby finished for her, sounding like doom incarnate.

CHAPTER 34

CHARLIE AND HER companions made it to Alamo, with a sheriff's car in not very hot pursuit. They bought gas and snacks and water and a pint of whole milk for Charlie's ulcer. The sheriff's car roared past as if the deputy didn't see them. Toby cleaned up his wounds in the men's room.

"My purse had my identification, lots of cash, and an extra metal stud on the bottom, which probably turned the lights out at the Hilton. Not too incriminating."

Bradone had left her purse, too large to fit in the pack, in the Jeep in the mine tunnel. Charlie certainly wished she had. "When Toby abandoned me, I put what I thought I needed to walk to the base in one pack. I'm sure not going back for it."

Toby came out of the little convenience store all smiles, hair dripping where he'd washed the blood out. They remembered to turn the license plates but never saw the representative of the Lincoln County Sheriff's Department again.

Merlin's tent office on I-15, just outside of Vegas, resembled a fireworks stand, striped with red, white, and blue. They turned the Cherokee in to a kid, maybe Libby's age, who kept glancing at Toby with suspicion but would give out no information on Merlin. He didn't even charge Bradone for the dents and scrapes that driving off the road in Area 51 had put on the Jeep.

Charlie should have suspected something right then, but she just wanted a shower.

They called a cab to get back to town, then looked at one another, undecided, when the driver wanted to know, "Where to?"

"Well, don't look at me." Charlie had no plan, no money, no credit cards, no plane ticket, no clean clothes, no ID to retrieve her belongings, which had probably been removed from her room at the Hilton. She might well lose her job and her freedom when that stud was found on her purse. And her eyesight. Her contacts were scratching again.

And her government, which she stoutly supported, could even now be tracing her life's history on the Internet using the information on credit cards, phone numbers, and the driver's license in her billfold. She wouldn't be hard to find. She'd have to rat on Evan to explain the stud.

Bradone suggested they try to retrieve Charlie's luggage anyway. "I expect the paparazzi have followed your Mitch Hilsten elsewhere."

But she sent Toby into the Hilton to use a house phone to see if Charlie still had a room and to do the same with Richard Morse. "I've got a card key to Richard's room. We'll see if we can't jimmy the connecting door."

Toby returned to say Charlie and her boss, still registered, did not answer their phones.

"Maybe we can move your luggage to Loopy Louie's until we think of something better. I'm not registered under my own name."

"Louie Deloese knows who you are by sight," Charlie pointed out, "and why wouldn't your paparazzi have followed Mitch to Loopy's? That's where he was staying."

"We'll go in the back way both places."

They rode up the Hilton's glass elevator on the outside of the building to avoid the lobby, Charlie wondering why the stargazer trusted the gofer, since she was so paranoid.

Charlie studied the interplay between Toby and Bradone. She kept slicing glances his way. He kept pretending he didn't notice. Charlie kept trying to remember who he resembled.

But they were all startled at the ease with which Toby triggered the dead bolt of the connecting door to Charlie's room. He looked at them and shrugged. "What can I say? I'm a magician."

Richard's room was a suite with a separate bedroom and a dressing room. Charlie's room was the extra bedroom to the suite. She checked the closet and found Richard's clothes still hanging there. In her own closet, the safe still held Charlie's computer, the wardrobe drawers all her panties. Her companions helped her cram everything into her luggage.

Showered, shampooed, shaved, deodorized, teeth brushed, contacts soaking, and wearing her glasses, which she never let anyone see her in but Libby and her neighbors in the condo complex. Clean jeans and soft gauze bandages, purchased in Alamo, under her shirt. And not arrested yet. Charlie savored the moment.

Nothing rotated here in Bradone's room at Loopy Louie's. No scimitars. The bed square, the TV on a corner table. This room was not as exotic as Mitch's, but the wallpaper featured endless lines of camels parading between endless palm-filled oases and rolling sand dunes.

Toby, showered and wearing one of Charlie's sleeping shirts and a pair of Bradone's shorts, opened the door to the room-service bedouin. Charlie could smell the coffee.

Bradone, dressed in two skimpy towels, one on her hair and the other wrapped around her body, barely, signed the tab, paraded to her purse and pulled out a bill that pleased the bedouin as much as her attire. "I know you aren't housekeeping, but could you see that we get more bath towels, soap, glasses, and whatever? And the evening newspaper? There's another one of these for you if they are all here in under ten minutes."

Everything was there before Charlie got her second sip of coffee. Rich people know how to get things done. Must have something to do with compounding.

Charlie had a creamy Allah omelette without camel fries. She and her stomach had begun to settle in when Bradone passed her a section of the newspaper and pointed out a small article at the bottom of a page.

> LONGTIME LAS VEGAS RESIDENT KILLED IN ROBBERY. Hilton Hotel food server, Ardith Miller, shot at bus stop, apparently for her tip money, authorities say.

"I told you so."

"Now listen to me, girl." Bradone shook a disciplinary finger at Charlie. "You had nothing to do with that death. People are robbed all the time, and sometimes it gets violent. She waited on thousands of people, who have no more reason to feel responsible for it than you do."

"Probably got killed for that hundred-dollar bill Art Sleem tipped her for my breakfast."

"You know how many hundred-dollar bills there are floating around this town? Tips all go in a pool and are divided up at the end of a shift anyway. The busers share in them, and the tax man too." Bradone's distress over her extraterrestrial rape had been replaced by an angry control.

"Shut up. Listen to this," Toby shouted, pointing at the TV.

"Metro spokeswoman, Camilla Hardy, has finally released some information on the triple murders at the home of filmmaker Evan Black." Different news team, different channel. Two guys this time, but they followed two identical replays of the Depends commercial, seen on Barry and Terry's channel.

"Police are now disclosing that the three victims, Matthew Tooney, Arthur Sleem, and Joseph Boyles were all murdered at different places in the house and then moved to one location in the family room."

"They have confirmed that not all three were killed with the same weapon," the other guy added. Both late forties, one in a blue blazer, one in a tan. "Sources say two were killed by the same gun and one, rumored to be Tooney, by a different-caliber weapon. Matthew Tooney has been identified as an investigator for the insurance company covering the casino at the Las Vegas Hilton." This was the tan blazer with the homey smile. So Tooney wasn't IRS. Maybe that's why he let Charlie keep the money.

The blue blazer had a squint that gave him a more serious demeanor. "The other two victims of last Thursday's shooting spree, Boyles and Sleem, had been employed as security for several casinos on the Strip, most recently, Loopy Louie's."

"Also, sources close to the Metro Police Department say that only a few thousand dollars of the money, stolen in the daring raid on the Las Vegas Hilton's cage in the wee hours of Wednesday morning, was missing."

"The money from the casino robbery, found near the door of the separate security building behind the hotel yesterday morning, had been stuffed into black plastic garbage bags."

"That's why all the reporters and TV trucks pulling up to the Hilton when I came to get you, Charlie. I thought it was you and Mitch that attracted them."

"There's Ardith, the waitperson." Charlie pointed at the stilled frame of black plastic bags lying up against a metal grate and several people walking away. One bag had bills spilling out of a tear in its side. "The one with the thick ankles. She'd come to work after all, but left with a stash." Poor Ardith. If Charlie had been her age in her job, she'd have grabbed extra cash too.

"Now you know it's not your fault," Bradone told Charlie.

"The real mystery to all this is why steal money and then return it?" The blue blazer tightened his squint on this one.

But Charlie knew. "Because Evan and crew made more

money for the conspiracy project by collecting on a bet that you couldn't pull off the robbery than if you'd kept the money, huh, Toby? You guys never planned to keep it, did you?"

The second-unit gofer gave her a bland smile and raised his eyebrows in a way that reminded Charlie of Bob, the limo driver.

"That's why that phony screening before Mitch got here. All those people were in on the bet or represented others who were, right? That's why the cash, only—Evan's going to fund the conspiracy project with bet money, he won't have to pay back from profits—it's free money, not a loan. It's probably all under the table, so no taxes either."

"They don't call the guy a genius for nothing. Nobody thought he could pull it off without hurting anybody. The odds were something else." He shook his curls. "It was beautiful. Even I was impressed."

"Is that why it hardly made the headlines?" Bradone asked.

"Word was out on the street for anybody tuned in. But nobody thought it would be the Hilton. It's got the tightest security. Most of the betting favored Loopy's or one of the casinos on Fremont. I didn't know until the last minute. They didn't let me in on anything much because of my uncle Louie. I figured they had you pegged to douse the lights for them, Charlie. Maybe they picked the Hilton because you had a room there. Only in Vegas, man."

". . . no new leads in the disappearance of heartthrob Mitch Hilsten and girlfriend, Hollywood agent Charlie Greene, who have been missing for over twenty-four hours.

"Friends say the two have been estranged recently and may simply be off making up in private."

"What friends? If Libby sees this, I'm dead. If Edwina's been saying that, she's dead."

"And now here's Greg Torpor with sports. Hey, Greg, how about those Atlantic No Doz, huh?"

"Yeah, Don," Greg wore a sports shirt, with hair trying to

grow out of the open collar, "it was a great weekend for football and the No Doz too. You know?"

Just as the music and all these huge black guys in helmets revved up, Bradone hit the mute.

"What is it with women?" Toby Johnson complained, and went back to his lamb curry something.

There'd been no news of Merlin's Caravan on the local newscast, but there certainly was on the national.

"Yes!" Toby raised his fork at the screen when their hostess unmuted the set. "Way to go, Merlin."

This segment made much of the fact that the supersecret air base was simply not acknowledged by the United States government and then showed the signs forbidding photography of this or any part of "this installation."

From then on, Area 51, or Groom Lake, was referred to as "this installation" and stills and videos of it appeared distant but from every angle imaginable. Many looked to Charlie as if they'd been taken from Merlin's Ridge.

The best shots of all were from the inside of some of the vehicles in the caravan and of the two Cherokees with light bars coming close to cameras, the men with threatening sunglasses motioning drivers to stop and then cursing when someone else in the line ahead broke loose.

"Told you they'd pack some of that stuff out in their sleeping bags," Toby purred.

Shots of the dark helicopters on the ground in front and back and of people, some of them kids, pulled from their vehicles and the vehicles searched. There did not appear to be enough searchers, several of whom were shown being bitten by family dogs.

A chuckling anchor, sitting in for Tom Brokaw, said, "Wait, this gets better."

More laughter from those working in the studio with him.

"Seems just as all forces were mobilized on one front and military Humvees of the plain old camouflage color came bouncing across the terrain to help out beleaguered security personnel, word came that another section of the perimeter had been breached the night before. And another caravan was now leaving from a different direction."

Somebody on the ground had videotaped a long line of four-wheel-drive enthusiasts heading through Rachel from a side road onto the paved highway. Studio jokesters added the triumphant score from *Star Wars* to accompany the sequence.

"They must have come out behind us." Bradone sat on the bed, holding her plate on her lap. "I wonder who cut ground censor wires for them? Could we have just been a decoy?"

Toby Johnson sat on the floor, eating off dishes perched on a corner of the coffee table in front of Charlie. He turned around on his tailbone to face their hostess, reminding Charlie of Evan Black exercising after the big screening.

"Merlin thinks of everything." He rotated his coccyx back to his dinner, Charlie hurting for him, and raised those eyebrows again. "But he tries to never be there when 'everything' happens."

"You know Merlin?" Charlie asked. "He's really Evan, right?"

"I've met Evan," Bradone insisted. She'd dressed in black again, pants and comfortable shoes. Black jacket and a black scarf around her hair. She looked like a cat burglar. "He's not Merlin."

"Toby, why did you go off and leave me on Merlin's Ridge?" Charlie asked.

"You disappeared over the side. I couldn't see you in all that orange. I was going to lug our unconscious hostess back to the tunnel and come look for you, but I tripped while still lugging."

"I never went over the side." If Charlie wasn't responsible for half the grief that was happening around her this week, Evan "Genius" Black had to be. There was simply no one else.

Though Bradone comes up in your doubts more often than you want to admit.

What could be her motive? Misled as she is, she's always trying to help.

Right now, she was staring murder at the back of Toby Johnson's head.

What motive could Evan have?

For that Merlin caravan thing, he could have a lot. Like Toby said, he could buy video and stills off amateurs—which some filmmakers wouldn't touch but which Evan could turn into gold. This guy had motive.

"Toby, did Evan Black set up this Merlin guy and his scam to entice all the UFO and conspiracy nuts out to Groom Lake? As a cover for something he wanted to do or to draw attention to its obvious existence?"

Toby batted those eyebrows this time. "Pure magic, right?"

"Oh no, is this the magic event Evan's been promising would get us all out of this mess?" It would make Charlie's government look silly if they went after him now for successfully invading and filming and making a motion picture about an "installation" that didn't exist.

Charlie looked at Toby Johnson and saw Bob the limo driver again. Add the fake eyebrows, the little round sunglasses, and cover the dark curls with a tam-o'-shanter . . .

Toby returned her look. "Got us a flashbulb here, do I see?"

What he didn't see was Bradone on the bed behind him pull a small gray pistol from under her pillow.

CHAPTER 35

BRADONE, HE GOT us out of Area Fifty-one alive."

Standing on the bed, the astrologer was doing that asinine stance you see on TV, legs spread, knees bent, both arms extended to steady the nasty little thing in her hands.

"Charlie, he's Merlin." Her lips drew back from her teeth. "And our murderer."

"Don't forget," Toby said, the little gun rising with him as he got to his feet and began to raise his hands in the air, "Merlin is also a magician." And before he'd fully straightened, he leapt with the ease of a gymnast, lifting and spreading his legs so his toes met his outflung hands. Bradone's shot merely creased the cloth of the saggy butt of her shorts, which he was wearing. When he came down, it was on Bradone, forcing her back on the bed, the little gray pistol his in an instant.

There was a frantic banging at the door to the hall. Charlie raced to open it, knowing it could be her government come to arrest her, but Toby looked like he might be considering using Bradone's gun. He yelled for her to stop, but by then the door was open.

Jerome Battista, two uniforms, and Mr. Undisclosed pushed past Charlie into the room and Toby threw Bradone's little pistol to the floor.

You could hear shouts and pounding now all up and down

the hall, the strident official voices of police and the confused voices of hotel guests. Loopy Louie's was being raided.

✣

"We know you were collecting great sums of cash for Evan Black. We know you helped him with the holdup at the Hilton casino by shutting down the electricity." Mr. Undisclosed drove out of the parking lot behind Loopy Louie's. A sea of light bars on cop cars strobed the night and, above it all, a harem girl and a camel jitterbugged in neon atop the hotel.

Who's we? Who, exactly, are you?

"We know that on at least two occasions you trespassed on high-security areas. That you stole top secret weapons. The charges against you are astronomical, Ms. Greene. And growing by the hour."

Why was she alone with him? Funny how dark it was once you'd left the Strip.

"We know that you were involved in the murder of Joseph Boyles, Arthur Sleem, and Matthew Tooney. What do you say for yourself?"

"Nothing until I see a lawyer."

"In my business, Charlie"—his voiced oozed condescension, made her want to hit somebody. She wished she had the nerve to make it him—"lawyers are not an option."

"If you're not with Metro or the federal government—"

"There are higher sources of power. Believe me."

"You work for God?"

The car braked, whirled into an Amoco station, and stopped just short of a parked eighteen-wheeler. Charlie was tempted to make a break for it, but he switched on the overhead light and grabbed her wrist, squeezing it so tightly, her hand went numb and floppy.

"You are in terrible trouble, lady." His expression was swearing even if his mouth wasn't. His teeth looked even more jumbled when he grimaced. "And you are not alone in it."

He released her and handed her an envelope. In it were four colored photographs. One of Libby Abigail Greene caught stepping out of her heap of a car to slap the obelisk in front of the gate to their condo complex. Even the still had captured the child-woman's fluid beauty. The obelisk was supposed to open the gate only to those with cards but often took extra persuasion. Damned thing seemed always to be on the blink.

Then a photo of Edwina Greene, who said things like "on the blink," which Charlie picked up through osmosis. Her mother was walking past Colombia Cemetery, where Libby'd been conceived. Edwina, her briefcase in hand, wore a stunning pantsuit and either wore a wig or had found a better hairstylist since Charlie last saw her. She was obviously on her way to her office and students at the University of Colorado in Boulder.

Edwina had turned into an angry but stylish late-late bloomer after her mastectomy. She'd never be good-looking, but she'd certainly experienced a transformation.

Then a photo of Larry Mann driving out of the underground parking garage at First Federal United Central Wilshire Bank of the Pacific in Beverly Hills, where Congdon and Morse Representation, Inc., had its offices. They'd caught Larry, gorgeous and fully aware of it, at the required stop onto Wilshire.

They had sent out intimidation photographers to the exact nerve centers of Charlie's life. They certainly did know where she lived. Whoever "they" were.

The fourth picture was of a man Charlie didn't know, but figured it was meant for Bradone's threatening envelope—he was young, dark-haired, well built—lounging in red swim trunks on a redwood deck, with two cats on his lap.

"So, do we deal?" the grizzle-haired man asked, and took the photos from her.

"Doesn't sound like I have anything to deal with. Even if you're with the CIA or the FBI, you have to let me have a lawyer, don't you?"

"Let's start with what you used to turn the lights out at the Hilton."

"It's attached to the bottom of my purse, which is not with me because I left it out at Merlin's Ridge."

"That's another strike against you, lady. You and your friends making a laughingstock of patriots. You don't deserve to inhabit the same planet with those intent on keeping sensitive information and weapons out of the hands of our enemies and keeping our country safe."

Even with the thudding of her pulse in her ears, the car was quiet after the sirens and panic and shouting and screaming at Loopy Louie's. What could have forced the Las Vegas police to go public on a gambling night on the Strip? "Why are you and Battista raiding Loopy's?"

"Battista's looking for that illegal gambling money you helped Black accumulate. My friends and I were looking for you and your coconspirators. You and Louie Deloese helped Black set up this Merlin business to make security at Groom and the objectives of the base itself a laughingstock. Now I'm going to let you out of this with your life on one condition—you're going to tell the truth to the press."

"I don't know what the truth is."

"You will."

"That's a very interesting ring. Is it real turquoise?" You weren't wearing it when I saw you last, but Battista was wearing his plain wedding band. Arthur Sleem wore one like yours, as did Eddie, the floorman, and, she'd be willing to bet, Joseph Boyles. Whoever murdered Sleem and Boyles took those rings. "Is it a wedding band?"

Charlie received no answer as they whizzed by the open gate to the Lakes subdivision, where Evan Black lived.

Charlie sat between Richard and Mitch on floor cushions, Evan's screening room pitch-dark. Mitch snorted like the red bull on the highway this afternoon. "Where the hell were you? I was worried sick."

"Out at Groom Lake with Bradone."

"Oh great, helping her detect, I suppose. Will you never learn? Oh honey, I'm sorry. I didn't mean to make you cry."

"I'm not crying. And I'm not honey."

"Don't these guys know it's against the law to kidnap people? I don't believe this." Richard and Mitch had teamed up to find Charlie and were in Mitch's room when the raid hit. "They hauled us out here without official or nonofficial explanations. Christ, Charlie, we were in a paddy wagon and the driver says he's neither police nor government, they just cooperate with each other sometimes. He says, 'I'm private, so your butt's mud, man. You don't have any rights.' "

"I think these are the ex-ARP reverse militia nuts Evan told us about."

"Quiet on the set," Mr. Grizzlehead said.

Only a select few of those rounded up at Loopy's had been brought here, led into the room in the dark.

"Ladies and gentlemen—"

Lights came on screen. Charlie and Bradone stood in the orange glare on Merlin's Ridge, hair waving in odd jags, as if electrified instead of windblown. Bradone covered her ears with the heels of her hands, her mouth open in a scream. As usual, there was no sound in Evan's screening room. Mel and Toby must have been behind them on the ridge longer than Charlie realized.

The camera couldn't begin to encompass the thing rising up out of the valley as a backdrop to Charlie and the stargazer or even to suggest its size. All the frames showed was a tiny portion, and that it was moving up.

The camera distorted the reality by making it look as if she and Bradone were actresses working in front of orange stage smoke. Charlie hit the dirt and grabbed her friend's ankles. The astrologer fell forward and both began their slide over the edge.

Mitch snorted again. Charlie had visions of him and his parts trotting down the highway to Rachel.

Before Bradone's rump tilted over the edge, the camera tilted up and the view was of what was inside the orange mist.

Spielberg figures, scrawny and long-limbed, walked in and out of view. One came up close and its benevolent oval-shaped head without hair or ears or nose came into focus. One of the almond-shaped eyes that turned up at the outer corners winked.

To Charlie, the message here was that everything was safe, all explained, under control, no threat the government couldn't handle. This is the version she was to tell if they were to let her leave. She figured she was a spokesperson because of the unwanted and inaccurate publicity about her being Mitch Hilsten's girlfriend.

Worked for Charlie.

She relaxed, began thinking of real life again. Libby and her damn Eric and car and employer. Keegan Monroe and his damn novel in Folsom prison, even Edwina and her hot flashes. And all the stuff coming down at the office. Ulcer thoughts. Oddly comforting.

But then memory images of what she'd really seen in that orange cloud intruded. The shapes barely visible inside the billowing orange gases had been vague rectangles and squares and a few triangles. Charlie's first thought was of an endless rotating array of office cubicles as seen from overhead, with small moving shapes inside each.

But hey, if it meant she could return to her life with all its demands and drawbacks and rights, Charlie could believe in little bald aliens with no eyelids who could wink anyway. Cool by her. Noooo problem.

Well, aren't we Little Miss Spineless? Where's your sense of integrity? Justice?

Got lost in the deep mud.

"Is that what you saw on Merlin's Ridge, Bradone McKinley?"

"No," Bradone's sense of integrity answered clearly off to the right of Charlie's little grouping.

"And you, Charlemagne Catherine Greene?"

"Yes." You betcha.

"Charlie?" Bradone sounded hurt and surprised.

"Was it really, Charlie?" Mitch sounded incredulous. But then, like Bradone, he too was an abductee.

Charlie's world was drowning in flakes. Who needed aliens? Different shots of the base, with the buildings cleverly cropped or clipped or somehow "disappeared" from the frames and the runways looking like geological anomalies, or riverbeds maybe.

But someone whose voice Charlie didn't recognize had the temerity to ask, "You the guys denying access to any new Groom Lake photos on the Internet? Blaming it on the provider?"

A light scuffle and the speaker was silenced. Could it have been Toby?

The next question sounded after frames of a plane aloft, dropping orange flares near the black mailbox (now white under its graffiti) for the Medlin Ranch.

"Is that the other orange thing you saw, Charlie Greene?"

"Absolutely." Charlie was a convert. Her government needed to do this stuff. In private. And it had some serious muscle in this room, official or not.

Next came a big orange balloon, which was not the fascinating thing she saw suspended over the forbidden air base, rising on air and not sitting still.

"I saw that too," she offered before Mr. Undisclosed could even ask. She'd confess to anything orange.

The show went on for maybe another half hour, very boring and inaccurate, but Charlie Greene confessed enthusiastically to the authenticity of every scam deployed. Bradone's sense of integrity had stopped complaining altogether, but Charlie'd heard no more scuffling and hoped her misguided friend had seen the light. Took more than a stock market to keep you afloat in this world.

The medium-sized screen was left lighted from behind, a tall, round dunce's stool placed before it. The screen light went out, and when it came back on, the shadow shape of a stocky man sat there, one leg extended so the foot could reach the floor, the other knee bent, its foot resting on a lower stool rung. Sitting straight, he had his hands placed somewhere in the darkness of his front.

But the slight repetitious movement of one arm identified him. The flexing of the hand—carpal tunnel syndrome? Some urge to strike out? Insane-behavior control?

"Name?"

"Edward G. Hackburger," Eddie, the floorman at the Las Vegas Hilton, answered.

"And your connection to the place shown on the piece of movie just played?" The questioner was not up on film lingo.

"I worked ARP on Nellis for twenty years before becoming head of Hilton security. The two ladies in the stage smoke were guests of the Hilton. And after watching *Starlight Express* two hundred times, I know stage smoke."

"And why are you here?"

"I'm investigating the robbery of our casino last week."

"Did you know Arthur Sleem, Joseph Boyles, and Matthew Tooney?"

"Yes, sir. Sleem and Boyles used to work ARP on Nellis with me. Matt worked for the company insuring the casino at the Hilton."

"Have you ever been employed directly by the United States government?"

"Not since the marines thirty years ago, sir. ARP service is provided by independent security companies."

Mitch was next. Even in shadow, he came over gorgeous, confused, and rumpled. He'd come to Vegas to discuss a film project with Evan Black and to see his friend Charlie Greene.

His friend Charlie Greene gnashed her teeth and her boss squirmed next to her. "Stop that, jeeze."

"Have you ever been to the place pictured on the screen just now?"

"Groom Lake? Just over the Internet, but once I—"

"That was not the question, Mr. Hilsten."

The question was repeated until the answer made no mention of Groom Lake, only "the place."

Made sense if Groom Lake did not exist. One up for Charlie's government and Mr. Undisclosed, who didn't work for it, just cooperated with it when it was advantageous.

Richard came to Vegas for a vacation and didn't give a fuck about "the place." He had an important business to run and had to get back to L.A.

Bradone came to Vegas for a vacation and went out to "the place" to look at the stars. She was a student of astrology.

"Did you have anything at all to do with the robbery of the Hilton casino?"

"I didn't know about it until the next day."

"You had other things on your mind that night," the questioner led. He might as well have said, "Ve haff veys . . ."

"I have other things on my mind every night." All in black, legs crossed, one heel hooked over the middle rung, voice dripping controlled rage, Bradone McKinley made the most impressive backlighted shadow yet.

Caryl Thompson was next. No amount of screwy lighting could hide her identity. The shape, the breath within the diction, the tragic yet lovely droop to the shoulders . . .

Give it a rest, Charlie. She'll get old too.

But the questioner's voice softened some. "Were you ever at the place shown on this film?"

"No," the well-stacked pilot answered.

Caryl Thompson wasn't asked about her brother's death or her flights over restricted areas for Evan Black. When asked what she did for a living, she said she worked as a beverage server at the Barbary Coast. Which was true, according to Evan, her day job was what paid the rent. Where *was* Evan Black?

Conspiracy may be maniacal, but truth could be slippery too.

By the time the lights went out on Caryl, Charlie was all too aware that neither Richard nor Mitch had returned to her side.

And figures too dark to see lifted Charlie by the arms, propelling her to the front of the room.

CHAPTER 36

CHARLIE HAD COME to Las Vegas on vacation, to play blackjack and to meet with clients Georgette Millrose and Evan Black. She had gone out to the place to see the stars with Bradone McKinley, whom she had met playing blackjack.

"And what did you see there?" Mr. Undisclosed was invisible from here too, but she directed her answers to a pinpoint of light at the back of the room.

"Lots of stars and orange stage smoke?"

"And the night of the robbery at the Las Vegas Hilton, where were you?"

Charlie'd so hoped he wouldn't ask this one. Actually, there were a number of things she hoped he wouldn't ask. And why hadn't he asked the well-stacked pilot/beverage server, Caryl Thompson, that question in the same way?

"I was returning from a burning airplane, in a van driven by—"

"Back to where?"

Shouldn't the question have been *from* where? "To the Hilton, I—"

"And what happened when you left this van?"

Charlie described the lights going out behind her and then the elevator stopping on the way to her room and then the lights in her room going out when she was in the shower. Funny how total intimidation can make you so eager to please.

The lights went out in this room and she was lifted back to her floor cushion. Still no sign of Richard and Mitch.

Toby Johnson took the stool next and now Detective Battista asked the questions. Even in shadow, Toby's jauntiness was gone. He leaned to one side, swaying slightly, spoke through a swollen mouth. His injuries had been added to.

He lived in Vegas and worked for producer Evan Black.

"Who else do you work for, Toby?"

"Sometimes I drive a limo for my uncle Elmo."

"Who else, Toby?"

"Sometimes I do magic."

"Who do you do magic for, Toby?"

Long pause here. An arm came out of the dark to prop him up on one side, another from the other to keep him from falling off the stool on that side, neither very gently. "I want a lawyer."

"Who do you do magic for, Toby?"

"My uncle Merlin."

"He *is* Merlin." Bradone's voice cut from behind Charlie.

Charlie listened for a scuffle again or, worse yet, a scream. She couldn't detect anything.

"What do you do for your uncle Louie, Toby?"

Toby Johnson didn't answer, even with more jostling.

"When Metro's Officer Timothy Graden tried to visit Evan Black to investigate the death of Black's personal pilot, you intercepted him with your uncle Elmo's limousine. And dumped the body on Highway One sixty, where your uncle Elmo's limo regularly delivers johns to the establishments out that way."

"Art Sleem stole the limo to kill Graden and cover his taking out Pat. He wanted me to get the blame."

"So you took out Sleem and Boyles."

"I want a lawyer" was all Toby would say.

"You're not in court. Elmo Johnson's limo service is licensed under the name of Tobias Johnson."

"I lent him the money is all."

"On a gofer's salary? And you don't have an uncle Merlin. You are Merlin, like the lady said. And every lease and rental place for hundreds of miles is out of white Cherokees."

"We got you on fraud and murder, got you locked tight. Want to deal and squeal? We want the guys you took your orders from, pimp." This was Mr. Undisclosed again, who co-operated with the government. Maybe he was a temp.

Charlie figured Toby got some of his orders from his "uncle" Evan. And did that same limo run over Patrick Thompson? Was Toby driving then? Sleem wasn't. But Vegas was full of limos. Toby had access to Evan's house, could have killed Art Sleem and Boyles. Because they tried to pin Officer Graden's murder on him. Or because Evan told him to. Or his uncle Louie did.

Before Toby could say whether or not he wanted to deal, Mel Goodall replaced him. Charlie couldn't tell if Mel had been roughed up or not.

Somewhere at the back of her exhaustion—this looked to be her second full night without sleep—Charlie wondered what Evan Black's role could be in this staged performance. It seemed too pedestrian for him. Maybe with Mel up there, she'd find out.

Mel lived in Vegas in this house and worked for Evan Black. He'd been to "the place" quite a few times. He had shot that footage from Merlin's Ridge even though he knew it was against Section 18 of U.S. CODE 795/797 and Executive Order 10104, which made it illegal to photograph the installation. And he'd done so for producer Evan Black.

Matthew Tooney had come to the house looking for proof that Evan was behind the Hilton casino heist after he'd seen the money that Charlie tried to give him. He figured Art Sleem was paying off Evan Black for the heist through his agent.

"It was paying off a wager, wasn't it? A wager that Evan Black could not pull off the casino robbery, and there were even odds on which casino the attempt would be made on."

"Yeah."

"What happened to the casino money?"

"Left it in black garbage bags at the back of the hotel."

Was all this being displayed for someone other than Charlie? Were there others who were supposed to tell the "truth" to the press?

Mel and Toby came home after the weird funeral service for Patrick Thompson while Caryl, Evan, and Patrick's parents distributed his ashes over Nellis, to find Tooney dead on the floor of the great room and Sleem and Boyles ransacking the house.

"And what were *they* looking for?"

"The real money."

"The money coming in from high rollers all over town who bet that Black couldn't pull off the heist. The money that would have paid for his next project."

"Yeah."

"So who shot Sleem and Boyles?" Charlie spoke up and then slapped a hand over her mouth. Dumb, that was dumb, Charlie.

"I don't know."

"I think you do, Mr. Goodall. And I think you know who paid them to find that money too. It wasn't Toby Johnson, was it? Where is Evan Black?"

"You don't know?" Genuine surprise on Mel's part.

"He's taken the 'real' money and left you holding the bag, hasn't he?"

"Evan wouldn't do that." Uncertainty, just a hint, but it was there, somewhere in the inflection.

"Where is he, Mel?"

"I don't believe he's gone. You're lying." Mel was apparently not as intimidated as Charlie.

"And he shot Sleem and Boyles, didn't he?"

"He never killed anybody in his life." Disdain now, and the hint of triumph this time. Mel knew his questioners didn't have all the right answers. He'd probably watched Toby kill Sleem and Boyles.

But instead of pressing the point to get at the real truth, they turned out the lights and Louie Deloese sat next on the stool.

Charlie decided that they already knew the truth, or that they didn't want to know the truth, or that they wanted to conceal the truth.

Loopy Louie wanted a lawyer too and he was about as loopy as a brain surgeon. His little body exuded fury. He would say nothing.

"Your nephew has confessed, Louie. Give it up."

"They're not convinced," Battista said, standing directly behind Charlie. "I'm not sure I am either."

"Then let's convince them," the mysterious Mr. Undisclosed said. "And convince you too."

CHAPTER 37

"BOY, DO THEY do their homework, or what?" Charlie had described the photos old Grizzlehead showed her. She and Bradone were now locked in a closet. "Was that dark-haired guy in a bathing suit—the one with the pecs—your houseboy?"

"Charlie, how could you lie like that about what happened at Merlin's Ridge?" Now Bradone was the one doing the whining. "About the orange spaceship?"

"I was hoping to get out of here with my skin. Don't you see? Those stills were meant to warn us that people close to us would be in danger if we don't cooperate and believe what they want us to. I'm supposed to reveal to the press what they want me to."

Funny, they hadn't shown a picture of Mitch, whom the press kept insisting was her boyfriend. Was that because he was here? Or because they knew her innermost thoughts? If Charlie lived, she'd never cheat on her taxes again.

"What do you think they're going to do with us?" Did they have everybody secluded off in closets? How many closets could this place have? "Maybe they're going to set the house afire and burn all evidence of what went on here. Mainly us."

"Just what was it that went on here?"

"Some fairly high-level secrets were either revealed or concealed here tonight." Grizzlehead might be private security with a tacit license to get done what needs to be done, but Battista was an officer of the law in this city. Charlie couldn't believe he'd stick his neck out that far.

They bumped into and away from each other, trying to slip past the shelves of thick towels at their backs, feeling over the doors in front of them.

"Now you sound like Evan Black. This is bigger than a conspiracy, Charlie."

"Where is Evan?" What's bigger than a conspiracy—other than World War Three or *E coli* from Mars?

"Off to Brazil or somewhere he can't be extradited. And carrying off with him the cash prize of a lifetime."

"I don't pretend to understand Evan Black, Bradone, but I can't imagine him leaving his work. I can see him blowing up the World Trade Center to get footage, but not cutting himself off from the industry. His identity is his work. Money just rewards it, shows him he's good."

"This is a linen closet," Bradone said suddenly.

"I know."

"Who has locks on a linen closet?"

"Oh." Charlie, instead of feeling for hinges or bolts she could pull out, pushed at the center of the doors instead, and it moved outward like those she had at home in Long Beach would if she'd ever thought to shut herself in her own closet.

"We are not dealing with great minds here." Bradone grunted, pushing her side open too. There was a little light out in the hall. Enough to see that the doors had not moved far. Something was stacked up in front of them.

Bodies. Still warm.

Charlie ran her hands over the wall, searching for a light switch. "Though I don't think they are either—working with great minds, I mean." She and Bradone hadn't even tried the doors, they'd been so intimidated. And exhausted. Charlie's ears rang with it.

"It's Richard . . . and Mitch. They're breathing but zonked. What are you doing?"

"Looking for a light switch."

"Charlie, there's all this starlight."

Charlie'd had it with Bradone and her stars. But when she reached the wall switches, they didn't work. The juice had been cut off to the house. She whirled to explain to the stargazer exactly where she could stick her stars, to see they were on the top balcony and the ghostly light of night shone on the lake outside through the window wall on the back of the house.

"You smelling what I'm smelling?" Bradone asked.

It was faint. But it was there. Smoke. "That's not cigarettes."

They tried to revive the men, with no success. So they dragged them down the stairs to the next-level balcony, which had egress to the outside by way of the front door on the street side. The deadweights nearly knocked them over backward.

When they reached the second balcony, Charlie dropped Mitch's armpits and raced back up.

"What are you doing, you total idiot?"

"Looking for others left lying about—Evan, for one."

"But he's run off with the bet money, I tell you."

With so little light, Charlie had to feel for doorways and closets and then determine by feel which were clothes and which had people in them. And try to remember the layout on this floor. Shoes with feet helped out a lot. Head hair was good. She didn't have time to discern dead from alive or identity or friend or foe. Which by now was a blur of the first order anyway.

Shit. Not only had she lost her mind, she'd lost her eyeglasses. She was so used to wearing contacts, had been kept in the dark so much, *now* she noticed.

But she'd found six bodies alive or dead and had dragged them to the top of the stairs before the density of the smoke panicked her. She screamed down for Bradone to come and help.

There was no answer.

CHAPTER 38

WHEN SHE GOT the first body down to the second balcony, Charlie knew why Bradone hadn't answered her call for help. The smoke was so thick, nobody could breathe.

Literally without thinking, she raced back upstairs, found the master bath by feel and panic, grabbed a towel from the rim of the Jacuzzi tub, soaked it in the stool, and wrapped it around her head. She felt her way out into the top hall, tripped over one of the bodies she'd left, and tumbled down with it to the really bad air on the floor below.

Charlie bounded back up for another, and this time just shoved it downstairs, knowing she had so little time herself. And then three more, hoping they'd land on one another for cushioning. Then the last, and she tumbled down after it, hoping she hadn't lost count or left somebody still up there.

She crawled over all the bodies on the second balcony to slide down to the first floor. The smoke was much less here and she opted for trying to push everybody down here and then pull them out onto the pool deck, because the way to the front door appeared to be what was on fire.

She envisioned countless dead and broken necks as she shoved every body she could find on the second balcony down the stairs to the great room.

And then she dragged them one at a time outside to air,

telling them to breathe, please, grabbing a breath herself and holding it before racing in for the next body.

Some body was stirring on one of her trips out. She'd become an automaton by now, hero or dupe. The last time in, she couldn't find another body but thought she could see flame.

No contacts, no glasses, no sleep, no mind—who knew what she saw? But she struggled back outside, and one of the bodies sat up.

"Charlie?"

Charlie would have sighed if she'd had breath. She'd saved Mitch Hilsten again and gotten caught in the act.

But he could see, so she convinced him to help her drag all the bodies on the patio to the boat.

He seemed to be coming to. She seemed to be going out. Next thing she knew, she was gone.

Charlie woke herself, coughing up the smoke in her burning lungs.

"You think you guys could keep it down?" Evan said from above her, and she realized she wasn't the only one coughing. He turned from the wheel of the small cabin cruiser to look at her and the mass of huddled bodies at his feet. "Thanks, Charlie. Already owed you one, remember? I was meant to go up in flames with my house. So now I owe you two."

Since one of the tinted lenses was gone from his eyewear and since Charlie was in her groggy state, plus had no eyewear at all, Evan Black appeared to wear two expressions at once—the tinted side obscure and blank, the naked one animated with mischief. No one else seemed to notice the ambiguity here.

"God, I hate heroes."

Mitch put a flask in her hand. "It's just water."

Even with her foggy vision, Charlie could see the others, sort of, because of the light. A little of it was dawn. A lot of it was flames in the sky.

"Oh, Evan, your beautiful house."

"That's okay—we got the can." Mel grinned at his boss. "Drink some of that, will ya? Then hand it to me."

Mitch, Evan, Bradone, Caryl, Mel—Charlie counted. "Not everybody made it, huh? I broke somebody's neck shoving you all downstairs, didn't I? I didn't know what else to do."

"Oh God, there she goes with the guilt again." Bradone grabbed the flask from Mel.

"Where's Toby, and Louie Deloese? Was there someone else?" Charlie had no idea how many people were in that house sending orange-red flares up into a dawning sky.

"Last I saw of Loopy Louie, he was dragging Toby 'Merlin' Johnson out around the wall to the next yard," Mitch told her. "I was so busy dragging people to the boat, I didn't have time to go after him. But they were on the pile of us you left out on Evan's pool deck."

"Don't worry, my men will get them." Detective Jerome Battista rolled over to face her.

"You? I thought *you* were with *them,*" Charlie said.

"Them. You. You sure you know the difference?"

Actually, she wasn't. She'd sort of hoped he knew.

All that questioning and public confession in the screening room was meant to show the whole story. There should be no need for inquiring minds, like Charlie's and Bradone's, for instance, to continue inquiring. If that didn't do it, the still pictures of loved ones should have made the point. And Battista had been in on it up to that point.

Everyone had been left with a terrible thirst and, except for Charlie and Bradone, with varying degrees of lost time.

"Could it have been that wand you used on the casino patrons at the Hilton?" Charlie asked Evan.

"It's possible they found it, turned the power up to black people out that long. What do you say, Detective, were we zapped with a fancy handheld laser developed at Area Fifty-one or stolen from aliens who landed out there in a giant orange?" The writer/producer turned his dual expressions on Jerome Battista.

Battista returned the look as calmly as he could with eyes still watering from smoke and coughing. "You all saw the film—there is no air base at Groom Lake, or Area Fifty-one, and that orange mist was stage smoke—thus there's no fancy laser either."

"They left me and Bradone conscious in a closet that didn't lock, with Richard and Mitch outside in the hall, in need of rescuing, tucked the rest of you and Louie Deloese and Toby away unconscious in closets to burn to death. Bradone and I would be so busy dragging Mitch and Richard to safety, we wouldn't have time to look for you."

"Give ya twenty to one ol' Loopy and his nephew land on their feet, somewhere out of the country," Evan said.

"You're on," Battista snapped back. "We got witnesses."

Charlie would never understand men. "What happened to old Grizzlehead, your undisclosed flabby sidekick? What about Eddie Hackburger? I mean, why did I get the feeling that the three of you were running that show? And Bradone and I had been given all this unsolicited information so we could be witness to the facts as they wanted them presented. What made them think we'd be chucking up all that misinformation to the press right now in Evan's backyard while the rest of you were burning with the house? I don't get the logic."

Evan and Battista took turns explaining that the retired ARPs expected to be believed no matter what, because their say-so should be enough.

"They are strangely out of the loop and can't handle people flaunting strict orders, questioning authority that has permission to use deadly force. Hey, they watch *Good Cops, Bad Guys* instead of *The X-Files.*" Jerome Battista added, "This is off the record you, understand. I'll deny any of it."

"Even with all these witnesses?"

"Yes, ma'am."

"All of which makes them wonderful tools for private and public security forces at all levels." Evan cut the engine and they drifted into a dock somewhere across the small lake from the burning house. The sirens and the helicopters did not sound that far away. "Even for police departments, casinos, and other corporations. And your government."

"They have an intimidating air of authority and can get things done faster than public institutions, which get so much press coverage." Detective Jerome Battista grimaced but met the eyes of a hushed and somber group of survivors. "The system could not function without them. There are so many limitations imposed on law enforcement."

Charlie couldn't see well enough to be sure that all the expressions on the boat mirrored the haunted one she knew she wore. But she couldn't see why they wouldn't.

"They do tend to meet untimely ends, if that's any consolation," he tried to reassure them.

"But they turned on you too."

"We've worked with these same freelancers before, to our advantage. Problem is, you never can be sure who else they are working for at the same time. In this case, they had their own agenda, and I should have seen it coming. They are highly patriotic and totally lacking in humor. Evan's project and everything about it would be a slap in the face to that crowd. I was not let in on the very last play in this particular game." Battista sat up straighter and clutched his ribs. "Which reminds me, Mr. Black—about the money from that illegal wager I've been hearing so much about—"

"All burned up," Evan said sadly, and he and Mel began handing Richard and Bradone onto the dock. "Charlie saved you but not the loot."

"It's still illegal—the wager itself."

Mitch reached down to help the homicide detective out of the boat next. And then reached for Charlie's hand, but all movement between dock and deck stopped when what was left of Evan's house exploded. Sudden bolts of lightning flashed from a cloudless sky.

"Jesus, what could have done that?" Richard grabbed Bradone as if to save her. She pushed him away.

"Must have been the water heater, huh, Battista?" Evan watched the smoke roil and billow—turn orangy like a volcano or— "Couldn't have been anything from an air base that doesn't exist, huh?"

"Talk about your conspiracy theory," Charlie told Evan as she left the boat. "You can't claim it was just our paranoia that created this whole last week."

"In a way, it was, Charlie. Somebody's paranoia."

CHAPTER 39

CHARLIE, ALL I can say is how sorry I am for doubting you." Bradone stood on the curb with the luggage she'd reclaimed from the lobby of an empty Loopy Louie's. Hotel guests had either taken planes out or relocated to other hotels after the raid. "I forgot in all the mayhem that you were a sensitive."

"Sensitive about what?"

"About lying in front of those people, about the orange spaceship and what we really saw on Merlin's Ridge. I should have known you knew the truth all along. And you saved all our lives."

"I didn't know any truth."

"But I wanted to simply get Richard and Mitch and us out of the house to safety when we smelled smoke, like the elderly ex-ARPs wanted us to. You ran back upstairs, looking for the others. You must have known something I didn't."

"No, I just figured that's what I'd do if I wanted to get rid of some of the people left unconscious in the house and use others who had been convinced to cooperate, by threatening their loved ones, to explain what happened afterward. That's why the silly confession staging to explain all the dead bodies ruining my vacation and why and how nothing of importance really happened out at Area Fifty-one. I was surprised they wanted to get rid of Detective Battista though." And Evan

Black had to know more than he admitted. What really happened to the real money?

"And burning down the house might also get rid of the true film shot by Mel on Merlin's Ridge."

"And any other secret goodies spirited out of Groom Lake by Patrick Thompson." Like lightning out of a cloudless sky. "Can't find what you want—burn the place down so nobody else can find it either."

"Mel's film in its real state might prove my abduction, and maybe yours too."

"Nobody was abducted, Bradone. I'm a sensitive and I know these things." Jeesh.

But they hugged good-bye as the stargazer's limo drew up to take her to the airport. It stopped right where the hunk pilot Patrick Thompson died. Charlie wanted to go home too. Richard was finding them tickets.

Back in the lobby, some guests still sorted through piled luggage. Others looked for someone to complain to because they couldn't find theirs. The news sources reported the raid as a massive drug bust and excused the closing and search of the casino on evidence that Louie Deloese was a drug lord.

Charlie figured it was Evan's bet money the authorities were looking for here too, especially if he'd taken Louie up on his offer to provide a conduit to get it out of the country. It would have been embarrassing to reveal Evan Black's successful stunt of the decade. Charlie wondered if Loopy Louie'd been had by the authorities, both official and non. If Evan was about to make his first-ever big-budget picture. Louie might appear small and inconsequential, but Charlie wouldn't want him for an enemy.

Was the undisclosed motive behind everything ultimately to ensure Groom Lake remained undisclosed?

"Well, guess this is it till next year, huh?" Mitch Hilsten, superstar, said behind her.

"Next year?" Charlie turned with resignation. I should be so lucky.

Fans still blew the gauzy veils around on the ceiling. The one above Mitch hid and then revealed a nasty-looking scimitar with regular and sad monotony. Loopy Louie's had been gloriously, unabashedly silly in a seriously silly town.

"My astrologer says your cycles are winding down as you get older and—"

"As *I* get older? You're the one who has to eat raw oysters and insure all your parts. Not to mention that you have well over ten years on me."

He put a finger to her lips and drew her close as cameras buzzed and clicked and whirred around them and mikes on booms lowered overhead.

"Yeah, but I'm a famous superstar." He had to whisper in her ear so she could hear over the rude chorus of rude questions.

"Jesus, wait till Libby sees this."

"I think it's about time Libby gets a life." And then the jerk kissed her for the benefit of the rude intruders. "Charlie, would you consider becoming my—"

"No."

"Agent?"

"No."

"Why not? I get more work and publicity through you than I do Lazarus."

"Tell me you and Evan aren't going through with the conspiracy project. Mel Gibson and *60 Minutes* and Oprah and everybody already has. It's going to take more than free money." They stood close, spoke low. Charlie hoped all the noise the reporters were making would cover their conversation.

Evan Black had waited until the rest were on the dock before he took off with Mel and Caryl and presumably "the can," leaving Battista shouting threats after the disappearing boat.

The detective had been duped by the freelance ex-ARPs and now by a real professional—a Hollywood producer.

"You bring charges against my client," Richard Morse warned, "you're going to open up a can of crocodiles. There are too many witnesses to Groom Lake and to your interrogation methods."

Mitch said now, "I wouldn't miss this one for anything. Not only do I get to work for the young genius but we got stuff in the can, Charlie, that will make Spielberg jealous. Trust me." And he was gone, half the cameras following and, damn him, the other half attacking Charlie.

She took a lesson from Loopy Louie and said nothing. Just lowered her head and pushed through the swirl around her, having not a clue where to go. She looked up once and thought she saw a familiar face behind one of the booms. When one of the eyes on that face winked, she recognized Toby "Merlin" Johnson, the dark curls disguised by a eunuch wig, the face still bruised, but both eyes open. She would have liked to thank him for saving her at Merlin's Ridge but didn't dare expose him. She'd saved his life too now, she supposed.

She walked on with her half of the pushy, increasingly insulting entourage, most demanding to know where she and Mitch had been hiding and if they'd secretly wed, until an arm pulled her through a concealed door into a Loopy Louie's security area, all its monitor screens black now. Mr. Undisclosed, with the close-cropped hair and crooked teeth, held out her purse. The freelance ex-ARP who evidently did not die in the fire that destroyed the house and its secrets.

He was so quiet after the paparazzi, she could barely hear him. "Since you've been cooperative, I'm going to make you a deal."

Just your small black unassuming strap bag with too many pockets.

"Your driver's license, Social Security card, business cards, keys to your home and car and office, your cash, credit and

ATM cards. Your identity really." He jerked it away when she reached for it and pulled an envelope from his shirt pocket. "I will return all to you for your promise and your signature on that promise."

It was an official-looking letter, nicely typed, but with the ubiquitous errors made so convenient by computers. It had an embossed seal—*THE GOVERNMENT OF THEY UNITED STATES*—and an eagle as letterhead, and various important and official-sounding departments listed across the bottom.

"Nice paper," Charlie said.

I, Charlie Greene, do hear here by swear upon my oak that I won't not reveal, promote, write about, or represent anyone who does.

The letter went on to describe what she would not reveal in lengthy terms that avoided mention of Groom Lake or Area 51. It did mention Nellis Air Force Base, which was sort of a pseudonym for southern Nevada. The thing was three paragraphs long, the last two all one sentence, phrases linked with semicolons and colons, but nary another verb until the last phrase, *So help me God.*

"Not even a mystery?" she asked in all innocence.

"Not even a mystery."

Charlie took the proffered ballpoint and signed the damn thing up against the wall. He reached for it. She reached for her purse. Neither blinked.

When they finally exchanged merchandise, he said, "You count to five hundred real slow and then follow me out that door at the end of the hall. Now you be a good little girl, Charlie Greene, and remember you signed a promise with Uncle Sam and he's watching you."

Charlie counted to fifty real fast and opened the door at the end of the hall. It led onto an alley. The man who thought she was dumb enough to keep her promise lay sprawled in the middle of it, a wicked-looking scimitar stuck in his back.

CHAPTER 40

CHARLIE SPRAWLED IN the comfort of first-class leather. Richard decided they'd earned some luxury after their vacation.

She took the blood-smeared envelope from her purse. The letter inside had an eagle and *GOVERNMENT OF THEY UNITED STATES* on its letterhead and was signed "Charles Greenwood." Toby had appeared from behind a Dumpster and handed it to her without a word.

But he'd held up his left hand, the back of it facing her. His ring finger sported three identical turquoise rings. Mr. Undisclosed was not wearing his.

Detective Battista had been right. Ex-ARPs tend to meet untimely ends. Thanks to Toby, his uncle Louie got revenge on one of his enemies anyway.

The extra stud had been removed from the bottom of her purse, leaving a gash in the leather.

Charlie reached into a zippered pocket stuffed with flattened hundred-dollar bills and checks. She tried to total her loot without taking them out.

"Jesus," Richard said beside her.

"And this was my worst trip ever to Vegas. Doesn't make sense." What really amazed Charlie was finding so much of the cash still there after the purse had been handled by all the nefarious "they." Maybe all of it. She'd lost count of her winnings among the dead bodies.

A portion of it would be donated to a fund set up by Barry and Terry's TV station for Officer Timothy Graden's children and his widow, Emily.

Richard's knee bobbed rhythmically. One hand held his scotch and water, the other drummed on the armrest between them in time to his knee. The night without sleep had taken its toll on his face in a series of lumps.

"She never loved me, Charlie. She was using me." Richard, not above using his position to entice young women to his bed, was hurting now. Charlie'd never known the agency to represent any of the hopefuls. He discarded them when he was through. "Not like you and Mitch."

"Bradone enjoyed you. That's a compliment."

"It's not right. Woman shouldn't lead a guy on like that."

"Hey, she wasn't after your money or trying to get the agency to represent her. She simply had a fling, like you've been doing for years." Richard's flings with the young discards was the reason Ann, his third wife and the only one Charlie had met, left him. But Charlie knew her boss to be unable to conceive that turnaround could be fair play when it came to women. "Mitch and I just had a fling too. Believe me, it was our last."

"Christ, the man's got everything a babe could want. What's the matter with women these days? Can't commit to anything. Thought what you might do when you get old?"

"Oh, I'll have hot flashes, watch my money compound and drip, live on a tropical island where nobody drops dead when I play blackjack, string a hammock between two palms near the beach, smear myself sticky with wild sweet potatoes, read only books I want to, maybe write one about what it was like to be a glamorous Hollywood agent at the millennium."

Richard Morse watched her with an almost fond expression. "You're full of shit, you know that, Charlie. But you're a good kid." He patted her hand. "And thanks for saving my life."

"Richard, won't the government go after Evan Black Productions if he tries to use illegal film from Area Fifty-one? Even shut down the project? Get an injunction, whatever?"

"They'll have to get in line. He's got pending lawsuits up the gills now. Won't be shooting it in the States. By the time the bureaucracy gets to it, thing could be in the theaters, and if the government tries to stop it then, they'll make it an even greater hit. They'll play right into his hands. He can shout conspiracy, First Amendment, censorship. That guy gets away with murder, don't he?"

Charlie wondered if he did. "Does Evan have any connections to organized crime?"

"Everybody does. It's big business now. International. We all brush up against it. Trick is to ignore it. Pretend you don't know. Safer that way."

In a way she didn't really want to inspect, Charlie knew what he meant. She'd wondered about Richard more than once too, but it's not that easy to question a paycheck.

"Richard, is Louis Deloese really Toby's uncle? Evan and Mel teased him so about all his uncles and Toby claimed he didn't know it was the Hilton that would be hit that night."

"*Family* has different meanings for different people. Toby Johnson was obviously for hire—Evan would know he had a relationship to Loopy's, and wouldn't want Louie to know which casino to bet on."

"For hire—you mean Evan could have hired Toby to kill Patrick Thompson and Officer Graden with his limo?"

"Charlie, what did I tell ya? Lay off Black. Somebody connected to Groom Lake, the Janet Terminal, and all that hired Sleem and Boyles to take out the pilot who was bringing secret stuff out of the base. They use one of uncle Elmo's limos to run him and the bicycle cop down so it'll be blamed on Toby."

"Who has connections with both Evan and Loopy Louie."

"So Toby takes them out when him and Mel catch them ransacking Evan's house. And look, Charlie, when Evan's project is on the screen, he's going to get even with the real murderers—the guys that hired Sleem and Boyles. You got to deal with what's out there—not what you wish was there. Okay? Is it clear now?"

No, it wasn't clear and it wasn't okay. But after two nights and three days without sleep, Charlie was fading fast. "Wake me up when we get there."

Charlie and her ulcer slept and ate and lounged at home for the rest of the week, trying to recover from their vacation. They had lots of help from the little condo community.

Betty Beesom showed up with her famous creamy chicken noodle supreme, which owed much of its flavor to Campbell's condensed soup and the baked-to-crunchy buttered crumb topping. Probably four thousand calories a bite, but soothing.

"Cut up hard-boiled eggs in it, knowing how you like eggs." Food from Betty came with Betty-to-dine, which once annoyed Charlie. But she'd come to depend on it in times of stress.

Mrs. Beesom's hair grew whiter, her paper-thin skin more mottled, her busy steps a tad slower. But her curiosity and her prominent tummy hadn't shrunk. They sat at the table in the breakfast nook, which was part of the kitchen but enclosed by high-backed booth seats that ended in a sunny window. It was Charlie's favorite part of the house.

Betty began with the news Charlie'd missed encountering dead bodies and not playing blackjack. Jeremy's latest live-in had moved out, and good riddance. Couldn't have been much older than Libby, sat around on Jeremy's patio picking her nose and reading filthy magazines. Maggie Stutzman came home two nights in a row real late during the workweek, and single-women lawyers ought to know better. "Just hope it's not some Mr. Candy Bar."

That nice Esterhazie boy appeared to be hanging around again. Betty, who had been not too fond of Doug Esterhazie several years ago, hoped his reappearance meant Libby would shuck that Eric, who drove such a noisy car.

And Tuxedo, when not busy peeing on Charlie's shoes, had apparently been busy fighting with Hairy, who lived across the alley from Betty. "Enough to wake the dead."

That last word, of course, leading back to Charlie's vacation. So she gave her neighbor a shortened version of her trip to Las Vegas and pushed her plate away, her stomach swollen with PMS and creamed chicken noodle supreme with boiled eggs.

"That was just wonderful, Mrs. Beesom."

"Well, I should think you needed every bite. Sounds like you spent most of your vacation throwing up." Betty motioned for Charlie to stay seated and rinsed their plates, put the glass lid on the casserole, and put it in Charlie's refrigerator.

Her hand on the doorknob, Betty Beesom paused to blink tired, watery eyes. "Seems to me, next time you take a vacation? You might consider just staying home. We won't tell anybody."

Jeremy Fiedler, who lived behind Maggie, dropped by when he saw Charlie on her sunken patio with yesterday's *Hollywood Reporter.*

He had receding reddish brown hair, a Ferrari, and a Trailblazer. Charlie figured he was a trust-funder. His job description changed often, but he never worked regular hours. Right now, he fancied himself a landscape architect but spent more time working out at his health club than architecting.

Tuxedo appeared from nowhere to jump on his lap when he sat in a chair facing her. "I understand from Mrs. Snoopy, you ran into some trouble in Vegas."

Charlie was halfway through describing her murder-filled vacation once again when the cordless bleeped next to her.

"Evan, tell me you're not in jail."

Evan was in Spain. So was Mitch Hilsten.

"How can you film *Conspiracy* in Spain? And you can't call it that. Too soon after the Mel Gibson one."

"You can film anything in Spain. It'll mix great with what we've got in the can. And we're going to call it *Paranoia Will Destroy Ya.*"

"That's the Kinks. You can't—"

"Recognized it right away, didn't you? We're talking immediate name recognition. It'll get out the baby-boomer gray heads even."

"Your critics will call it 'exploitive.' "

"My fans will call it 'derivative.' And the kids will love it. We're going to blow up Vegas. Well, the Strip—one casino at a time, and maybe Fremont, and for sure McCarran. We're talking *Independence Day* meets *The Godfather* here, Charlie. Louie has these fantastic craftsmen making sets and miniatures. Vacated two of his horse barns for it. And Toby's going to finally get to strut his stuff." The second unit got to do all the dangerous explosive stuff.

Somehow this didn't sound like the "quiet, creep up on you and you'll never forget it" film Evan pitched to Mitch on the boat moored on Lake Mead.

Louie Deloese was putting up the production crew and cast on his estate there. He had a certain grudge against Las Vegas and the U.S. Government for some reason. Toby, Mel, and Caryl sent their hellos. Did she want to talk to Mitch now?

"No, but remember those two favors you owe me, Evan? I don't want any harm to come to Mitch over there, okay?"

After a prolonged pause, he said, "You got my word, Charlie." He knew what she suspected, and here was old trusting Hilsten filming at a Spanish villa with a gang of thieves and murderers. "What's the second one?"

"There's been a fund set up for Officer Timothy Graden's family that could use a healthy donation."

"God, you're not only beautiful and have a great imagination, you've even got a heart."

"More like a conscience—"

"Don't worry, I already thought of it, and so did Louie. We

wired healthy chunks—through laundered donors, of course. So you still get another one."

"I'd like to know who killed Ardith Miller, the waitress at the Hilton."

"I'll see the word gets out on the street—but that's a long shot, Charlie. Probably just some addict at the bus stop saw her stuffing money from the heist into her purse. But I'll be in touch."

Charlie came back to Jeremy and Tuxedo, squinting at her with doubt.

"So there were eight bodies? The pilot, the cop, Hanley from Wisconsin, the two enforcers—Boyles and Sleem—and the insurance investigator—Tooney—and then the waitress and the grizzle-haired guy who got a scimitar in his back."

"Actually, there were nine. They found the body of Eddie Hackburger, the Hilton security chief, in the ashes of Evan's home." Charlie had received an envelope with the tiny newspaper clipping from Detective Jerome Battista.

"So, who set the fire?"

"Probably Eddie Hackburger—didn't get out in time. But he was part of a patriotic vigilante group with Mr. Undisclosed and his boys."

"And Ben Hanley?"

"Much as I hate to admit it, probably too many cheese balls."

"And the waitress at the Hilton?"

"Somebody saw her with a wad of hundred-dollar bills stolen from the black plastic bags. They could have grabbed the money. Why'd they have to kill her?"

"Didn't want to be identified. And you saved all those unconscious people from a burning house." Jeremy looked impressed. Tuxedo didn't. The sleek black creature sat up to wash his white chest fur. "But here's Toby Johnson, responsible for at least three of the bodies, perhaps countless others, alive and well in Spain. Modern-day justice for you."

"No more responsible than the official agencies that hire ex-armed response personnel to take care of problems they deem dangerous or embarrassing to national security. And Toby was the last person you'd ever think a hit man. Young, wiry, carefree, not totally selfish."

"So what was that humongous orange thing between Merlin's Ridge and Groom Lake? Another secret government invention?"

"I sure hope so." If anybody in the universe has that kind of power, Charlie wouldn't want it to be somebody else's government.

CHAPTER 41

THURSDAY, CHARLIE GOT through to Keegan Monroe in Folsom. He'd thrown out his novel and started over. Charlie wasn't surprised. It was a habit of his. But she did remind him that his was not a life sentence and when he got out, if he didn't start back on screenplays, his career was in the toilet. If he couldn't finish a novel with all that time on his hands, he never would.

Thursday was also the day Richard called. He was home too and not a happy boss. "So, Charlie, tell me again what happened between you and Millrose?"

"She fired me and signed on with Jethro Larue. You know that. You said not to sweat it, that she wasn't worth it."

"You haven't seen the trades today." It wasn't a question. "Larue started the bidding at two mil for a trilogy. First one's written. Rumor has it the ante's just reached seven mil."

"You're kidding. Nobody takes a chance like that anymore. They steal best-selling authors from another house. Who would—"

"Pitman's and Norseman are still duking it out. Face it, kid, you didn't pay attention. Like I told you before, you were coasting with Georgette Millrose. Look what happened."

Friday, Charlie discovered the source of the threatening E-mail she'd received in Las Vegas. Edwina had decided to go modern. The strange address resulted from the fact that she used the university as her server. The strange message was due to a suicidal impulse, from which she'd recovered—and Edwina notified Charlie of that in a subsequent communication she'd thought to sign.

Friday was also the day Libby told off Perry Mosher and quit her job at Critter Spa and Deli, then promptly rear-ended a semi and totaled her already wreck of a car.

Neither of these events came as a surprise. Libby's reaction to her accident, however, did.

She took responsibility for it.

"I tell you, Maggie, I'm just stunned," Charlie told her best friend and neighbor that night.

All four houses in the complex were identical originally. It was interesting how they'd been individually modified. Maggie Stutzman had taken the wall out between the kitchen and living/dining room. Which only proved she didn't live with a teenager.

"Well, you should be proud of her, for godsake. You're always complaining she blames her problems on other people. And the best part is that nobody was injured. If she'd been driving a small car like yours, they could have been beheaded. That big old rusty Detroit steel you carried on about so could have saved a lot of grief in your household."

"I am proud of her and grateful all the kids were belted in." Eric had a cut on his cheek, Lori broke a finger, and Doug and Libby came through without a scratch.

Maggie set the bowl of fresh-popped corn on the coffee table and gave Charlie a hug that needed no explanation. After all Charlie'd been through, Libby's accident was what had made her knees shake.

They curled up on the ends of a couch, facing each other, with their shoes off and toes stuck under the center cushion, a ritual that had grown with friendship.

The popcorn was hot and salty. Charlie sighed. "Mrs. Beesom says if I ever go on vacation again, I should just stay home. Sounds good to me."

"Jesus, Greene, there goes the neighborhood." Black hair, pale and perfect skin, blue eyes that flashed mischief. God it felt good to be home. "Don't think we could handle it."

"You're one to talk, Stutzman. Hear you've been keeping late hours on work nights." If you get a man in here, which you need to do and is right for you, I won't be able to come over for popcorn and soul talk.

"Betty Snoop strikes again." Maggie wrinkled a seriously silly nose and grinned. "Charlie, he's the most delightful, wonderful, gorgeous man I've ever met, and you can breathe now—he's married."

"You're dating a married man? You know better than that. I can't even leave town but what you—how married?"

They crunched corn and stared each other down.

Maggie broke first. "Well, he can't compare with Mitch Hilsten, but—"

"Maggie, that's cheap and you know it."

"Okay, he's married, but separated from his wife, and he's—"

"Where have we heard that before? Where'd you meet him?"

"He's my stockbroker."

"You too? Like dripping and compounding and everything?"

"Charlie, I've been investing for years. You just never wanted to discuss that kind of thing. Now, I've heard some from Jeremy and Betty Snoop, but I want to hear about your Vegas experience firsthand."

"Not till you fill me in on Mr. Married Dow Jones."

Another impasse, but Charlie couldn't buffalo Maggie Stutzman twice in one evening. So, she sang for her popcorn.

Maggie thought Bradone sounded fascinating and wanted to meet her. "Living in Santa Barbara with a houseboy, traveling around the world, enjoying guys and then dumping them first, and all that money—makes my life sound so dull."

Charlie didn't comment for once. Unfortunately, Maggie's life *was* dull.

Maggie must have had a window open, because a piercing scream brought them to their feet. Another took them out the kitchen door barefoot and into the middle of the concrete courtyard ringed with patios and parking.

"Was it Libby? Didn't really sound like her."

"She's not home. It didn't, like, sound human. . . ." Charlie had stood and then raced out here so fast, she felt dizzy.

Mrs. Beesom turned on the light over her door and stuck her head out. She wore a funny nightcap to protect her curls between weekly visits to the hairdresser. Even with her glasses off, she spotted them.

"It's them cats in the alley again. I was sure hoping now you're home, Charlie, you'd put a stop to it."

"It's okay, Mrs. Beesom. I'll take care of it. You can go back to bed."

"I don't know how she can go to sleep so early and still keep track of her neighbors like she does," Maggie complained as they headed for the metal gate at the back of the courtyard.

Before they reached it, Tuxedo Greene insinuated himself between the bars, his body all a shadow except for his white chest and toes. And his eyes, which refracted the dim light from Jeremy's windows.

For a moment, Charlie imagined she saw them through a residual smear of orange.